THE VIRIDIAN CONVICT

THE
VIRIDIAN
CONVICT

SAM YORK

North Star
—EDITIONS—
Mendota Heights, Minnesota

First Edition
First Printing, 2018

Book design by Sarah Taplin
Cover design by Sarah Taplin
Cover images by HypnoArt/Pixabay; PellissierJP/Pixabay; G4889166/Pixabay; ThePolovinkin/Shutterstock

This is a work of fiction. Names, characters, places, and incidents are either the product of the author's imagination or are used fictitiously, and any resemblance to actual persons living or dead, business establishments, events, or locales is entirely coincidental. Cover models used for illustrative purposes only and may not endorse or represent the book's subject.

Library of Congress Cataloging-in-Publication Data (Pending)
978-1-63583-904-3

North Star Editions, Inc.
2297 Waters Drive
Mendota Heights, MN 55120
www.northstareditions.com

Printed in the United States of America

For Mike and Paul, in hopes you will read this book.

ONE

The call came in just as I was about to clock out, but then, munis in my position never really clock out. Not on the moon of Viridian. Not when they work for Granny.

"This one's for you, Tig," Marmot said with a smirk as he handed me the slip.

Annoyance fizzled and spat.

God, I hated that rat-faced, weasely piece of Scard excrement.

Too bad he was my boss.

Well, technically, my shift supervisor. Granny was the real boss and everyone knew it.

No one was more powerful on Viridian. Except the Fed.

But then, Fed agents, those Blue bastards, rarely came on planet.

For one thing, this place was a shithole that made *Lord of the Flies* look like Disneyland. For another, there really wasn't much to police here. Nothing they cared about anyway. Their job was to sit up in their luxurious space station and make sure none of the cons escaped the planetary shield.

Occasionally one of them would drop down—usually to indulge their darker appetites—but they never stayed long. Just long enough to fuck shit up.

My gut clenched as the memory of my last tangle with a particular Fed scorched my brain. I tried to push all thoughts of Mia from my mind, but it was hard to forget what that Blue bitch had done.

"Well?" Marmot's pointy nose quivered.

"What is it?" I snapped.

He grinned. His razor-sharp teeth glinted in the light. "DB. Out in Harleytown."

"Awesome." I scrubbed at my face. My day beard scratched at my palm. I was tired. I wanted to go home and take a load off. Maybe get shitfaced. I glanced at the other munis lounging in the lobby: a couple Trogs, a Raven, and some random Frogs. They all avoided eye contact. With a sigh, I dropped the annoying assignment. The paper fluttered onto the desk. "I'm off in two."

Marmot pushed the slip right back at me. "Special request. Asked for you."

Yeah. I loved being popular. "Who?"

"Jimmy Bluenote."

Well, hell.

That Dink had saved my ass last week in a sting that went sour—way sour. I'd be rolling around in an Ozzie stew about now if it hadn't been for him. I owed him. And here, on Viridian, a prison moon filled to the gills with all manner of vengeful species, you always paid your debts.

"Fine." I snatched the slip from Marmot's bony fingers and wheeled away.

"And, Tig?"

I glanced back at him. His nose wiggled. His whiskers quivered. His beady little eyes glinted. "Take the Skeeg."

"Seriously?" I'd spent most of my day trying to shake that tail.

Marmot waggled his furry eyebrows. "Take the Skeeg."

Each flatfoot working for Granny was assigned a Skeeg for "protection," which was a fucking joke. Those Frogs could barely protect their own eggs. I suspected Granny was just doing them a favor, offering them a place in his kingdom in exchange for licking rights. Some creatures on this rock would kill or die for Skeeg pglet. In addition to having rumored regenerative properties, it was, apparently, a most excellent high.

I'd never been tempted. The thought of licking one of those repugnant creatures made me want to vomit. Besides, I had my own dark cravings to deal with. Last thing I needed was another addiction.

At any rate, on Granny's behest, I spent my shifts being trailed by a tall, skinny, green douchebag with one eye on a stalk. It creeped me out, the way he looked around, that stalk all bendy like it was. The way he smelled wasn't orgasmic either. But Granny was God. We did what he said. No matter what.

We knew we were damn lucky to have the job. Some vestige of power in a world where power equaled survival.

Viridian wasn't a penal colony so much as a Federation garbage dump. A first-uni Australia of the nineteenth century . . . only with aliens. Who wanted to eat you. Loads of fun.

Got a problem you wanna make disappear? Send it to Viridian with the scumbags and lowlifes of the uni. Let nature take its course.

I'd been somebody's problem.

I suspect we all had been. At some point.

For many, a conviction and transport to Viridian was a death sentence. Pity it wasn't for most. Fact was, the ones who thrived here were the most brutal, pitiless, soulless creatures in the known universe. Savages who would do anything to survive.

No one expected me to make it a week.

Soft Earthie? Pretty boy? I didn't have venom, no spines, no secret weapons. To make matters worse, of all the creatures in this universe, humans and Feds looked far too much alike. Except for my non-blue skin color, I could have been one. That alone made humans exceedingly unpopular.

Yeah. I shoulda died. Expected to.

No one could have predicted I'd land on my feet, first day out the gate. I sure as shit didn't. But fortune fell in my lap in the holding cell in intake, up on the Fed station orbiting this moon. My dumbshit noble sensibilities clicked on when I saw two Ozzies making a move on a kid. A young, stupid Ferrod, with velvet still on his antlers. He was utterly out of his league here in this hell hole, but connected. The Ozzies wanted to chow down—they'll eat anything, and they have these long, razor-sharp teeth to make the job easier. You could call them fangs. Or straws.

Any rate, I snapped a couple off, saved the sniveling kid, and got him through the gate. To daddy. I had no idea "daddy" was Big Jogn. That furry, fat fence set me up with his capo and that led me to Granny. I'd been working under his banner ever since. Ten years. Or what passes for a year on this rock.

My official title was Enforcer, but we all knew we were errand boys. Bag men, cleaners, muscle. Whatever Granny demanded, we did it.

Even consort with Skeegs.

I glanced over to my office where my partner sat slumped in a chair at his desk, wiping the slime from his green skin. Great. He was oozing again. I knew what that meant.

Of course, I was assuming One Eye was a "he." Skeegs didn't have a gender—not until it was mating season—then they'd do whatever Skeegs needed to do.

God. Skeeg mating season. What a mess.

"Hey, Frog," I called. One Eye's earhole twitched. He looked up. His long, stalky eye settled on me and he blinked, slow, steady, like he did. I waved the slip. "We got a call."

I crossed my arms and watched as he unfolded his long, leggy body from the chair and made his way through the station house toward me, his flat, webbed feet slapping wetly on the hardwood floor. He left a trail behind him. The other munis curled their noses—and other various appendages—when he passed. When Skeegs started going into musth, they stank to high heaven. And dripped.

He moved like molasses in winter, but I was in no hurry. I owed it to Jimmy to respond to whatever emergency he had, but seriously, there was no call to go overboard. At least tonight I'd be able to clear an annoying debt.

And Jimmy was annoying.

We headed down to the garage and hopped into my skimmer, but I took the precaution of pulling some towels out of the trunk and draping them over the passenger seat first. I didn't have a fancy ride, but it was mine, and the last thing I wanted was to get Skeeg cum all over the leather.

I was assuming it was cum.

One Eye and I weren't close enough to ask.

I never wanted to be that close.

Point being, it was a wise precaution. You could never get that stank out.

Once we were both settled, I flicked on my hovers and headed out onto the street. It was a dark night, but hardly quiet. There were few quiet nights in this town. In fact, nighttime was when it came alive, started to hum, sometimes scream. When I'd first arrived here, I'd hated it, the constant thrum of excitement, expectation, and malicious intent. But you get used to everything. Eventually. And sometimes you even start liking it.

We hit a snag in the Prospect District. Some riot in progress. I switched on my lights and a path cleared through the melee. It wasn't like back on Earth, where people had respect for the law and pulled over when they saw a unit coming. Here, they cleared a path because they knew if they didn't, I would blast my way through them.

I didn't miss the snarls they flashed me as I flew by, but I didn't care.

They all knew whom I worked for, and no one pissed on Granny's parade.

We turned onto the flyway and I jetted into gear. One Eye gasped and grabbed the handgrip as I accelerated, which sent a curl of annoyance through me. Skeegs never liked going fast and One Eye had never been a fan of my driving.

"Chill, Frog," I muttered, as I shifted gears and roared into seventh gear. The skimmer shot forward with a howl.

One Eye didn't respond, other than to level that big, glassy orb on me. I hated when he stared.

I angled my skimmer up to the top lane where we could really fly. Aside from the speed, I liked the view. Nothing overhead but the great expanse of the city dome—the dome that kept out the brutal storms of the Barrens and served as climate control for the settlement. Tonight, the sky was clear and myriad stars speckled the firmament.

I turned on the radio and let the Earth tunes wash over me as we wailed along the flyway. It helped me ignore my partner's unnerving, silent stare. When he didn't quit staring, I turned the volume up and sang along.

I smirked when he grimaced.

Yeah, I'm pretty tone deaf.

"Call?" One Eye asked over the cacophony. A croak.

"DB."

One Eye let out something that might have been a burbly sigh. Yup. I hated dead bodies too. Freaking pain in the ass. Way too much paperwork. Not that anyone cared, but Granny liked to keep tabs. On everything.

Viridian was his kingdom.

We came to the Harleytown exit and I veered onto the ramp, a glittering, silver beam of light ribboning off into the darkness.

The howl of the flyway receded as we whipped down into the bowels of the city.

As we slid onto the street in one of the dirtiest districts of town, One Eye turned off the radio. I shot him a glare as I hovered to the address on the call and switched off, tugging on my gloves in an almost-automatic motion. One Eye did the same. His took a little more work on account of the slime and everything. But no way was I helping him. No way was I touching that.

It might have been my imagination, but he seemed to be seeping more than usual.

"You ready?" I asked.

He did a quick weapons check and then nodded to me. Together, we eased from the skimmer.

The buildings towered over us, shutting out the light of the night moons. The streets were quiet. Eerily quiet. It was odd for Harleytown, which was usually crawling with johns and hookers seeking out depraved companionship, drug dealers, predators, and not-so-petty thieves. But tonight it was as though something, some dark whisper in the night, had spooked them all back into their hidey-holes.

A shiver danced down my spine and I gave my gloves a tug.

This was a perfect place for a crime.

But, hell, what was I saying? Any place on this rock was the perfect place for a crime.

A rat skittered through the garbage piled on the street, and someone peered out at us through the curtains of a window on the first floor of a seedy brownstone. When they noticed my attention, the curtain fluttered closed. Light flicked off.

Yeah. No one in this part of town wanted to tangle with one of Granny's munis. They'd lose.

"Oh God, oh God, oh God." Jimmy's nasally voice echoed through the shadows, bouncing off the stones. "You're here. Thank God."

God had nothing to do with it.

I narrowed my eyes against the gloom and spotted him, hunkering in a debris-strewn alley. Jimmy was a jumpy gecko, but the way he was shuddering, the way his gaze kept skipping over the empty street, the way his left eye twitched, made me think this was something more than his usual paranoia. "What is it, Jimmy?" I called.

"Here. Come 'ere." He waved me over, a frantic flutter of fingers. "Pflerg, Tig. Hurry."

I shot a glance at One Eye and sighed. My partner held up his scanner and pointed it at the slender slit between the buildings. A beam of iridescent light walked its way over the crumbling bricks and scattered refuse with a low hum. The scanner beeped, a harsh intonation. One Eye nodded. Clear.

Nice to know the Dink wasn't leading me into an ambush.

I headed toward him and One Eye took up position at the mouth of the alley, facing out, watching the street. Granted, we were Granny's munis, but experience had taught us never to let down our guard. There was always someone watching. Always some shit in play.

I strolled down the long alley to Jimmy, adjusting my gloves. Not to make a point or anything. His gaze fixated on them, his slit pupils dilated, and his throat worked. Sweat beaded his scaly forehead . . . and Dinks sweated in pus. Great, gooey globs of it. And they were green. Great, gooey green globs. Rolling down the side of his face. Jesus, it was gross. Almost as bad as the Skeeg.

"What is it, Jimmy?" Goddamn it. I knew this was going to be a pain in the ass, whatever it was. Just knew.

He stubbed out his draw and scuttled over. "I swear to God, Tig. I didn't know." His eyes bugged out. His way of emphasizing his innocence—or his ignorance. Hard to tell. He had little of one and a lot of the other.

"You didn't know what, Jimmy?"

"Oh pflerg, Tig. Over here. Pflerg."

Damn. I'd seen the little lizard in a wad more than once, was used to his mouth, but this—this was weird.

I shook my head and followed him back into the corner of the alley barely lit by a faint streetlamp. It was a dead end, a box-in. Stone walls on all sides. No escape but the mouth of the cave. Ideal for a surprise attack. The body lay at the far end, a jumbled pile of clothes draped over a stack of wooden pallets.

"We was just, you know, tanging a little. Just playing around. It got a little rough and . . . I swear. I swear, Tig. I didn't know."

I leaned closer and shined my light on the scene with a tsk. "Jimmy, Jimmy. What did you—?"

Oh. Fuck.

The first clue I had that my life was about to swirl down the crapper was a dark puddle of blood. Ah, but not just any blood.

It was blue.

Fucking. Blue.

The sight of it made my gut clench. My belly heave. Made me wish I hadn't eaten today because it was now all churning acid making a bitter incursion back up my gullet.

"Shit, Jimmy." Forced out, though tight lips. I spun around, raked my hair. Panic whipped through me like a storm.

"I swear! I didn't know it was a Goon!"

I clapped my hand over his slimy mouth. "Shut the hell up, Jimmy," I hissed in his ear. "You want someone to hear?"

He made some response—no idea what it was; didn't care—and shook his head.

But we both knew. One call to the Fed, and we'd all be dead. In the blink of an eye.

No one killed a Goon.

No. One.

Well, except Jimmy, apparently.

I pulled him down lower, out of One Eye's line of vision. Yanked him closer and snarled, "What the hell happened?"

"I told you. Things got rough." God, I hated when he whined. I smacked him on the back of his scaly head. Hard.

"Are you telling me you tanged a Goon to *death*?" *Seriously?*

Jimmy shrugged. "There might have been some knife play."

"God damn it, Jimmy." Jesus.

"You're going to protect me, aren't you, Tig?"

My mind spun. It wasn't a question of protecting Jimmy. This was worlds bigger than that. If the Feds got wind that an agent had died on Viridian, they'd quark the whole planet. Just drop a Q-bomb and let everyone fry. They'd done it at the Epsy colony, back in '02.

Being ripped to shreds, molecule by molecule, was not the way I wanted to die.

We had to hide this. We had to dispose of the body. Dispose of it in a way it could never be found. And no one—no one—could know.

Especially not my partner.

If Skeegs had one fatal flaw—aside from dripping on every freaking thing—it was their inability to tell a lie.

I glared at Jimmy. I wanted to deck him, shiv him, shoot him, but I couldn't. I needed his help. Maybe later. "Stay here," I spat, and then I sucked in a breath and casually strolled to the mouth of the alley.

As I leaned against the brownstone, One Eye's stalk curled down and he stared at me with that unblinking orb. Damn, I hated that.

"Yeah," I said, pulling out a smoke and lighting it. "Just a dead hooker. I can handle this." I offered him the cigarette. He just kept looking at me. I knew he wouldn't take it. He hated the smell. Besides, Skeegs couldn't indulge. Couldn't get in a puff before their ooze crept down and extinguished the ember. I patted him on the shoulder, then surreptitiously wiped my palm on my duster. "It's late. Why don't you head on home?"

"Home?" he croaked. Might have been the pulse thrumming in my ear, but it sounded like his voice was getting . . . froggier.

"Yeah. See you. Tomorrow?"

He glanced meaningfully at the skimmer. Skeegs weren't chatty guys to begin with and One Eye took this to a whole new level, but he'd been my partner for a while. I knew how to read him. "Yeah. You take it back to the station house. Jimmy and I are going out for a drink after we—" I flourished a hand. "You know. He'll give me a lift home."

The Frog stared at me for a moment, then he curled his eye back into the alley and studied Jimmy, who was trying like hell to act casual. The pus probably ruined the effect, but One Eye seemed to buy it. He nodded and headed to my skimmer.

I watched as he levered into my car, and tried not to grimace when he slid wetly over my Corinthian leather. I waited until he pulled out and headed back to the skyway before I stubbed out my cigarette and turned back to the nightmare my evening had become.

Jimmy made it just that much worse by lighting up a god-damn huff just as I approached him. "Draw?" He held out a slender cylinder of hell wrapped in soaked papers.

My mouth watered. My fingers twitched. I lit another cig-arette to drown the urge. It didn't help. It took a second or two to dredge up my resolve. "Nah. I quit."

His buggy eyes bulged. Thick, scaly lids quivered. "Since when?"

"Since I did."

"Okay . . ."

I sucked in a breath. "I'd appreciate it if you would put that out."

I didn't think my voice was that snarly, but Jimmy's Adam's apples bounced as he swallowed. "Yeah, Tig. Sure, Tig." He dropped the huff onto the pavement and ground it out.

I still wanted it.

It took a lot of effort to focus my attention on the body. I tugged at my gloves. To remind me who I was. Who I had been.

Jimmy sidled up next to me. It pissed me off that he still smelled like it. It pissed me off that for some species, draw wasn't like heroin. Some species could just enjoy the high and walk away without a thought.

The universe was fucking unfair.

But at least it had a sense of humor.

"So what we gonna do, Tig? How we gonna handle this?" Jimmy asked.

I glared at him. "*We* are not going to handle this. *I* am. You're going to shut up and do as I say."

"Sure, Tig. Sure."

"You still tanging that Nard, Chinga?"

"I'm tanging everyone," he said with a chuckle.

Ain't that the truth? He was sure tanging me tonight.

"Call her. We need her skimmer, that old beater. No questions asked."

Jimmy puffed out his chest and blew out a scoff. "She never asks questions. I got her trained."

"Well get that skimmer here, ASAP. Gonna need a tarp too. Black one. And some sulfuric acid."

"On it." He headed for the street. He moved with a little too much alacrity.

"Oh, and Jimmy?" I called.

"Yeah, Tig?"

"You bail on me, and I'm leaving this mess here, with your name on it. You got that?"

He paled. Might have paled. With Dinks it was tough to tell sometimes, what with the rippling scales and all. But his throat worked. "Ah, right, Tig. Sure thing."

Little fucker.

He would have. He would have run.

Son of a bitch.

As I waited for the Nard to show up with our wheels, I studied the scene. The dead Goon, the knife, the blood. I tried to ignore the pile of draw butts Jimmy had huffed as he waited for me to waltz in and save his ass, but it tugged on my consciousness. It took a hell of a lot of focus to keep that shit at bay.

The scene was your typical toss and floss. From what I could tell, Jimmy had screwed the Goon and then knifed him where the sun don't shine. Kind of rude, but Jimmy was rarely polite. The thing that got me was the Goon's skin color. It was easy to see why Jimmy didn't finger him as a Blue. He was as pasty as me.

I pulled the knife from the body and a flap of skin peeled back, like latex, revealing the true skin beneath. Yeah. A suit.

The Goon had disguised himself as a rubberduck to come on planet and get his rocks off. He'd just picked up the wrong sick lizard. No doubt, he and Jimmy had come here for a little playtime and then everything had gone south. Pretty standard story. With one, big, fat Blue twist.

"It's all set, Tig," Jimmy said as he sidled up to me. "All set. She'll be here in a tick."

"After she drops off the skimmer, get rid of her. She can't even suspect what we're doing. Got it?"

"Right. I'll tell her it's a delivery."

Whatever.

I stayed in the shadows as Jimmy met the Nard. She didn't even glance in my direction. Probably knew better. But if she was tanging Jimmy, she would. She took off and Jimmy loped back into the alley carrying the tarp and the acid. Together, we rolled up the Goon, nice and tight. A little Fed burrito. One that could get us both killed.

We dumped the body in the trunk of the beater and headed back to clean up the scene. Not one drop of blue blood could remain.

As I approached, my gaze landed on the pile of draw butts on the ground. Anger roiled. Surely not because I wanted them. I smacked Jimmy on the back of his scaly head. "What the hell is wrong with you?"

His nostrils widened. "What, Tig?"

I pointed to the mess he'd made. "Each and every one of those has your freaking DNA on it. Clean that shit up."

"Oh, right, Tig. Sure, Tig." He scuttled over to the butts and scooped them up. I stood and watched with my arms crossed. When he looked at me expectantly, I quirked a brow, because shit. No way was I helping.

I wouldn't touch a draw butt if my life depended on it. And it did.

When he was done, I poured the acid over the pallets, the pavement, everything. It sizzled and popped, eating everything in sight. When it was all pretty much liquefied, I shot a beam over the site to check it out, just to be sure any evidence was gone. Nothing left. Just a puddle of goo.

"What are we gonna do with the body, Tig?" Jimmy asked as we headed for the Nard's beater.

I shot him a look. He knew. We both knew. There was only one place it could go.

"Jesus, Tig. The Kase?"

I snorted and slid into the driver's seat, turned the key, and the skimmer powered up.

Jimmy slumped into the passenger seat. "Pflerg."

Thank God Sandman was home. He probably wished he weren't. I knocked on his door and waited while he hid any incriminating evidence of his profession. I always did him the favor of respecting his, ahem, privacy, and in return he did me favors.

I needed a favor tonight. A big one.

He opened the door and greeted me with a huge, toothy smile. "Tig."

"Sandman."

"Come in. Come in." He ushered me into his shithole apartment. His old lady peeped at me through the cracked bedroom door, but when our gazes clashed, she melted away.

Sandman strolled into the shabby kitchenette, leaving a dusting of grit in his wake, and slid into one of the chairs. I took the other. "Come by for some chud?"

I frowned at him. "I told you, I gave that up."

"Still?"

"Yeah."

He leaned forward and the table groaned against his weight. "Never pegged you as a quitter, Tig."

I snorted a laugh. "Some things are good to quit."

"Everybody needs a little playtime," he said with a chuckle, one that sent a spray of sand over the tabletop. "You shouldn't be such a preacher."

"You know it ain't playtime for me." It was my all. My everything. *That* was the problem with it.

He smirked. "Gotta love a righteous convert."

Hardly. "I just know what's best for me."

He offered me a show of teeth. "How is being clean good for anybody?"

There was no response to that. Not to a dealer. "Look, I need a favor."

His grin faded. "Really? You? Coming to me? Asking for a favor?" He drummed his fingers on the table, making the thin layer of grit there dance. "Kinda lopsided, isn't it?"

"Is it?"

"Seems to me, you owe me already."

What? I glared at him. Adjusted my gloves. He wasn't cowed. "What for?"

He cleared his throat and said, in a gravelly tone, "You know. That tip on Brimms."

Seriously? "Dropping a dime on your competition was a favor to me?"

"Got you a nice, fat collar. Made Granny happy."

"Right. Same way it'll make him happy to know you're dealing chud in Roxy? Last time I checked, that was his territory . . . at least, according to the accord."

Sandy shifted in his seat. His eyes flicked around the room. His back plates bristled. All signs he was gonna bolt.

I held up a hand. "But look. That's not what this is about. I need to borrow your pass key to the gate." We both knew which gate I was talking about.

His eyes widened. His lips worked. Before he could ask, I shook my head. "Better you don't know."

"Right." He stared at me for a while and then stood and loped over to his safe, which was sunken into the floor. It took him a second to punch in the code and pull out a fat key on a chain. "I need it back by morning."

"Won't take me that long," I said. "I'll have it back in an hour."

All I needed to do was dump a body.

Sulfuric acid was nice. It destroyed almost anything. But it was always possible for some nerdy, techass Fed to find something. Some evidence. Some clues. Some DNA.

The Kase was a different story altogether. It was like a river of antimatter snarling along a groove in the space-time continuum. It ate up anything it touched. Disappeared things in a very permanent way. Particle by particle.

When they'd first settled this planet, the Fed had contained the leak in a millennium shield, turning it in on itself like a caustic ouroboros. No doubt they used it as their own garbage disposal.

Naturally, none of the cons were allowed through the gate. But hell, we were cons.

We were kind of here because we did what we wanted regardless of the rules.

We all knew that if you wanted something to go away forever, the Kase was the place. But it was dangerous. One drop of that shit on you, and you were toast. It would crawl all over you, expanding as it chewed you up, eating you alive until nothing was left. I'd seen it happen. Not something I wanted to see again. The trick was to drop in a body without any splash back.

As one of Granny's enforcers, I'd been to the Kase more than once. I knew where the walls were highest, where the drop was safest.

Granny had his own key to the back gate, the one no one guarded, but I'd already made up my mind not to tell Granny about this. This was too big for even him to handle and there was always the chance that to save himself, he would roll over on me. And that was not going to happen. I wasn't anyone's patsy.

So I would handle this myself.

If I were really smart and heartless, I'd make sure Jimmy tripped and fell into the river too, but I figured this favor far outweighed what I owed him, and this was a string I could tug whenever I needed to. Could be useful.

No doubt these thoughts were flickering through his reptilian brain as well, judging from the way his eyes danced nervously around as we made our way through the back streets to the Rursus Gate, past squalid tenements, empty warehouses, and dilapidated speakeasies silenced by the early morning hour. Jimmy's fingers were twitchy too. His tongue flickered in and out, tasting the air.

"Relax," I said as we pulled into the shadows next to an industrial dumpster waiting for tomorrow's burn. I cupped his cheek and made him meet my eye. "It's gonna be cool, Jimmy. I got your back."

He narrowed his eyes and studied me. His Adam's apples wobbled. It was a weird thing to watch because Dinks had two gullets and they swallowed at different intervals. "You sure, Tig?"

Holy crap. I hated reassuring people. Just on principle. But this was important, or Jimmy might panic and I might be the poor schmuck taking a swim in eternity. "What you did for me? Last week? I owe you, brother." That didn't seem to convince him. Not wholly, so I added, with a snarky grin, "Besides, I like having a little more dirt on a snitch."

His eyes flared. "I ain't no snitch, Tig."

I patted his cheek, a little harder than necessary, steeled my expression. "After this? You're my snitch. Got it?"

His scaly mouth fell open, but he nodded. I saw the relief flicker though his eyes and I knew he'd swallowed my so-sincere reassurance, hook, line, and sinker.

I fixed a confident smile on my face and tugged on my gloves. "Let's do this thing, shall we?"

"Right, Tig. Right."

It was a good thing I was being honest, because he was far too trusting. If he kept that sentimental shit up, it would probably get him killed.

TWO

Jimmy and I worked together to haul the tarp-wrapped body from the trunk, but I think it's fair to say I did most of the work. Jimmy mostly complained about how heavy the Goon was. When I told him to shut up, he proceeded to whine beneath his breath, which was even more annoying.

We both silenced and froze when, just as we were about to round the dumpster, a wheezy laugh drifted toward us on the night air.

I eased the body to the ground and peered around the corner, and my gut clenched. Shit. Two munis, a Raven and a Rat, had exited the gate and were heading right for us. What were the odds that someone else would be making use of this cosmic garbage dump?

I left the body where it was, hoping the dark tarp would render it invisible in the shadows, and shoved Jimmy back behind the dumpster. He issued a high-pitched yip and I almost strangled him then and there. If those munis heard and investigated, I'd have no choice but to take them on, which would only complicate things.

Especially if they killed me.

I hunched there, holding my breath and counting the heartbeats as the Raven and Rat paused to light up some chud. The smoke found me, of course, making my pulse thunder. I clenched my teeth and ignored it. I tried to focus on their conversation, some pointless banter about a whorehouse they'd visited on the Strand. It seemed to go on forever.

Finally—finally—they moved on. Far too slowly, as it happened, shambling away down a side street as my heart beat a painful tattoo in my temple. Even after they'd disappeared from sight, even after their voices ceased to echo off the cold stone walls, I waited.

Jimmy tugged at my jacket. "Let's go," he hissed.

My instincts, awake and screaming, knew we needed to wait. Knew we needed to let those munis have more distance from the Kase. I smacked Jimmy away. "Shut up." I peered into the shadows for a good ten minutes longer before I felt comfortable emerging, and even then, I did so stealthily.

I headed out first and, using Sandman's key, opened the gate, then went back for Jimmy and the body. We carried it up the ramp and onto the tungstanium bulwark containing the caustic swill of the Kase.

We both knew better than to throw things into the Kase all willy-nilly. With supreme care, we gently rolled the wrapped body into the inky, viscous waters of the Kase. The river writhed with what seemed like pleasure as it undulated over the Fed's body, bubbling and spitting as the darkness consumed every atom. We didn't leave until the body was completely submerged, not until the very last blurp.

When it was done, I turned to Jimmy and adjusted my gloves. "Not a word," I growled threateningly, even though I knew he would never tell. At least not intentionally. But I wouldn't put it past Jimmy to get skanked and brag to his friends about offing a Fed.

"I ain't gonna talk, Tig" he said in a whiny little voice.

"I'll gut you from stem to stern if I so much as suspect you talked. To anyone."

His nostrils flared. Probably in response to my menace. Not that I was dubious about his ability to keep a secret, but I was.

"I won't. I swear."

"You'd better not. It's both our asses if you do."

"I know, Tig. I know."

I adjusted my gloves again, just to make a point. Jimmy nodded in my direction—not making eye contact—and then he scuttled away into the night.

After taking a moment to collect myself, to calm my still-thudding heart, I eased into the skimmer, returned the key to Sandy, then headed back to the office to check out.

The station house was smack dab in the middle of town, where Granny's tentacles could reach far and wide. It was an unremarkable brick brownstone taking up an entire unremarkable block, but don't let the mundanity fool you. Lots of nasty shit went down inside.

The bottom floors were muni offices. The Skeegs all lived in dorms on four and five, and Granny's place took up the entire top floor. He lived there. Rarely left.

It was way past my bedtime, hours past in fact, but Granny got twitchy when his munis didn't check in. It should have taken me five minutes tops, but Boggs met me at the door. I grimaced. Boggs always complicated things.

He was Granny's muscle, a big bulging Trog with a row of spikes running down his back to his stumpy tail. We had a grudging respect for each other, but only grudging. Trogs weren't the sharpest tong on the pitchfork, but then, they didn't need to be. A Trog could flatten a man with one fist. Literally. I'd seen more than one perp pancaked like that. Hell of a mess to clean up. Took a spatula.

Boggs was usually right there at Granny's side, but tonight he sat at the front desk next to Doris, picking his teeth with an Ozzie fang. Called it his toothpick. His idea of a joke. The fact that he wasn't on the top floor guarding Granny's back should have tipped me off. When he saw me, he straightened. "Hey, Earthie. Where you been?"

I handed my laser pistol to Doris, the duty clerk, and glanced up at Boggs. "Cleaning up shit."

"Yeah. Granny's been lookin' for you. Got a job."

Hell. I shouldn't have gone back to the office to sign out. Should have gone straight home and sunk into a bottle of Lurian Ease. Too late now. When Granny snapped his fingers, I jumped. We all did. I followed Boggs to the elevator. The door closed with a metallic clang and we lurched up to the top floor. The whole while, he kept his beady black eyes on me, like I was going to escape or something. It was damned unnerving.

Scale was waiting for me in the foyer that served as Granny's reception area. It was late, so the clerk was gone, but Scale sat at the desk, overpowering it with his bulk, sharpening his knives. Not that he had it in for me or anything. He just liked sharpening his knives. More than one guy who'd come up against Granny had gone for a swim in the Kase, but those were the lucky ones. The unlucky ones got to have a chat with Scale. And his knives.

Scale really enjoyed his work.

I didn't even like to think about that sick bastard.

He was a Dargum, a species related to Dinks, with the singular distinction that Dargumi were vicious as hell. They were larger than Dinks and had sharper teeth, longer claws, and sadistic proclivities. I had adopted the policy to avoid Scale as much as humanly possible.

I nodded to him, trying to ignore the incessant, menacing slide of metal on whetstone.

He narrowed his eyes and growled.

Such a socialite.

I lifted my arms. "Granny wants to see me."

Scale dropped his knife on the desk in a clatter and patted

me down. It was just procedure and I knew it, but it pissed me off. I was a loyal muni. I didn't appreciate the distrust. But then, distrust was why Granny was still alive.

The pat-down was rough—rougher than usual. That, combined with Scale's malicious glower, only increased my trepidation. The thought flittered through my brain that Granny might know about my recent crimes, that I was heading into something nasty. I tried to ignore the prickles on my nape and act casual, but it cost me.

Once Scale was sure I wasn't carrying anything, he waved me into Granny's office and then, to my dismay, followed me in.

It was a plush room, with mahogany furniture and damask fabric stretched on the wall. It looked like a bordello from a 1900s Western. But then, Granny had always been a fan of Earthie vids.

The boss was standing by the window and staring down at the street; his bulk blocked out the light from the windows, sending shadows skittering in the dim lamplight.

When the door slammed closed, he turned. His fat jowls shuddered and his thick, froggy lips pursed when he saw me. He waddled over to his desk and sat with a huge gust. Granny was six hundred stones if he was an ounce. Rolls of fat draped over the arms of the chair and his chins dribbled down his chest. He jiggled like Jell-O with every wheezy breath, but don't let the visual fool you.

He was a tough motherfucker. I'd seen him take twenty bullets from a semi-automatic and just spit them out. Aside from that, he was smart. The smartest con on the planet. He'd arrived here with nothing, just like the rest of us, and built an empire on sheer will alone. There was nothing—*nothing*—he wouldn't do to keep all that safe.

Back on his home planet of Creel, Granny had been a mafia kingpin. He got sent up on some bogus tax evasion charge, though everyone knew he'd done much worse.

Didn't take him long to seize power. Once he got control of the weather dome, he practically had it all. You don't mess with a guy who can make it rain on a desert planet. After that, he quickly unified all the banners—except those on the outskirts, in the Barrens, who weren't worth worrying about. Capos who wouldn't sign the accord simply disappeared in the Kase.

The result was something that—most days—resembled actual peace.

The upside to Granny's reign was that there was less bloodshed. The downside was Granny's reign.

He was damn near omnipotent, and we all know that absolute power corrupts . . . absolutely.

He studied me—a silence punctuated only by his rasping breath—and then flicked the ash of his stogie. God knew where he got Cuban cigars. "Sit." He gestured to the chair on the other side of his desk. He nodded at Scale to take the other.

My heart thrummed. My throat tightened.

If Scale was in on the convo, this wasn't a casual check-in.

"Busy night, Tig?" the boss man asked in that low, rumbling voice.

A snarl of panic howled through me. I swallowed heavily and fixed a blasé expression on my face. "Every night is a busy night, Granny," I said with a forced laugh.

"I understand you got a *personal* request call?" He spat the word. Granny had little use for personal relationships. Not if they didn't put gold or power in his pocket.

"Yeah." I adjusted my gloves. Sucked in a deep, calming breath. "Jimmy Bluenote called in a favor. He, ah, wandered into a swamp. Needed a tow."

Granny studied me for a long, hard moment. I hoped he couldn't see my thrumming pulse. "So . . ." A croak. "Does a Dink owe us a favor now?"

I blinked and then relaxed a little at the turn the conversation had taken. If Granny knew the truth about tonight, that question would have been very different. But, I was not a fool. I didn't relax too much. I smiled and said, "I believe he might." And then some. But Granny didn't need to know the deets. No one did. This one would go with me to my grave. Hopefully, not too soon.

"And the DB?"

"Taken care of." That wasn't what he was asking, but it was all I was sayin'.

Granny's gaze burned me. I let it. Not crackin'. Not for all the chud in Chinatown.

Yeah, Granny was my boss, and a vicious motherfucker, but he didn't respect a man who couldn't give him a little pushback. Trick was, not giving too much. And the line was blurry.

Thank God, he relented. His lashes lowered. "Well. Okay then." He tapped the stogie on the ashtray. His heavy breathing bubbled through the room. His tongue slid out and wet his thick lips. "Hear you sent the Skeeg home."

Oh, hell. "Yeah."

"Why?"

I snorted. "He was stinking up the place." Yeah. And that eye. Watching me.

Granny's eyes narrowed into slits and he hissed a little. Might have been some Creel profanity. I didn't take it personally. After a minute of that steely inspection, he shook his stogie at me and grated, "Don't do that again. We keep the Skeegs for good reason."

I forced a grin. "Because they smell nice?"

"You need to be a little more tolerant of other species." This, he said with a smile. It was mostly teeth. "That's the trouble with you Earthies. Only one dominant species on the HP makes you think you're hot snot."

Yeah. I wasn't hot snot on my home planet, or any planet. And I knew it. I grinned anyway.

Granny took another puff on the stogie and studied me through the smoke. "Your Skeeg is dealing with some . . . health issues. I can get you another partner if you want."

Don't know why something tugged in the region of my heart. Couldn't imagine One Eye faring well with Tularney or Boggs. They'd chew him up and spit him out. He was a stinky, slimy Frog, with only one eye, but he'd saved my ass more than once. Besides, better the devil you know. Last thing I wanted was the hassle of breaking in a new partner. "Naw."

Those fat lips might have quirked up. A little. "All right. But it's on you. I don't want to see you without your backup again."

I would not—if I lived to be a hundred—understand Granny's love affair with the Skeegs. Sure, they both came from the same home planet, but all that shit went out the window when you came to a place like this.

Not that I would know. Earthies were rare. Hardly ever made it past intake. It sucked being all soft and squishy.

"I want to hear it, Tig."

"Yes, sir."

"No exceptions. Understand?" His intensity was a little unsettling.

"Sure."

"I mean it."

Blood-chilling, hard-ass mob boss or not, he was starting to tick me off. "I got it."

He stared at me for a long while. Sending a message, perhaps. I think I got it. *Keep the Skeeg in my back pocket.* Right.

I made a mental note to stock up on fresh towels.

When his perusal got a little too uncomfortable, I shifted and said, "Boggs said you had a job for me?"

Granny grunted and sifted through a jumbled of slips on the desktop. "Yeah. I want you to pick up a package arriving on the 215 tomorrow."

Oh, super awesome. Now I was a delivery boy. I tried not to let the bile seep into my words. "What is it?"

"Sweet meat."

"A novitiate?" That should piss off the Sisterhood.

"It's an important package, Tig. Make sure she gets here."

"Mother Superior won't be pleased if you detain one of her babies."

Granny barked a laugh. "That ship has sailed."

Oh. Holy. Fuck.

I hadn't known that. The accord with the Sisterhood had been broken? It was not good news. When one accord fails, others are bound to tumble behind it.

Granny must have seen the look on my face. He leaned closer. His fetid breath washed over me. "This is important, kid. This is the big one. It was worth the risk."

"Those nuns are mean sons of bitches."

His brow rumpled. "Not *sons* at all." They weren't. Female, each and every one.

I sighed. "It's an expression." But female or not, they were mean sons of bitches. Most had been consigned to Viridian for political dissent against the Fed, but to assume they weren't just as dangerous as the hardened criminals on this rock was a fatal error. No man had ever ventured into the Hive and escaped their clutches alive—including the slaves they kept for God-knew-what-purpose. The sisters would not appreciate Granny detaining one of their girls. Our only saving grace was that they were too far away—out in the Barrens—to find out. At least, for a while.

Of course, they probably had informants here. And I had to assume they were sending someone to meet her. This shit could get tricky.

Granny slid the slip and a photo across the table through the draw ash and the crabnut shells.

I slid it right back. "Can't you get Boomer on it?"

"Boomer's on a job. Besides, this one is tailor-made for you. Just look at this, honey." He held up the pic. My gaze lit on it, and something in my chest pinched. She was gorgeous. Blonde hair, curvy bod, truly epic rack . . . humanoid. And her face. Ah, hell. Her face. She was a freaking angel.

I shook my head. The second to the last thing I needed was a hot piece of ass.

"Look, pretty boy." Shit. Granny only called me that when he was about to go on a rant. And yeah. Here it came. "Remember who saved your ass. If it weren't for me, you'd be takin' it up the tube in some pleasure house on the Strand about now."

Not true. I'd be dead. I'd have gutted any Krill or Oakie who tried to ream me and been gutted in return.

Granny grinned, a huge, toothy monstrosity. His tongue lapped at his fleshy lips. "Come on, pretty boy. This one is a piece of cake. We need her." His expression darkened and he glared at me. Making a point, I guess. "And we need her whole."

That pissed me off big time. "I am not in the habit of carving up women."

No idea why Scale snorted a laugh. But then, I didn't want one.

"Of course you're not." Granny sucked on his stogie. "That's why it has to be you. I know she'll get here in one piece."

I glanced at the pic again, and a shiver skittered down my spine. It might have nested in my balls. Yeah. A delectable little nugget like this? Even one of Granny's hardcore munis would be tempted to take a taste. Hell, even I was tempted.

"I may not be your best guy for this," I muttered, shifting in my seat. Yeah. Something was getting uncomfortable.

Granny snorted in a wet spray. "Tig. You're practically a monk."

Scale chuckled, a filthy rumble. "What better *man* to escort a nun?"

I glared at him. He had no idea. No idea who or what I was. He had no clue what had led me here. No concept of how dangerous I could be.

"Do the job, Tig. I . . . trust you." Granny's tone was silky. Way too silky. "And as insurance?"

"Yeah?"

"Take the Skeeg."

Right.

With One Eye watching me, no way any of this could go the way my fantasies were tugging.

But it hardly mattered, did it? She was a novitiate of the Sisterhood. From everything I'd heard, they were celibate and eschewed men as a general rule. Killed them as a matter of ritual. Maybe even sucked on their bones. And not in a good way.

Even if I wanted her—and I did—she would want nothing to do with me. Not the muni charged with seizing her and delivering her to the enemy. It was all good.

"Okay."

"And you'll be there? Meet the transport tomorrow?"

"Wouldn't miss it for the world."

He glared at me. I guess he didn't appreciate the humor. "Don't be late," he grumbled. And then, as I stood to leave the room, "And don't forget the Skeeg."

Right.

I was beat to hell as I pulled off my gloves and made my way home. It had been a helluva day. I wanted nothing more than to collapse into my bed. Maybe with a belly full of booze.

For the first time in a long time, the thought of a draw didn't even interest me.

That was damn tired.

I clomped up the stairs to my third-floor apartment nearly in a daze. But shit, I wasn't so gone I didn't notice the fact that the light was out on the landing. I went on instant alert. All my malaise and exhaustion washed away. I pulled out my pistol (not the muni piece, the illegal one) and crept closer, peering around the bannister to see if anyone was there. It was clear but—hell—my door was open a crack.

Pretty sure I hadn't left it that way. Pretty sure I never did.

My heart thrummed up into my throat. My vision went a little blurry as my pulse ticked. I sucked in a breath and eased up one step, two. I skipped the one that creaked and scuttled onto the landing, then, holding my piece up before my face, I opened the door with the barrel.

The creak of the hinges seemed to scream into the night.

I winced and waited, listening, scanning.

Nothing.

Slowly, I eased in. One step. Two. Constantly checking and rechecking the shadows for movement. For something. But all was silent, still. All was—

"Tig."

Hell. That voice, sultry and low, slid over my skin. I dropped my head against the doorjamb and drew in a calming breath. It didn't help. I flicked on the light and turned. She sat at my piece-of-shit table in my piece-of-shit apartment, sucking on a draw stick. I should have smelled it. I should have known.

I should have run.

It was a goddamn shame she looked so damn gorgeous, with that leather bustier thrusting those big, blue boobs out like that, her slick latex uniform cupping every curve with an intimacy that should be reserved for the bedroom, her features, exotic and flawless, fixed in an ever-innocent mien. It was a goddamn shame because I wanted to put a bullet in her.

"Long time, Tig."

Not long enough. I pushed into the room and dropped my piece onto the table. "What do you want, Mia?"

"Want? Me?" She shot a look at her partner, a stick-up-the-ass stiff who sat next to her with one of my beers open in front of him, stroking the sweating bottle with azure fingers. Guess they'd been waiting a while. "What makes you think I want anything?"

"You're here?" I snorted.

She held up a slender stick. "You still on the draw?"

Like she didn't know. I frowned at her. "Haven't huffed in six months."

"Six whole months? Wow, Tig. Pretty impressive." Her tone belied any sincerity she was shooting for. But then, she always had been a bitch of the first order.

"Look, Mia. I'm tired. It's been a long day. Just tell me what you want and get out. Okay?"

She put out a lip. Her seductive expression told me what was coming. Weird how I could read her so easily when it didn't really matter. On the big stuff, she always blindsided me. "Is that any way to talk to your lover, baby?" She stood and tried to wrap her arms around me.

I unwrapped her. "You're not my lover. And I'm nothing to you but a tool in your toolbox. Let's not pretend this is anything but what it is."

"So cynical."

I offered a grin, something with teeth. "That's what happens when you get fucked over one time too many."

"Only one time?" A pout.

God, she was gorgeous. It should be against the law for a woman to be that beautiful and so filled with evil.

I headed to the icebox, pulled out some Lurian Ease, and poured myself a couple fingers. None for her. Then I dropped into the chair by the table. "What do you want?"

She looked at her Goon. He nodded and shuffled from the kitchen into the living room. I kept an eye on him. Didn't like the idea of him riffling through my shit.

"Word is, the Sisterhood has a shipment coming in."

She said it all casual and slick, but it still sent a shard of alarm up my neck. I took a real nonchalant sip of my drink and grunted.

"Word is, there are a lot of interested parties."

Good to know.

The Goon in the living room started flicking through my vids. I cracked my knuckles one at a time.

Mia sidled closer. It did not enhance my calm. "We know Granny wants you to pick her up. Bring her in. But, Tig . . ." She waited until she had my attention. It took a while.

"We don't want you to take her to Granny."

Shit.

"Why don't you just pick her up yourself?" Hell, they were the Fed. They could tap anyone they wanted.

Mia sighed. "It's not *her* we want, Tig. It's what she's carrying."

"And what is that, exactly?"

Mia shrugged. "Intel? Maybe?"

"You don't fucking know?

"Watch your fucking tongue." She grinned so I'd know she was kidding, but I hardly needed the clue; her mouth was like a toilet. Especially in bed. She got really dirty there.

I forced those thoughts from my mind. It took some effort.

Apparently this abstinence thing wasn't working for me. Apparently I needed to get laid.

"What exactly are you asking me to do here, Mia?"

She shrugged. "Pick the girl up, like you're supposed to do. Just . . . don't take her to Granny."

Oh, sure. Right. Just kind of disobey the biggest, meanest

mob boss this side of the Crab Nebula? On a whim? "Where the hell do I take her? Can't bring her here."

Mia looked around. Her nose curled. "Nah. You can't. This place is a dump."

It wasn't that bad.

Or maybe it was.

Point being, "What do you want me to *do* with her?"

"Isn't that obvious?"

"Not really." With Mia, nothing ever was. Her plots and plans folded in on each other like an Escher drawing. I never really knew what she was up to, what her angle was.

She sighed. There might have been impatience threaded in the sound. "Escort her to the Hive."

What.

The.

Actual.

Fuck.

I gaped at her. "You want me to help the novitiate make it to the Sisterhood?"

Worse, she wanted me to walk into the Barrens? On purpose?

Mia fluttered her long, blue lashes.

I shook my head. "Those bitches eat little boys like me for breakfast."

She made a derisive moue. On her perfect features, it was still goddamn pretty. "They won't eat you. You're . . . doing them a favor."

Right. "Like leading the Fed to their door?"

"This is bigger than a simple bust. They're doing something out there in the desert, Tig. I know it, my bosses know it. Everyone knows it. If I can figure out what it is, if I can bust them, this could make my career. And that little girl is the key. You pick her up. Transport her safely. Deliver her to the Sisterhood in one piece."

"And then what?" How the hell was I supposed to live on this planet if I betrayed Granny? He decided who drew breath each day. Who got rich and who starved. Hell, he decided when it fucking rained. Nothing happened without his say so. Nothing.

Mia patted my hand. "You leave that up to me."

I eyed her cynically. "Last time I trusted you, someone ended up dead."

Mia paled. "None of that was supposed to happen—"

"But it did."

"And it's beside the point."

"Is it?"

"Look, Tig. We need your help, and you're gonna help us."

"Really?" I'd helped her before. Got jacked. Not likely to happen again. And she knew it. Which begged the question, what the hell was she doing here? Slumming? Groveling?

She picked up her lighter and fiddled with it, insouciantly, sexually, as though she was giving it a nice, slow hand job. When she circled the tip with her blue-tinged nail, I had to look away. "What's the sentence for offing a Blue again?" she asked softly. "I forget."

My gut lurched.

Goddamn bitch. She hadn't forgotten what happened to a poor soul who offed a Blue. No one ever did. Not here.

I swallowed and raked back my hair. "I have no idea what you're talking about, Mia."

"Don't you?" I was getting tired of her cooing voice. She finally lit her draw, and as she did, watched me over the flare of her flame. Hunger crawled in my belly. She was the devil's spawn, for sure.

"I didn't off a Blue," I snapped.

"No. You didn't." Her smile sent prickles all over my skin, like Scards in mating season. "Jimmy did."

Oh. Fuck.

Her lips curled in a heinous smile. "And what do you suppose the sentence is for aiding and abetting?"

"I didn't aid—"

"Cut the crap, Tig." She stubbed out the draw. I stared at it. Tried to silence the wailing hunger. "We have it on wire."

My gaze snapped to hers at that. And my heart lurched. My ass clenched. Fuck Jimmy and his fucked-up shit. I'd really screwed the pooch this time. Her hot gaze sizzled into mine. Silence, intense and virulent, snarled through the room as a horrible realization settled in my gut.

I'd been set up.

Played.

Like a patsy.

I swallowed, slow. Tried to form the words, though my lips were numb. "So . . . Jimmy's workin' for you?" Hard to think I'd been set up by the stupidest lizard-brain in the lockup.

But Mia blew out a laugh and tipped her head to the side. "Nah. That, my friend, was a lucky accident."

Right. A lucky accident they happened to get on wire. Just when they needed me to do them a favor.

I was so screwed.

I was gonna kill Jimmy next time I saw him. No doubt.

Mia sent me a too-sweet smile. "It won't go over well with the PTB when it comes out that a convict shivved a Fed on planet."

"A Fed who came down for a little playtime."

She sniffed. "No one cares about that. But a citizen? Murdered by a con? Now that will make the news on the home planet. That will stir up some shit."

No kidding. They would probably nuke the whole shebang. And sit back and watch. Maybe roast some marshmallows.

"But no one needs to know. You do this one little thing,

and I'll make the vid of you and Jimmy dumping a Fed in the Kase disappear."

I settled back and crossed my arms. "Why should I care? I cross Granny and I'm a dead man anyway."

"Granny won't be around forever."

What the hell did that mean?

"When he steps down, someone has to take his place as boss."

I stared at her. I had no idea what she was saying. It sure as hell wouldn't be me. And I wouldn't want the gig. Hell, I'd be dead in a week if I tried to step into his shoes. I must have shook my head because she blew out a sigh and tried another tactic. "We can keep you safe."

"From the mob?" Seriously? Was she talking about witness relocation or some shit? On Viridian? What a joke. Might as well take a swan dive into the river myself. "It's a small planet, Mia. They will find me."

She shrugged. "Technically, it's a moon."

"Don't go getting all technical on me, baby," I smirked. "That never ends well."

Her eyes narrowed at the reference to the last time we'd "worked" together. The debacle still burned at the edges of my soul.

"We can relocate you to another colony."

Oh, awesome. Where I could start over. At the bottom of the heap. Like a dream come fucking true.

Her expression hardened. "With cred."

"You are a crazy bitch, Mia."

"I don't know why you're being difficult here, Tig. It's not like you have a lot of choices. You escort the girl. I lose the paperwork on tonight's clusterfuck, and when it's over, we set you up. Nice and tidy. Somewhere else."

"Yeah. Right." I didn't look at her. Couldn't stomach it. We both knew it would never, get that far. The second I didn't deliver the package to Granny, he would call in the infantry. Maybe even put a bounty on my head. Everyone from the Ozzies to the Swan Cartel would be after me.

I would never make it to the Hive.

Hell, I'd be lucky to make it out of town.

And Mia knew it.

She set her hand on mine. "Don't fret about it, Tig," she said in that soft, cooing voice. "You know I have your back."

I met her eyes at that. Stared at her. Thought about Ella and Skinny and the clusterfuck-that-was. "Do you?" The words came out harsh, grated, like my soul.

Mia stared right back. She gave my hand a squeeze. "Meet the 215. Don't be late." And then she stood, nodded to her partner, and strolled out of my apartment, leaving a nuclear blast zone in her wake.

She always did.

I sighed and glanced at the plate she'd been using as an ashtray. It was littered with butts. The residual smell curled through my nostrils and made my heart thump hopefully.

But I steeled my spine. I dumped the ashtray and the goddamn butts in the toilet. As much as my body screamed for it, I couldn't afford to indulge. For one thing, it had cost me a lot to get clean. And for another, I was in deep shit, and I had some serious thinking to do.

THREE

I laid awake all night, playing the scenarios.

Stupid of me because I really needed the sleep, and in the morning, I was right where I'd been the night before. There was no smart move here. No brilliant exit strategy. No escape.

Both of my options came with lethal consequences.

Do as Mia asked, and Granny would flay me alive.

Stay loyal to Granny, and Mia would see me executed.

No matter how I looked at it, I couldn't see a way out.

A better use of my time would have been writing my last will and testament. Pity no one gave a damn if I lived or died. Also, I didn't have anything worth the ink to write a will. Barely a pot to piss in.

I had no idea why all this was falling on me, but I had to believe it was probably karma. My past was bound to catch up to me at some point.

I was fuzzy as I dressed for work, so I set an alarm on my watch for 2:00 so I wouldn't miss the transport. Then I went into the kitchen and made a pot of go-jo. Kind of like coffee, but coffee in hyperdrive. A couple snorts of that and I was all good again. When it wore off, I'd crash and burn, though. I set another alarm, so the crash wouldn't catch me off guard. I had a good ten hours before the swirls would hit me.

If I decided to deliver the package to Granny, it wouldn't be a problem. That was a quick drop. But if I decided to make a run for the Barrens . . .

The conflict blew through me again. I didn't like the way it twisted up my bowels. Didn't like the crawl of acid in my throat. Sure as hell didn't like the hum it set up in my head. I needed to be clear, today of all days.

I blew out a breath and raked back my hair. Either way, it was going to be a shitty day. I had several hours before I had to be at the depot, before I had to make a real hard choice, so I decided to just play it out and see where I was when the time came.

Maybe I'd get lucky and catch a bullet before I had to make up my mind.

A guy can hope.

I sent one quick look around my apartment. It wasn't lost on me that, no matter what happened, it was probably the last time I'd ever be here. I had a hard time feeling any regret over that.

With a sigh, I pulled on my muni gloves and headed out.

Just another day in paradise.

As I came up to the station house, it was clear that something had hit the fan. I could only hope it was shit. The place was crawling with Trogs and Ravens. There were even a couple Rats sniffing around. I parked my skimmer and pushed through the crowd, heading for the door.

Boggs was stationed at the top of the stoop next to the thick, wooden double doors, ostensibly to discourage unauthorized personnel from entering. I sidled up next to him. "What's going on?" I asked in an undertone.

His spikes riffled. He banked his thick head toward the lobby. "Someone left us a present last night."

I shoved my hands into my pockets, scanned the street. The intensity of the milling crowd was manic. "Nice of them."

"Yeah." A snort. "Five bodies."

Really? Delivered to the station house? To Granny's doorstep?

This was not normal. Not at all. No one would dare. No doubt it meant one of the rival gangs was getting antsy. No doubt it meant one of the accords was about to go south. Oddly, I didn't give a whole lot of shits. I had other things on my mind today. If everything blew up on Viridian, it only worked in my favor at the moment. You know. Distract everyone.

"Any idea who it was?"

Boggs shot me a look. "No. A weird collection, man. No rhyme or reason."

"And the security footage of the drop?"

"Static."

Holy hell. Who had that kind of pull? Get in. Get out. Wipe the evidence? In the most highly guarded bunker on the planet? A shiver prickled at my nape. This was getting weirder and weirder. "Inside job?"

Boggs sucked on his teeth. "Maybe. Granny is asking us all to come in."

Yay. I knew what that meant. Interrogation. The craptastic icing on my shitcake. "Right." I nodded to the Trog. "Better get to it."

"Have fun."

I snorted and headed inside.

It wasn't any better in there. The lobby, usually quiet and calm, was filled with munis, pacing, grumbling, and muttering among themselves. I noticed that they'd all polarized. The Trogs were with the Trogs. Ravens with the Ravens. Skeegs with the Skeegs. Not a good sign. As munis, we had one rule: All for one. A muni was a muni. It didn't matter where you hailed from. Didn't matter the color of your skin or whether you had a tail or eye stalks. We all protected each other. Everyone respected the glove.

This kind of division wasn't good for anyone.

Especially me. Because I was the only Earthie. In this mix, I was all alone. All. Alone.

I put a swagger in my gait as I headed for the desk, ignoring the creak of the old hardwood floors beneath my feet and the rising scent of alien angst. I was aware of the eyes following me but pretended I didn't have a care in the world as I leaned on the front counter and shot a flirty grin at Doris.

She was a . . . large woman, a Capuchin with a furry face and sharp teeth. It was her job to check us in and to hand out and collect our laser weapons before and after shift. She graciously turned a blind eye to the illegal pieces most of us carried. In my case, it was a rare Earth Glock that I'd confiscated on a raid. I loved that weapon.

Doris was a tough cookie, but she had a thing for me. More than once, she'd cornered me in the break room and tried to get something going. I'd always kept it light. Playful. Capuchins could be vicious if crossed. Or insulted. Or mildly irritated. Especially the females. But if anyone knew anything about what was going on, it was Doris, so in this situation, a little light flirtation was worth the risk.

"Morning, darlin'," I said on a purr.

Her lips stretched over her fangs. The fur on the back of her neck rippled. "Morning, pretty boy."

"I, uh, hear there's been some excitement."

"Hmm."

"Five bodies?"

"Stiffs." She waggled her bushy brows and conspiratorially glanced in the direction of the conference room.

My pulse ticked. Nothing that happened in the conference room ever ended well. I cleared my throat in a rumble. "Anything I should know?"

Doris blew out a banana-scented breath. "No one knows anything. Everyone is on edge. Granny's on a rampage."

"I can imagine."

Her gaze flicked over the lobby. She leaned closer and set her paw on my arm, squeezing tenderly. "Watch your back, Tig. This is dangerous."

Yeah. And so was flirting with a Capuchin. But it was a means to an end. And when all was said and done, I really did like Doris, even though her infatuation sometimes gave me cold sweats.

The door to the conference room slammed open and Granny poked his head out. "Is that Tig?" he roared. "Get your ass in here, boy."

"Hell."

Doris nodded. "Indeed. And, Tig?"

"Yeah?"

"Good luck."

Right.

I nodded and headed for the CR. I was hopped up on go-jo, but that probably wasn't why my heart was slamming the way it was. On that long, slow walk, I tried to calm myself. I tried to remind myself that no matter what all this was about, I was already a dead man, thanks to Mia.

For some reason, the reminder didn't help.

I stepped into the room and glanced at Granny, then Scale, the only two occupants. The long conference table held five covered mounds. The shrouds were spotted with a mélange of colors. Green, black, yellow, brown, and white. I tugged at my gloves—force of habit, I guess—and settled my gaze on Granny. "What we got?" I asked in what I hoped was a blasé tone.

"We got bodies," Granny snarled. "A shitload of them." He leaned closer. "One of them is yours."

What? I blinked.

Granny nodded to Scale, and he whipped off the shrouds. My heart stopped. Stopped. I stared at the bodies. Studied them, one after the other. And with each one, my angst kicked up a notch. Or six.

Likely no one else knew what it meant. No one else got the significance of this particular collection of convicts. No one else realized that this was a message. A message for me.

Jimmy was the first one I saw. Throat slit. Tongue pulled out. Necktie. His sightless eyes stared up at the ceiling.

Sandman laid next to him with a bullet between his eyes.

They really hadn't needed to kill the Nard and Sandman's squeeze to make a point, but they had.

And the point was made.

Clear as day.

There was no one left to back up my story. No one left who'd so much as brushed up against this Blue fiasco.

I was in this all alone now.

With the Feds watching my every move.

Goddamn Mia.

Scale gave me a suspicious stare. His scaly fingers stroked the hilt of his knife. "Any idea who they are?" He asked in a low, rumbling voice.

My gut clenched. How much to tell them? Not much. I couldn't risk it.

"Jimmy's my PI."

Granny's slimy chins juddered as he nodded. He knew this. "And the others?"

"Sandman. My dealer."

My boss' walleyes narrowed. "I thought you were off the draw."

"I am. But he and Jimmy were working a deal. Met through me." A complete and utter lie. But I had to tie them together somehow. Could hardly say, *Yeah, we all went on a little jaunt last night and offed a Blue.*

Scale glanced at Granny and then glared at me with his

trademark suspicion. His plates rippled ominously. "And the others?"

I shook my head. "Maybe they were C.O.W.? Wrong place, wrong time?"

Happened all the time, casualties of war. Innocents getting in the way. Although none of us, really, were innocent. Not here.

Scale snorted and Granny frowned. "Why would anyone dump them here?"

I shrugged. "Maybe Jimmy and Sandy were making a play against you? Maybe this is a warning?"

Granny blew out a shuddering breath. "They were small time. Way too small for that. And not connected. It doesn't make sense."

I looked at the fifth body, the only one I didn't know. He was a White. His feathers were ruffled, bloodied. Something on his neck caught my attention and I pulled back his leathers.

Aw, hell. The little hairs on the back of my neck rippled. "A cygnet?"

Granny crossed his arms, though they barely reached over his enormous chest. "Yeah. I saw that too."

A flicker of trepidation skittered over my skin. "Do you think the Swans are rising up?"

"That was my thought."

"I thought we squashed that, back in '05."

"So did I." Granny's tone was grim. And for good reason. If the Swan Cartel decided to make a move on Granny's turf, it would be bloody.

But that still didn't explain why Mia—or whomever she'd sent to do her dirty work—had dropped a chicken into this shit stew. A familiar annoyance at her and the sick games she liked to play rose within me, but I swallowed it down. I could deal with that later. For the moment, I needed to deal with Granny and set his suspicion at ease. Best way, as always, was to play dumb.

Fortunately, that wasn't a stretch for me. "Okay," I said on a gust. "Where do we go with this?"

The Creel's eyes narrowed. "*We?* We don't go anywhere with this. You have a job to do today."

"You still want me to pick up that package?" Yeah, it was probably delusional of me to think I could squirm out of it that easily.

"Business as usual, son." He lanced me with a speaking gaze. "That is your only priority. Meet that 215. Bring me that package and—"

"And what?"

"Watch your back."

"Right." I scanned the table again, the mystery of the Swan circling in my brain. "Anything else, boss?"

"Naw. You're free to go," he said, but when I reached for the door, he called me back. "Tig?"

"Yeah?"

"Don't forget to take the Skeeg."

I had some time to kill before the pickup, so I grabbed the Skeeg from the dorms over by the station house, picked up my laser pistol from Doris, and headed out to snag a coffee.

And damn if One Eye wasn't even gooier. I gave him the once-over as we headed out of the station house to my skimmer. "What is going on with you?" I asked.

He shrugged and followed me, those Froggy feet slapping a tattoo in my wake.

Thanks to Mia's heads-up, I knew other parties were interested in my package, so I took the precaution of reaching out to Mooney and calling in a favor. Mooney ran the clothing emporium just off the depot. I knew he'd have what I needed.

I took a seat at the coffee shop against the wall and waited for him, sipping an espresso. One Eye took up position at my back.

A few minutes after we sat down, a brood of Whites flocked through the door, losing feathers in their wake. Naturally, they caught my attention, especially after this morning. Aside from that, Whites weren't fans of coffee—made them tweak a little—and I didn't like the way they were eyeing me. They took a table at the far end of the shop and tried to look inconspicuous.

And did I mention they were staring at me?

Fortunately, it didn't take Mooney long to respond to my summons. The bell dinged over the door as he pushed through. As he leaned forward and scanned the shop, his fish eyes squinted. Squigs came from a water world, like my Skeeg; they couldn't see well in the dry.

I decided to help him out and raised a hand so he could see me. He tipped up his chin and waddled over to my table. God, he was dripping. Must have just come from the pool.

Couldn't blame him though. I can't imagine what it would be like to be imprisoned on a desert moon when water was your very life, the air you breathed. Mooney squished into a chair and dropped a wrapped package on the table. He smiled. It was a forced grin. No one liked doing business with a muni. Especially not a guy like Mooney. He liked to keep his nose clean. And wet.

"That it?" I asked.

He nodded and eased the package across the table.

"Is it sterile?"

"What?" His flippers flapped in offense. "Of course it's sterile, Tig. What do you think I'm trying to pull here?"

I shrugged. "Just want to make sure you didn't lift this from some poor leper."

His fat fish lips pouted. "No, Tig. I'd never do that to you. I wouldn't. Not ever."

"Good." I dropped my hand on the package. "Because it's for a special delivery. To Granny." The Squig's throat worked.

"G-G-Granny?"

"Yeah. And I wouldn't want to hand him over something crawling with Scards, now would I?" Those flesh-eating trilobites were the scourge of the planet. We'd pretty much contained them in town, but they were around. And once they crawled under a man's skin, they ate him from the inside out.

Mooney's gaze flicked to the package. His gills frilled out. He made a wet noise and slid the package back across the table. "I'll be right back," he muttered and then scuttled out of the shop.

I leaned back and lit a cigarette, glancing at One Eye. "Miserable, lying fish," I said.

One Eye snorted in response.

I sipped my espresso and smoked my cig down to a nub before Mooney returned. And, aw, he was contrite. How cute.

He handed me the second package. The sterile package. "Here you go, Tig. Sorry, Tig. Sorry for the confusion, Tig."

"Confusion?"

"Yeah. I . . . I thought it was clean . . . but—"

I stood up and glared down at him. "Let's get one thing straight, Mooney. Ain't no one gonna believe you got confused. I report this back to Granny, or Scale, that the Squigs are pushing back, and there's gonna be some kind of fish fry, understand?"

"No. No. Not pushing back. I swear, Tig. It was an honest mistake."

I looked him up and down, took in the sweat on his slimy brow, the wild look in his eye, the tremble of his dorsal fin. There was a lot of sincerity in his fear. I didn't trust sincerity, but I did trust fear.

I tugged at my gloves. "Well, okay then."

"You believe me?" he gushed wetly. "You believe me?"

I frowned at him. Nodded. A tiny tick of my head. "No

clue why. But if I ever, ever, hear of you dicking a muni around again, I'll gut you like a . . ." Well, there was no need to finish that threat. He got it. In fact, I think he pissed a little on the floor.

A damn shame.

This was my favorite coffeehouse. I probably wouldn't be so welcome here after this.

It took a minute to remind myself it didn't matter much because I'd be dead soon.

I nodded to One Eye, who took the wrapped package, and we headed out the door.

Together, we stepped out onto the busy street and headed for my skimmer. I had an appointment to make and I didn't want to be late.

Too bad I never saw the blow coming.

FOUR

I woke up in a warehouse God-knows-where, dangling from some chains. I had no idea how long I'd been out. My head hurt like hell, and my fingers were numb; it had probably been a while. The cavernous building was empty and shadowed. As far as I could tell, I was all alone.

The first thought that flicked through my mind was, *Good.* The decision had been taken from my hands. Let Mia escort her own piece of trouble. Maybe whoever had ambushed me would kill me now.

A muted howl caught my attention and I cracked open an eye. Scanned the room. I stilled as I spotted One Eye tied to a rack. Three Whites, those tall, nervous, bird-like creatures, stood over him jabbing him with forks and then licking madly when his body produced the pglet. They were also giggling like little girls. Apparently they'd been at it a while. They were high as kites.

One Eye was starting to foam.

Shit.

Skeegs only foam when they're in severe distress. My partner was a pain in the ass and probably Granny's stooge, but he was my partner and a muni. I hated to see him suffer.

So I moaned.

The Whites whipped around, dropped their forks.

Given half a chance, I swore I'd jab them a time or two. Just to even the score.

"Come on. He's awake."

"Get Warb."

One of the Whites headed out, his gait decidedly unsteady. Looked like he'd taken one lick too many.

"Hey, Earthie." One of the others gave me a push. I swung back and forth. The chains creaked. It hurt like hell. Still, I kept my cool and stared him down.

"Keep away from my Skeeg, White."

He snorted. Cocked his neck, a White's way of throwing out his chest. "Or what?" Clearly he thought he was hot snot. I was chained up and he was walking around free. He was a delusional bird.

"Or you die."

My tone stopped him in his tracks. His beady eyes blinked. He ruffled his feathers and glanced around at his buddies. I liked that they all took a step back. The one still standing over One Eye eased away.

The dumbshit waddled up close to me and dragged his fork over my chest in a painful rake of tines. "You gonna tang me up, Earthie?" he smirked. "You don't look in any condition to take me."

"No, I don't." But I didn't get the reputation I enjoyed by being a pussy. I let him move closer and then I kicked up my legs, wrapped my thighs around his shoulders, and squeezed. Didn't take long to snap his scrawny neck. The sound echoed through the room.

The others squawked. Their heads started to bob. Manic clucking filled the room. I eyed them all as I let the dead bird fall. "Anyone else?" I asked sweetly.

They all took another step back.

"What the—" A large White swept into the room and stared at the clucker on the floor and then assessed me slowly. He glanced over at One Eye and the other Whites hovering around him. Pglet coated their beaks. He muttered an imprecation beneath his breath and turned to his second in command, a rooster who'd followed him in. "Get these nuggets out of here," he snapped. When one of them passed, in a flurry of feathers, he smacked the back of his head.

He sauntered over to me and looked me up and down. "So. You Granny's Earthie?"

I tipped my head.

"Yeah. I heard about you." He frowned down at the dead chicken at his feet. "Guess it's true. Tough mother scratcher . . . for a Hume."

I suppose that was a compliment. "I do what I can."

"Do you know who I am?" he asked, smoothing down his pompadour.

I narrowed my eyes, focused on the ink on his neck. "Swan, I'm guessing." Not so much of a guess. The cygnet was a dead giveaway. What I was really wondering was, what was the connection between this shit and the dead White back at the station house?

"Name's Warble."

Oh. Hell.

I'd heard of him. Cock of the Walk. King of the Hill. He'd taken over after Caw had bought the big chicken farm in the sky. The only chicken that outranked him was Crow, who was as much of a recluse as Granny. The birds lived on the other side of town, not my district. That was why I didn't recognize him on sight. "Okay. And what do you want from us . . . Warble?"

He nodded to the rooster, who lowered me down. He unlocked the cuffs on my wrists and watched as I massaged the blood back in. "Just some intel. Sorry for the kerfuffle. The boys are a little on edge. Very jumpy."

I glanced at One Eye, who was still oozing pglet. "That should calm them down a little."

Warble sighed and nodded to rooster, who headed over to

release One Eye. My partner was pretty pissed. Once he was free, he backhanded the cock and sent him flying across the room.

I blinked. I'd never seen that kind of reaction from One Eye, the calm, sedate son of a bitch. The birds must have poked him pretty good.

"Some water?" I asked Warble. One of his minions hurried over with a large ladle, gingerly handed it to One Eye, and fretfully sprang away. My partner upended it over his head, sighing as the balm flowed over his skin. The pockmarks bubbled a bit, and then closed.

"You okay?" I asked.

He glanced at me. Then nodded and turned his glare back on the rooster. He picked up a fork one of the birds had dropped and fingered it thoughtfully.

Warble watched, his expression dark, then he turned back to me. "Look, we don't want a beef with Granny."

"Really? Because this ain't the way to go about it." When Granny found out they'd tortured his favorite Skeeg, he'd probably fry up a batch of thighs and wings.

"I know. I know. I'm sorry. Like I said, the boys are jumpy. We, ah, lost one of ours last night."

Right.

"A Swan?"

Warble nodded. "We're just trying to figure out what it means."

"So are we. Someone dumped a Swan on our doorstep. Along with four other DBs. No one has any idea why."

No one but me.

I crossed my arms and stared at him. "What are you into, Warble?"

"Me?" he clucked. "Nothing. We're just simple boys, trying to scratch out a living here on this rock."

Yeah. Protestations of innocence didn't go too far. Not on

Viridian. "Come on, Warble. Toss me a bone here. You must be up to something. Someone wanted to point at you, or your man wouldn't have been included in the party."

His beady eyes flicked around. His head bobbed. His long neck undulated. "We, uh . . . might be in the market for some contraband." This, he whispered.

"What kind of contraband?"

He leaned closer. His voice dropped even more. "Word is, the Sisterhood is bringing in something valuable."

Christ.

"How valuable?"

"I don't know. Really. I don't but there's talk."

"What do the *talkers* say?"

"It's big. Very big. Huge. We want a piece."

"You want a piece, but you don't even know what it is?"

He shrugged. "Gotta stay ahead of the curve, man."

"Right." This was starting to smell worse and worse.

Worse than my Skeeg, who had sidled up next to me and was wiping the pglet from his skin. He had the package from Mooney under his arm. It was soaked.

I blew out a breath and focused on Warble. "Yeah, well, I don't know anything about this, whatever it is."

The White shot me a smile. "If you did, would you tell me?"

I sent him a sardonic look.

"Okay." He blew out a breath. "If you find out anything about our missing guy, will you tell me that?"

I stared at him. "Depends."

"On what?"

"On whether or not you get in my way again."

White as he was, he paled.

It wasn't even satisfying, because just then, my alarm went off.

It was 2:15.

Warble had his guys give us a ride back to the depot. It wasn't far, which was a shame because all the way, One Eye poked the Swan sitting next to him with a fork. It was kind of fun to watch. The White didn't dare complain, but he did squawk. With each jab.

Yeah, I kind of liked *this* One Eye.

I shot him a grin. "Tenderizing the meat?" I asked.

His lips quirked. Another howl rose from the back seat.

The Whites dropped us in front of the depot and drove away in a squeal of tires. I scanned the ramps. My stomach dropped right away because the busy station was nearly deserted. I knew what that meant. I'd missed my window.

But I also knew I couldn't return to Granny empty-handed.

And without the novitiate, a run to the Barrens was pointless. I had to get her back. Damn the Swans for their bad timing. Or my bad luck of being the first muni they spotted. But even though this cluckerfuck had come at a bad time, and even though it had made me late, maybe completely screwed me over, at least now I understood why there had been a Swan in that dog pile of DBs.

It was a warning from Mia.

The Swans were the other interested party.

Or, one of them.

She had such a sweet way of sending a message.

The depot was a modern, airy, domed building that looked like something from a dated Tomorrowland ride. It was clean and bright and white-washed fresh, but to add insult to injury, it was the only clean and pleasant spot on the entire moon. The last decent place a new convict would ever see.

It had six landing pads, though more than one was rarely

used. At the moment, all the pads were empty. The shuttle had already dropped its load and departed.

Awesome.

I headed up the ramp and hailed one of the Ferrod officers milling by the gate. "I'm looking for a nube," I said.

He waggled his bushy brows and huffed a laugh. "Ain't we all?"

Without warning, One Eye body slammed him against the wall; the Ferrod's eyes bugged out.

"This one is special," I growled. "Came in on the 215."

"I, ah, right." The Ferrod's wet nose quivered. "What-what did he look like?"

Blond hair, angelic features. Curves out to here. "She. A novitiate."

"Oh, yeah. Her." One Eye let him down and the officer tugged down his shirt, shot the Skeeg a glare, then fixed his attention on me. "Quite a looker."

My fingers curled. That flat face probably needed a pound down. "And?"

"She got picked up by a billygoat."

Fuck. Granny would have my hide if I didn't get her back before someone took a taste. And Mia? Hell, Mia'd have my balls. "What house?"

"Greek."

"Awesome."

Not.

I pulled out my laser pistol and checked the clip. Fully charged. Excellent. I was going to need it. I didn't have any friends in Greek. Hell, I didn't have any friends on the Strand at all. I shot a look at One Eye. "You ready, bro?"

He didn't respond, other than to stare at me with that one unblinking eye. Probably in shock. I'd never called him "bro" before. He nodded slowly and made a low gurgling sound I took as agreement.

"Okay," I said, holstering my pistol. "Let's do this thang."

The Greek House was located on a shitty street in a shittier part of town. The whole district was known for one thing. Pussy. And I'm not talking about kitty cats. The Strand was *the* place to go if a guy wanted to get his rocks off. Or have them flogged. Or whatever. You could get anything at any hour. If you knew the right people.

Judging from the teeming crowd, a lot of convicts knew the right people. All manner of creatures strolled the streets, peering into display windows advertising the kinkiest proclivities. Hookers of all species catcalled potential customers from their corners. Slimy pimps accosted willing strangers, whispering of the delights to be had for a handful of coins.

Aside from the pleasure houses, the Strand offered a myriad of decadent pursuits from chud cafes, to peep shows, to gambling rooms where there was no maximum bet. More than once, a convict had bet his life and lost on the Strand.

This wasn't my usual beat, and I sure as hell didn't imbibe—in any of it—so I wasn't very well connected. As we headed for the Greek House, I glanced at One Eye. "Think we should tell Granny we lost her?" I asked.

The look he sent me might have been a pitying one. But hell, I had to ask. He was Granny's snitch after all. Relief scuttled through me when he shook his head.

For the first time since I'd drawn him as a partner, I had the feeling that we were on the same page. Maybe even a team. For better or worse. 'Til death do us part. Or some shit like that. I clapped him on the shoulder. Friendship and respect.

And then, all clandestine-like, I wiped my hand on my

duster. Yeah. He was still oozing. Somehow, I didn't mind so much.

The Greek House had about the same fanfare as Granny's station, but hell, it hardly needed it. Everyone knew what kind of establishment it was, and anyone who wanted something knew just where to go.

Very few secrets on Viridian.

I paused at the top of the steps to the brownstone and shot a look at One Eye. "Ready?" When he nodded, I puffed up my chest and pushed through the door, trying to look as ominous as I could.

The bouncer, a big Trog, rose up to block my way. I casually put my hands on my hips, easing back my duster to show my gun rack.

I should have known he'd snort in disgust. This was hardly a house of delicate repute.

Guns were illegal on Viridian, except for badges, like me. But this *was* Viridian.

The ban on weapons was pretty much a joke to anyone with any steel in their spine.

"Help you?" the Trog growled.

"Lookin' for a new arrival."

He eyed me up and down. "Feelin' horny?"

"Not lookin' like that. One of your Billygoats snagged my collar."

The Trog snorted and turned away.

It pissed me off, his disrespect. So I sucker-punched him in the kidneys. Or, where I thought his kidneys might be. The blow landed with a dull thud. I think I broke a finger. I surreptitiously shook my hand and then clasped them behind my back.

The Trog turned slowly, his scaly face hard, his eyes narrowed. He made a sound. A snarl. It resonated on the air.

And, shit.

I was probably dead.

Might as well go in full bore.

"No one turns their back on me," I hissed.

The Trog cracked his knuckles. All twenty of them. "Tang you, Earthie."

I forced a grin. Something smug and snarky. "Sorry, troll-boy. Not in the mood."

His snarl swelled. I bunched my muscles, preparing for the blow I knew was coming. I'd give him that. Then I'd blow off his nuts. Wherever they were.

"Wait." A slick slither. A Viper—obviously the house mother—snaked across the foyer, her coils undulating in a sensuous slide. Half of her looked human, if one could discount the fangs, but her lower half consisted of a thickly scaled tail that corkscrewed beneath her and tapered to an ominous rattle. A shiver danced down my spine. Vipers always creeped me out. This one was even creepier because her upper body was a perfectly proportioned torso with magnificent tits that captured and held my attention, utterly against my will.

She shot a look at One Eye, then glanced at me. Her tongue flickered. "Who are you working for?"

"Who the hell are you?"

She rearranged her coils. "Boa." A sultry whisper. "And who are you?"

"Tig."

"Mmm. Nice name. Short and sweet. To the point. And who do you work for, Tig?"

"Granny."

Her gaze narrowed. "We have an accord. Granny don't run this part of town."

"I'm not running diddly. I have a collar to nab. Your billygoat snatched her first."

"Really?" She looked me up and down. "And where were you, pretty boy, when the transport came in?"

Annoyance riffled. "Detained."

"Pity."

Holy crap. Was she really giving me pushback? I leaned in and snarled, "If you don't give up this girl, your accord won't be worth the paper it was shit on. What's that going to look like in the future? When munis start raiding your parties? How many johns are going to want to tangle with that?"

She glanced at One Eye again and then studied me for a long while, her forked tongue flickering in a restless dance. "I don't want a war with Granny."

"No. You do not."

"If I give you this girl, you tell Granny he owes me one?"

I gaped at her. Snorted a laugh. "Your billygoat fucking snagged her."

Boa shrugged. "He was just doing his job."

"Right." Picking up any wide-eyed innocent who landed in the depot. Turning them into whores. Enslaving them. "Nice job. But this one belongs to Granny."

"Hmm."

Yeah, I didn't like her hesitation. Something Granny probably needed to know about . . . if I ever saw him again. I still hadn't decided how all this was going to play out. There might be a chance I could do what I needed to do for Granny and still drop off Mia's grid.

Might be a moot point anyway, with the Skeeg on my ass. If I wanted to blow into the wind with the girl, I'd have to shake him first.

"All right. I'll give her up." Boa studied her nails. They were long and sharp. Probably ripped out a throat or two in their time. "I give you the girl, but Granny owes me a favor."

"I'll be sure to let him know."

"And you . . ."

I swallowed heavily. I didn't like her expression. The way her eyes glinted. The way her tongue tasted the air. Like she wanted to eat me. Or something.

She leaned closer and hissed in my ear, "You owe me too."

Awesome.

"Okay—" I jumped when her hand caressed my belly. Those talons? So close to Mr. Happy? Not soothing.

"I've never had a Hume before." The tip of her tail curled around my leg, walked up my thigh and wedged in my crotch. Stroked. Her rattle rattled.

Yeah. Nothing.

"And you're such a pretty boy." Hardly. I had my scars. Some of them were visible.

I tried to un-wedge the tip of her tail—it was starting to tickle—but she pushed back. She was stronger. And the landscape down there was . . . delicate. I settled for a contrite smile. "You and I are definitely not DC."

Her tail tightened around my leg. "Just because we aren't DNA compatible don't mean we can't have a little fun."

"Right. I just prefer to mate with someone—"

"Well?" Her tongue flicked into my ear. I eased away.

"Someone I can . . . mate with."

Her warm gaze went a little colder. I knew I was pissing her off, but, hell. A Viper? I couldn't do it. Just couldn't rouse the interest.

Her tail dropped away. "Asshole."

I shot her a grin. "Yeah. I don't go for that either."

She reeled back and glared at me, which could be dangerous because Vipers are known to spit acid on occasion. Apparently, I hadn't pissed her off that much. All she spat was, "I can't stand self-righteous pricks."

That was hardly fair. "Darlin, I ain't any kind of righteous.

I just like to know the juice is contributing to the better good."
When I screwed someone, I didn't want to be thinking about the
weird-shit offspring we could produce. I'd been to the mutant
boneyard. None of those babies lived past a year.

Besides . . . ew. Just ew.

She tipped her head to the side. "There are ways to prevent
any . . . unfortunate complications. I am a madame, you know."

"I know. And thanks. Tempting offer. But I really gotta grab
the girl and go. Granny wants her bad." I decided to throw her
a bone. Just not that kind of bone. "Besides, I'm afraid you're
too much woman for me, baby," I purred.

This seemed to mollify her. "Fine." She ticked a finger at
the Trog. He grunted and jerked his head. I took that to mean
Follow me. When One Eye started after us, the Viper held up a
hand. "Not the Skeeg."

I leveled a glare on her. "He's my partner."

Her lashes flickered and she gestured to the expensive,
hand-woven Daneurian carpet. "They drip."

I glanced at One Eye, waited for his acquiescence, and then,
with a nod to Boa, who was still pouting, I headed up the stair-
case after the Trog. Not going to say it was with alacrity, but I
did kind of haul ass out of the nest.

Because, fuck.

The upside of the whole situation was that Boa had effec-
tively separated me from the Skeeg. Since I still hadn't made
up my mind which way I wanted to die—I'm wishy-washy like
that—I took this as a sign from God.

The Barrens it was.

Unless something else changed.

And the way this day was going, it probably might.

The Trog led me up the stairs and down a long, narrow
hallway. Amazing he could negotiate the breadth of it because

he was so freaking massive. His shoulders brushed against the walls and he had to dip his head to miss the light fixtures.

It was a pretty cushy hallway. The carpet was thick and plush, and there was a rich, velvet baize on the walls with hardly any cum stains. Muffled moans, cries, and the occasional scream emanated from the rooms we passed. I didn't even want to think about what was happening behind those doors. There were some sick bastards on Viridian.

We reached the end of the hall and he pushed through a green door marked *Private*. And when I say pushed through, I mean it. Dude barely fit. He had to turn sideways. The door led into another hallway, this one more utilitarian, another wing of the establishment. We stopped at a door with a fading sign that read *Holding*.

"Here," the Trog grunted.

The door swung open and my heart surged. Cock too. Because there she was, my angel, tied to a hook on the ceiling, buck naked. Well, almost. She wore her chastity belt, a golden bikini bottom designed to keep a man out of heaven, keep his intentions burning in hell. But the rest of her? The rest of her was bare.

And man, was she a sight to see, all creamy skin and long legs. Her tits were high and full, her ass when she turned to avoid a groping hand, was absolutely fricking perfect. Made my mouth water. Her hair was long and blond and silky, and her face—God. A cameo. So beautiful, she stole my breath.

She was surrounded by handlers, Boa's men, prepping her for service. The truth of it made my gut churn. I didn't want anyone touching her. Anyone but me. Especially any of those Scard-eaters.

But still, I was on the job. First things first. "Where's her package?" I growled.

"Her what?"

"She came in with a package."

The billygoats looked at each other, some bullshit confusion written on their faces. I punched one of them. To help with his memory. When that didn't work, I decked another. The leader glared at me and said, through a spittle of blood, "I swear. No package."

I turned to her. Pinned her with a steely gaze. "Where is it?" Granny wanted that package. Wanted it bad.

Her eyes went wide. She trembled.

"Where is it?"

Her mouth opened. Lips worked. "I . . ." She swallowed, looked down, and whispered, "I am the package."

Holy. Hell. Her voice was like a song. It sent heat boiling through my gut.

Not looking at her was one thing, but how does a man close his ears?

I pushed down my lust and tried to focus on business. "Cut her down."

The handlers all turned to stare at me. One of them scoffed. I lifted my laser pistol and put a hole in him. Musta stung because he howled like a banshee. The others lunged forward to take me out, but the Trog lifted a hand and they skidded to a halt.

"Do as he says," he grated. "Boa's orders."

"But . . ." one of the billygoats sputtered. He glanced at the angel. Her eyes were closed. Her face wan. She looked defeated. The sight tugged at my heart. I took a deep breath, and ignored the sensation.

"But what?" I snapped.

"We can't release her."

"No?" I pulled back my duster, showed them my other piece, the illegal one, that could end them in a hail of metal.

The billygoat's pointy beard quivered. He shook his head, sputtered, "No you . . . don't understand. She's . . ."

"She's what?"

"A handful."

I nearly snorted. Really? Warning me? *Me?*

This tiny thing could hurt me about as much as a kitten batting a ball of yarn.

I glanced at her again. My anger riffled. She looked like a handful. A handful of heaven. Maybe two. But hardly a threat that needed to be restrained. No doubt these freaks wanted to have a little playtime before Boa handed her over to the real customers. The slimy pieces of dung. It curdled my gut to think what they might already have done to her to make her appear so crushed.

"Cut. Her. Down. Or I will."

One of the billygoats bristled. All his spines went on point. He stepped between me and my prize. "Wait. Wait. This is my catch."

I tried to step around him and he shifted again, blocking the way. "You take her, I don't get my bounty."

I holstered my pistol and bumped up against him. "Get your billygoat ass out of my way."

I should have expected he'd lunge at me. Should have expected the blow to my gut.

But hell. After the day I'd had, I was in the mood to pound the crap out of something, and this peckerwood had just had his hands on *her*. That his buddies decided to come to his rescue was just an added bonus.

The melee was orgasmic. Blood and teeth and broken spines flew everywhere as I worked out my angst about the dead Fed, Jimmy, the Kase, Granny, Scale . . . and yeah, Mia.

The Trog, of course, just stood there, leaning against the doorjamb with his arms crossed, watching. Not that I needed his help.

All in all, it was kinda cathartic.

When they were all sedate, groaning and bleeding on the floor, I turned back to the Trog. "Help me get her down."

One of the billygoats opened his mouth and started bleating something. I kicked him in the teeth. When the Trog released the angel's wrists from the chain, she slumped against me with a moan.

And God.

God.

The feel of her soft, warm body in my arms, her silky skin against my palms. Something shot through me, an electric jolt. The little hairs on my arm stood on end.

Da-ham.

I'd been hard since I set eyes on her, but touching her sent my libido into the stratosphere. I knew I needed to get a handle on this, and now.

I couldn't afford the distraction of wanting her.

But damn, it was hard.

Really hard.

I lifted her into my arms and nodded to the Trog. "Is there somewhere we can clean her up? Get her dressed?"

He nodded and led us to another room.

Gently, I laid her down on the cot and glanced at the Trog. "Can you find her something to wear? Oh, and my Skeeg has a package I need."

He nodded and eased back out into the hallway, closing the door behind him.

And we were alone.

My gaze skimmed over her face, the delicate twin arches of her collarbone. Her breasts. Her flat stomach. She was as close to a human woman as I'd seen in years, if I didn't count Mia. My fingers twitched, but I managed to keep myself in check. It would probably be a good thing if she trusted me, and if I gave into the temptation to feel her up? Yeah. Might not be productive.

Her eyes flickered open and my thoughts stalled.

Because, hell.

They were incredible eyes.

Greener than green. Verdant. Warm. Like a forest in spring. Or some shit like that. I'm hardly a poet. Point was, they were mesmerizing.

"Hi," I said. Yeah. Not a poet. "I'm Tig."

Her lips turned up, but it was a shaky smile.

"Are you, uh, okay?"

I hated the sudden fear that flared in her eyes. The way she reached to cover herself. Her retreat.

"Hey. I'm not going to hurt you. All right?"

She gazed at me with a dubious expression. "You aren't?"

"No. I'm here to . . ." *What? Collect you for Granny? Help you do Mia's dirty work?* "Help."

"Help?"

"Help you get out of here." I stood and turned away, so she wouldn't feel threatened by the creep ogling her bare breasts. "You really should be careful who you trust on this planet." Surely, that wasn't a warning. About myself. "That billygoat was going to sell you to this whorehouse."

She made a distressed noise and I had to look at her. She'd curled herself up into a ball, hugging her knees and peeping at me over them through thick, long lashes. Damn shame her breasts were hidden. Or not.

"And you?" God. Her voice was like a melody. It sizzled through me on a skein of lust.

"Me?"

"Who are you going to sell me to?"

And yeah. That lanced me through my gut. Her soft question, threaded as it was with despair and certitude. And vulnerability. It was the vulnerability that got me. Did I really look so treacherous? What kind of man had I become?

"Obviously, someone is paying you to rescue me," she said softly. "I deserve to know who it is."

Hell, I wasn't even sure.

I was spared the indignity of answering, when the Trog opened the door and thrust some clothes at me, along with the package One Eye had been holding. I tossed the latter onto a chair and examined the outfit.

Holy hell.

I tipped my head and sent the Trog a derisive glance. "Seriously?"

He shrugged. "Sorry. It's all I could find."

"Black latex and chains?"

Another lift of those muscular shoulders. "This is a whorehouse."

"Right." I shook my head and turned back to the angel, handing over a very kinky outfit. "Sorry."

She took it with an unsteady hand, staring at it dubiously. Slowly, she stood and began to dress. Then she stopped and stared at me.

"What?" I asked.

"Turn around."

Seriously? I'd seen her almost naked, but she didn't want me to watch her dress?

Chicks.

With a huge sigh, I did as she asked, trying not to wince as the clink of chains and the slick slide of latex covering nubile thighs filled the room. Or maybe it didn't fill the room. Maybe it just filled my imagination. Whatever.

I whipped around at her moan. It was a moan of disgruntlement but seemed to fit right in with my fantasies and—

Oh. My. Holy. God.

Remember that old cartoon, where some dude's tongue

unrolls onto the floor and his eyes pop out all *a-ooga*? Yeah. Like that.

She. Was. Freaking. Hot.

She was gorgeous in general, but dressed like this? Like some dommy mommy? In shiny, form-fitting black latex?

There oughta be a law.

She held out her hands and sighed. "I can't wear this."

"It, ahem, fits." It did. And how. I tried not to fixate on her boobs. On the pebbles of her nipples poking through the latex like targets.

She snorted. "Not what I meant. I would attract too much attention—"

"Got that covered." I tore open the package we'd picked up from the Squig and whipped it out with a snap. A long black cloak unfolded. "You can wear this. It'll cover you. Make you practically invisible. But don't look anyone in the eye."

Her brow rippled as she took the cloak. "Why not?"

"It's a leper cloak."

She dropped it like it burned her.

I chuckled and picked it back up. "No worries. It's clean. Brand new. But it will give you the, ah, anonymity you require."

Her gaze met mine. She studied me silently for a moment and then nodded, just a tip of her chin. But she smiled—a little—and took the cloak. "Okay." Her lashes fluttered and she looked up at me. Her eyes were limpid and wide. "And, Tig?"

Heat snarled through me at the sound of my name on her lips. "Yeah?"

"Thanks." A sigh. A smile. A real one. It lit a fire in my soul, my heart, my belly. It was a challenge to remind myself I was on the job.

A flush crept up her cheeks and she lowered her lashes. "Would you mind . . . ?"

"Mind what?"

She peeped up at me. Her face scrunched ruefully. "Turning around again?"

Oh, God. She was shy.

But then, she was a novitiate. Planning to spend the rest of her life as a nun. Probably never even been kissed.

Ah hell. I never should have allowed *that* thought.

She blinked. "Well?"

Right. "Sure."

I turned away again to face the blank wall while she pulled on the cloak . . . and I entertained lurid fantasies of being the first man to hold her, to have her, as she oohed and cooed and came apart in my arms, crying out, wailing what a big manly stud I really was.

And yeah, when the blow came—from behind—I hardly even felt it.

It was a shower of bright lights and a flash of insight that I was probably the dumbest, most gullible piece of shit on the planet and then, blackness.

A universe of it.

FIVE

I woke up with a headache and a gut full of regret and rage. Not rage at her. Not really. It was probably self-directed.

I should have known better. This was Viridian. Nothing was what it seemed. Not even sweet innocents just off the turnip truck from Iowa.

This was on me for making assumptions.

But it hardly mattered anyway.

She was gone. It was doubtful I would ever find her. Especially with the handy-dandy disguise I had given her.

Did I mention what an idiotic piece of shit I was? A horny, led-by-his-dick, certifiable *ma-roon*?

Now both Granny and Mia were going to kill me. They'd just have to arm wrestle over it. The worst part was plodding down the long hallway and through the house to the foyer where One Eye was waiting for me. And yeah, explaining to him how a tiny little sprite who looked like an angel and had a right hook like the devil had gotten the best of me.

It didn't help that he snickered.

I glared at him. "Come on," I said. "We should probably get back. Granny will want to know."

Untrue.

Granny would not want to know. But he needed to. I wasn't quite sure how I was going to explain it.

In the end, I didn't need to. As I dragged ass into the station,

One Eye turned to me and put a hand on my shoulder. "Got this," he said in a croaky voice.

I frowned. "You're not the one who lost her," I hissed. Not too loud. Lots of ears around.

One Eye patted me once. "Got. This." And then he padded to the elevator—leaving a slimy trail in his wake—and headed up to face our boss and explain why we lost his important package. Why I lost it.

In a whorehouse.

Shit.

Completely defeated, I tossed myself into a chair in the lobby and hung my head.

At any moment, Granny would come tearing out of that elevator and haul my ass down into the basement for a flogging. Or maybe just shoot me.

A cup of java appeared beneath my nose. I sucked in a trail of fragrant heaven. Then glanced up. Doris gave me a smile. "Rough day, baby?"

"Yeah. Pretty shitty." I took the cup and sipped. Heat trickled down my gullet. Invigorated me. "Thanks."

She settled into the chair next to me. Filled it up. But I kind of liked her fuzzy warmth next to me. "Chin up, buttercup. It can't get any worse."

I looked at her. Just looked. I didn't want to think how much worse it could get. Was probably gonna get. Didn't help that the elevator dinged just then and Scale leaned out and bellowed in his harsh, grating tone, "Earthie!"

I shot Doris a wan smile. "You were saying?"

She patted my knee. Nearly crushed it. "Hang in there, Tig. It's all gonna work out."

Was it?

I shot her a smile anyway. Kind of a smile. "Thanks, Doris."

I sighed and stood. Couldn't resist a parting smirk. "Nice knowing you."

Her chuckle followed me all the way to the elevator, where it was subsumed by Scale's growl. He glowered at me as he closed the cage and pushed the button for the top floor. "Granny wants to talk to you."

Yeah. I figured.

There was nothing to say, so I said nothing. Just folded my hands before me and watched the lights ding by on the header. Hummed along with the elevator music. Sad, that would be the last song I ever heard. What I wouldn't have given for some nice, smoky blues right about then.

And thoughts of her?

I evicted them.

Hell, she was probably halfway to the Huggas by now. From there, it was only a stolen skimmer and a day or two run to the Hive. I'd never see her again.

Not that I wanted to. She was too much trouble.

But still . . .

Damn.

The door opened and for some reason it caught me by surprise. I knew it had to open at some point. Still, it kind of startled me. Just another hint at how bemused she had me. How she had, within minutes, tied me into knots. It was probably a good thing that I'd never see her again because she was one dangerous nun.

Scale pushed me into Granny's office. I don't know why he had to be such a dick. It wasn't like I was trying to escape or anything. I knew what was coming. I was ready.

But I wasn't. I was not ready for what happened next.

Granny was sitting at his desk and glanced up as I crossed the long, dim room. He frowned. "You lost her."

"Yeah." I shot a look at One Eye, you know, to see if any parts were missing. Though he was slumped over—his gangly arms resting on his knees with fingers folded, his head hanging low—his eye was up and alert and on me. He blinked.

Granny's gaze flicked to One Eye, then back to me. "Unfortunate."

Yeah. That would describe the situation. "It's all on me," I said.

Granny turned to the Trog. "Give us a minute?" Scale frowned, but nodded and then clomped from the room. When we were alone, my boss waved to a tray on the table. "Drink?"

Well, hell. Don't mind if I do.

I poured myself a couple fingers of the lavender liquid and offered it to One Eye. He looked like he could use a slug, but he shook his head, so I took a sip.

"Sit."

I did that too. Not just because my boss told me to, but because I didn't think my knees would hold me up. Even the bump from this morning's go-jo wasn't enough to buoy me after the day I'd had . . . and it wasn't even close to over yet. I dropped thankfully into the chair and fixed my attention on Granny. I had no idea where this conversation was headed, but he should be the one to take the lead.

Still, I couldn't help saying, "I'm sorry, Granny. I—"

He cut me off with the slash of his hand. "Don't worry about that."

"She got away. Escaped."

"She won't get far. When you and One Eye left this morning, I closed down the city gates."

My jaw dropped. First, because that never happened. Ever. And second of all . . . "You don't trust us?"

"Of course I trust you." Not exactly oozing with sincerity there. "But there are things you don't know."

I narrowed my eyes. "Like what?"

He readjusted his chair—it creaked as he arranged his fat

folds—and then he sighed. "I can't help thinking this is my fault, Tig."

My chin snapped up. What? "Why?"

He folded his sausage fingers and blew out another sigh. "I didn't tell you everything. It's clear now, I should have."

I glanced at my partner with a question in my eyes; he shrugged.

"Like what?"

He shrugged. "Like the Fed may be on her tail."

Yeah. I kinda knew that, but still, I feigned outrage. Because, shit. "What the hell, Granny?"

His lashes flickered. "There's more." There was? Awesome. "She wasn't just any novitiate."

Again, not a surprise. Not totally. "Who was she?"

"A member of the Sisterhood's elite military team. Special ops. One of their best."

I gaped at him. Special ops? Special fucking ops? "And you let us go in, not knowing that?"

He scrubbed at his jowls. "A mistake. I see that now." He gored me with a dark glower; it was tinged with something that looked like desperation. "You gotta get her back, Tig. You've got to find her and bring her in. We need to know what she's carrying."

"She wasn't carrying anything." I knew. I'd seen her. Almost naked.

Granny snorted. He opened his desk drawer and fished around, and then tossed something onto the desk. It landed with a clang. "This is what Scale extracted from the last one."

"The last . . . novitiate?" And then, oh hell . . . "There have been more?"

"Lots of them. We've only been able to intercept one. She was carrying this."

I picked up the chunk. Studied it. Weirdest thing I'd ever seen. "What is it?"

Granny shrugged. "You tell me."

It looked like a cog. A machine part. But to what? "You say a novitiate was carrying this?"

"Yup."

"Where? How'd she get this through scan?"

"It was hidden beneath her chastity belt."

"Shit." The Sisterhood did like their chastity. Those loons would die for it. No one would suspect they would *use* a belt to smuggle contraband. "In the belt?"

His expression firmed. "In her body. Beneath the belt. Imbedded in her . . . well, imbedded in her."

Christ. "How'd you get it out?"

Granny lifted a brow. "How do you think?" A mutter. "Goddamn shame. She was a pretty thing. Would have been a great asset to the lineup." Right. Like a novitiate of the Sisterhood would take well to turning tricks for a mob boss. Granny grimaced. "Scale had fun though."

"Bet he did." There was nothing Scale enjoyed more than carving up meat. I tossed the cog onto the desk. "And you think today's arrival was carrying something like this too? Why?"

Granny shrugged. "Intel is they're building . . . something. This piece seems to back that up." He picked up the mystery cog again and studied it. Then he tossed it into his drawer and closed it with a slam. "Could be a weapon. They could be prepping to make a move. I need to know what that bitch Mother is up to. I need you to find that girl and bring her back here so we can . . . investigate."

Something went cold in my chest. Might have been my heart. "Gonna carve her open too?" A casual query. Somehow it scraped through my throat. Visions of my angel under Scale's knife seared through my brain.

Granny's stubby lashes flickered. "Most likely." He gored me with a sharp look. "You find her, Tig. Find her and bring her back."

Awesome. My favorite thing was delivering beautiful innocents to their doom.

One Eye's stare was a little unnerving as we rode the elevator back down to the ground floor. I tried to ignore him, but couldn't. When our gazes met, he leaned down and asked, "What now?"

I blew out a breath and wiped my face.

What now, indeed?

"I guess we reach out to our PIs. See if anyone has seen her. Canvass the streets for a very clean-looking leper. You have any ideas?"

He shrugged. "Sounds good."

"Yeah." I leaned back and stared up at the ceiling. "What a clusterfuck."

His chuckle was an annoyance.

I pushed out of the elevator when the door opened and strode through the lobby, One Eye following in my wake. Might have been my imagination, but the Skeeg seemed more sluggish than usual. I frowned back at him. I'd never find the girl with him slowing me down.

"Hey, how about you take east, I take west?" Sounded fair.

His brows lowered. "Granny—"

"Granny said find her." Screw this *Always keep your Skeeg with you* shit. "If I get a lead, I'll call you and vice versa. Okay?" When he dithered, I leaned in and hissed, "We need to move, man. This way, we can cover twice the territory."

He didn't answer, so I slapped him on the shoulder and headed out.

Even if he wanted to, he could never catch me.

Besides, I needed to lose him. I needed to lose him because when I found the girl, no way was I taking her back to Granny's. No way was I going to deliver her to Scale and be responsible for her death.

Even though she'd clocked me.

Maybe because of it.

You had to respect a woman who could get the better of a muni with nothing more than her fists and clever brain.

My first stop was Maltby's nest. It was a skeezy piece-of-shit place down on the Skid. The narrow street was dark and damp in the shadows of the towering brownstones, and it was lined with lepers and junked-out cons who were clinging to life by a thread. The scent of old draw butts hung on the air, stale, rancid, and alluring.

Somehow, that was easy to ignore. I guess having something a little more pressing than a quick high—something that was immediate and visceral and life-or-death—did something to a man's blood chemistry. I barely felt a flicker of need.

As I made my way down the street to the hole the Rat called home, no one even glanced at me. Not because I was a muni in a place no muni bothered to patrol, but because they were too beaten down to even care. This was a place cons came to die when they wanted to die quietly.

It was a place I came for info.

Maltby had never let me down yet.

As slippery and weasely as he was, he had a pipeline. He usually knew what was going on before it happened. And if he didn't know, he could find out. Maltby was my best bet in all this. I just knew it.

I checked my six as I slipped into the alley leading to his

place. No one following. No one watching. The street was quiet, still. Dodging the piles of strategically placed "refuse," I made my way to his door.

Rats didn't like living in apartments. They didn't like walls and doors and refrigerators. Shit like that made them nervous. They liked living below, underground, in the sewers and tunnels of the city. They liked the stank.

Maltby was no exception. His nest was a series of interconnected caverns and pipes from which he ran his vast network. But for all his connections, he was a simple guy. For the most part, he lived alone and spent his days passing information for profit. The dude was all about business—didn't have scruple number one. I liked that about him. You could trust that about him. For a sparkly trinket, he'd give up his mother.

When I visited him, I always carried trinkets.

He answered my knock like he'd been waiting at the door. He nodded to me, and then his beady eyes scanned the shadows; his whiskers quivered as he sniffed the air. When he was sure no one had followed me, he opened the door and let me in.

"Tig. Tig," he hissed as we exchanged one of those man-hugs that were neither sincere nor affectionate. We were surreptitiously patting each other down. Or not so surreptitiously. His wariness relieved mine. There was some charm in honor among thieves. "Good to see you, brother."

"Been a while."

"That it has. Come in." He scuttled from his "foyer" to the tunnel that led to his office. I'd never seen past this one room, but then, I didn't really want to. This one was bad enough. It was piled high with crap. Littered with junk the little hoarder had collected over the years. This was his favorite stuff, stuff he liked to keep close. No doubt there were countless caverns holding mountains of other crap.

And it was crap. A Nardian trumpet bent out of shape,

the arm from a plastic baby doll, a box of ratty feathers. In the corner, a pile of stinking rags. Who knew what it all meant to him, but it meant something. Or he was just a nut job.

I didn't care.

"Some draw?" he asked.

Hunger hit my gut. Low and hard. My head went woozy and my vision blurred. I wiped the sweat from my brow and shook my head. "I quit."

His eyes widened. Quite a feat for a Rat. "When?"

"A while ago." Not long enough ago. Too long ago.

He nodded. "Gets in the blood, don't it?"

Not for everyone. Just those of us with warm blood. "This isn't a draw buy, Maltby," I said, but I was pretty sure he already knew. I could see it humming around him, a tension. I could see it in the tic of his fuzzy cheek. He knew why I was here, and he had information to sell.

"Ahem. What then?"

Yeah, he knew, but he needed me to ask. "I'm looking for a girl. A nove. Wearing a leper cloak."

The whiskers went into overdrive. Maltby's little Rat feet started shifting, dancing. I knew he had my info. Slowly, I pulled a necklace, one I'd snagged from impound just for this purpose, from my pocket. The crystals caught the light of his one dim bulb.

Maltby fixated on it. He might have drooled a little. "Ah . . . hot little number in latex?"

My pulse flared; it thrummed in my neck. "Yeah. That's the one."

His gaze flicked to me, then flicked away. "I don't know where she is." *Shit.* "But I know who does."

"Who?"

He notched his head at the bling. Shuddered. "Even trade?"

"Even trade."

Without warning, he snatched the piece and skittered off down some long, dark tunnel. I didn't bother following. For one thing, it was a long, dark tunnel in a Rat hole, and it stank to high heaven. For another, Maltby always delivered. I knew he'd return with what I needed.

I didn't have long to wait, but Maltby didn't return.

I felt her presence behind me—smelled her presence behind me—even before she spoke. A wave of nausea washed over me. It was flecked with an inconvenient and long-lost lust. "Lose something?" A low, slow drawl. A voice that always sent shivers down my spine.

With a sigh, I turned. "Mia." Shoulda known. I crossed my arms over my chest. A protective gesture and I knew it. I also knew it was futile. Nothing could protect me from her.

"Tig. Tiggy, Tig, Tig, Tig." She slithered up to me like a snake—far more lethal than Boa—and sidled in. I tried not to lurch away when she threaded her fingers through my hair. But hell, I didn't like being this close to her. Didn't like her breathing in my face. "I really thought you could keep your hands on her a little longer than that."

I detangled myself and glared at her. "You should have told me she was S.O."

Mia huffed a laugh. Her slender shoulder lifted. "Where's the fun in that?"

"I thought she was a sweet, innocent, helpless nove."

She settled her gaze on me. There was derision in it. "You always did have a habit of underestimating your women, Tig."

"No shit." I sure as hell had underestimated *her*. But then, no one could have suspected she could be as conniving and cold as she was.

She picked up a Skeeg cross and toyed it. Somehow, she made it sexual. Somehow she always made it sexual. "I heard she took you out."

"My back was turned."

"Smooth move."

"I *trusted* her."

She ticked her tongue. "Always a mistake."

"I thought I was helping her."

"Taking her to Granny?"

"I wasn't taking her to Granny." Almost not a lie.

Mia's blue brow rose. "Really? You decided to play ball with me? Over your big boss?"

"Did I ever have a choice?"

"Only the one you imagined you had." Her smile was a smirk.

"Granny would kill her."

She dropped the cross on a pile of jumbled-up jewelry. It landed with a soft clang. She dropped her gaze as well. "Probably. You, ah, don't want that to happen?"

My response was a glare.

"You know, noble intentions will get you killed, Tig."

"Either way, I'm already dead. We both know it."

"I promised you an out."

I snorted. "Right."

"You gotta trust someone, baby."

"Trust will also get you killed."

"Such a cynic."

"Comes with the territory, darlin'." But this foreplay was getting us nowhere. "Do you know where she is or not?"

"Of course I do."

My pulse stuttered. "Where?"

Mia tipped her head to the side. "Our feathered friends picked her up just outside the Greek House."

Hell. "They followed me?"

"Probably. Hardly matters. They caught wind that something's up and they want in. They're holding her in their warehouse." She flicked a look at me. "Same one you visited earlier today. Word is, they'll offer her to Granny tomorrow for a nice, big ransom."

Great. I needed to get there. Get her free. Get out of town before . . . "Tomorrow?" Why wait? Something skittered through my bowels. "What happens tonight?"

Mia's tongue danced out. She didn't meet my gaze. "Birds always wanna . . . have fun."

Something prickled at my nape. The thought of those Swans playing with my angel made me want to vomit. Or rip out someone's throat. I must have snarled or something because Mia laughed. "Oh, Jesus. Relax, will you, Tig? She'll be fine. You just need to get to her. And soon."

"And if she won't come with me?" That was always a possibility.

A shrug. "We'll let her stew for a little while, then set it up to look like you're rescuing her. Be her big, bad hero."

I liked that idea, well, the hero part. Not the part about letting her stew. Who knew what the damn Swans were doing to her, even now. My blood hummed with angst. Red curtained down my vision and I blinked my eyes to clear them.

"The Bronson Gate will be unguarded. Get the girl, then get her out of town. Get her to the Sisterhood. Find out what they're up to. And remember . . . we'll have eyes on you."

"Don't you always?"

Her smile was reptilian. "It should be comforting, knowing you're not all alone."

Comforting, hell. I shot her a glare as my patience waned. "Why don't you just take her?" I snapped.

She made that annoying tsking sound with her tongue. "You know I like to keep a low profile, Tiggy."

Right. More likely, she just wanted someone else to take the fall if things went south. That was her *modus operandi*, after all.

"Fine." I dabbed at the sweat beading my brow. I steadied myself as dizziness hit me. I forced myself to focus on her face. "Just keep out of my way, Mia."

"I'll try." A smirk. "And you?"

"Yeah?"

"Just get your baby out of town. Before it's too late."

"Right." I turned away from her and headed for the exit with one thing—and one thing only—on my mind. I needed to get to the Swan Cartel's warehouse as soon as possible. I had to rescue Angel before they started poking her with forks . . . or worse.

I might already be too late.

The thought made my neck crawl. Made my pulse thrum. Made me—

Hell.

Good timing had never been my forte, and today was no exception because just then, my alarm started to beep. My gut lurched and I whipped out my cell and stared at it.

Shit. I'd completely forgotten.

My go-jo was wearing off.

A crash was imminent.

Like *now*-imminent.

My vision blurred. My lips went numb. My muscles started to fold.

Shit. Shit, shit, shit.

I shot a look at Mia; her amusement at my predicament was annoying as hell. I had the sudden suspicion she'd known I was fading all along. Then again, I would have noticed the signs, if I'd been paying attention.

She caught me when I staggered and eased me to the floor. "Sleep well, baby," she said, pressing her lips to my forehead. "And, Tig?"

"Yeah?" I murmured through the descending fog.

"I really am sorry about Ella." A whisper.

Fury raked me, body and soul. I lunged up at her, though it was a boneless effort. Couldn't even hold her in my enraged clutch. "Don't ever say that name. Not ever. You hear me?" I wheezed. I was already half gone.

She stepped back, out of my reach. Easily. "Okay. Okay. Right. Chill. I . . ." Her expression was one I'd never seen before. It was almost remorseful. Almost sincere. My brain was too fuzzy to interpret it. "Yeah," she whispered. "Just that."

It took everything in me to keep my eyes open a crack, for a second more. The blackness and bliss descended. I sank into it.

I had no choice.

It consumed me utterly.

SIX

Everything hurt when I woke up. Everything. Even my ass. But then, I'd been sleeping on something sharp for hours. I leaned to the side and pulled it out. The damn Skeeg cross. Probably had the imprint on both cheeks.

That was the thing about the crash. It would take down an elephant in mid-charge. A Rhino. A Mack truck. When the go-jo wore off, it *wore off*. It probably hit me faster than usual because of all the adrenaline I'd burned up running around town on this collar. I should have expected it. I should have known.

I checked my cell for the time and winced. Hell. I'd slept for hours. And all that time, my angel had been in the hands of the goddamn Cluckers. I lurched up and then stilled, waiting for my head to stop spinning. I knew from past experience it was going to take me a while to reorient, but I didn't have the time.

For one thing, she was in danger at worst and exposed at best. For another, I knew One Eye was hunting her too. And that Skeeg was one damn good tracker. I'd be lucky if he hadn't already found her and delivered her to Granny.

I'd be lucky if she weren't already dead.

Damn Mia. Damn her to hell. It would serve her right if I failed because she let me crash. We both knew she could have stopped it when she saw it coming. I had no idea why she wanted me to wait before heading for the warehouse, but I was damn clear on one fact. Mia Dominios never did anything that wasn't highly calculated and deliberate.

Holding onto the cavern wall, I stood and tested my knees. When they were sturdy enough to hold my weight, I staggered out of the Rat hole and into the alley.

The night had fled during my slumber, and the weak light of the morning moons filtered through the buildings, illuminating the landscape. It was even uglier in the daylight. But then, I expected it would be. I didn't expect my skimmer to be where I left it. I certainly didn't expect to find it unmolested, but there it was. There should, at the very least, have been a gang tag or a polite *"tang you, muni"* spray painted on the side.

I guess I could thank Mia for that.

I hopped in and powered up. It was a short run to Chickentown and thanks to Warble and his boys, I knew just where they were holding her. The skyway was jammed with commuter traffic, so I turned on my lights to clear a path. I hated to make a spectacle of myself, especially now, but I really needed to move. The trepidation was gnawing a hole in my gut. What I wouldn't give for a tall, cold glass of milk. Too bad the cows on this planet weren't cooperative. I missed milk, but it wasn't worth all the horns.

When I hit the off-ramp, I turned off the lights. Wouldn't help to let the birds know I was coming. I parked away from the warehouse and strolled in. Didn't bother to skulk. Skulking would be far more conspicuous.

There was no one in the yard, so I made my way through the chain link gate and headed toward the door. The big roll-up along one side, which had been open earlier, was closed.

I paused at the door and glanced around—not a soul—then stealthily checked my laser pistol. They were known for draining down unexpectedly and I needed to make sure I had some firepower if there were some birds that needed to fry. With relief, I saw it was fully charged.

With a deep breath, I pushed through the door. It led to an

office—empty—which in turn, led into the bowels of the warehouse. I stilled as I heard the rumble of a muffled conversation. I scanned the room. Saw nothing, but my sight was obscured by pallets of feed. Holding my weapon up, I danced over and scuttled behind one. Using it as cover, I popped my head up, grabbed a glimpse, and then dropped down.

My heart surged into my throat. The vision was burned into my retinas. My angel was laid out on the same rack where they'd tortured One Eye. Her latex playsuit had been peeled back to bare her belly all the way to her belt.

There was blood.

Somewhere in the foggy recesses of my mind, I also registered the fact that there were two birds guarding her. Just two. And they were both distracted by their cells. Probably scrolling for chick porn or schlocky avian memes. I peeped around the pallets, assessing my options.

I decided to rush them. I could pop off one shot and get a bead on the second before he could grab his weapon. But I didn't want to bring down the whole flock on my head, so I screwed on my silencer. It was going to have to be quick and brutal.

There was no contrition here. Not with the sight of her blood still burning in my brain.

Her blood was red. Just like mine.

Fury raged.

Sucking in a breath, I watched, waited until one bird clucked a laugh and showed the other his screen, and then they both chuckled. While they were engrossed in the vid, I made my move. Bounded up. Took aim.

Pop.

Pop.

They both fell before they knew what hit 'em. I waited a tick, just to make sure there wasn't someone else lounging in the shadows ready to squawk, and when nothing stirred, I scuttled out and over to the rack.

Damn. They'd scratched her up good.

All the cuts were around the lip of her belt. It was pretty clear they'd been trying to get a peek beneath it. Fortunately none of the cuts looked very deep. I wiped away what blood I could with my thumb, ignoring the jump of my pulse at the contact. I tried not to think about how warm and soft her skin was. How tantalizing.

At my touch, she moaned. Her lids fluttered open.

"You okay?" I asked softly.

Her pupils dilated as she focused on me, then her eyes widened as she recognized me. She thrashed. A little. I set my hand on her shoulder. "Relax, hotshot. I'm here to help."

She frowned.

I have no idea why she frowned.

I frowned right back. "You do want me to help you? Don't you? Or should I leave you here?"

"No," she snapped.

A vague response, considering I'd asked more than one question. I tipped my head and shot her a quizzical glance.

"Don't . . . don't leave me here."

Still, I hesitated. "You going to bonk me over the head again?"

She glared.

"Are you?"

"Probably not." A reluctant mutter.

"Probably?"

"Oh. All right. I won't bonk you over the head." And when my gaze turned cynical, she added, "I promise."

I had the sense that she kept her promises—a matter of personal integrity. I also had the suspicion that she kept them verbatim. She'd worded that promise awfully carefully. No doubt she was planning to bonk something else.

"All right then." I shot her one more warning glance and released her from the manacles. She sat up slowly, as though she'd been there for a while. Still, I didn't help her. Simple courtesy hadn't worked out well for me with her so far. I sure as shit wasn't turning my back on her again.

"You okay?" I asked.

"Fine." She levered her legs onto the floor and dropped her head into her hands for a minute.

"They cut you pretty bad."

She frowned at me and tugged the latex down over her wounds. "It's nothing."

"Should get that looked at."

"I said it's nothing."

I held up my hands, as though that could hold off her ferocity. "Okay. Okay. Fine."

She groaned and straightened, then stretched her neck. Worked her hands. And then, she shot me a contemplative glance. "All right. So you found me again."

"Yep."

"Probably feeling kind of full of yourself."

"Not really." I shot her a grin. It seemed to surprise her. "Now I get to explain to the boys how I was taken down by a half-naked woman in a whorehouse."

Her lips tweaked up. I had the sense it was her first real smile. Too bad she quashed it so quickly. It was . . . pretty.

"Did I mention I was sorry about that?"

"No. You did not."

Another smile. This one, she could not quash.

"I—"

Whatever she'd been going to say was drowned out in a flurry of flutters as a swarm of Cluckers surged into the warehouse and surrounded us. Probably the whole flock. They closed in, watching us with those beady eyes, their heads bobbing with aggression.

Angel stood, and without discussion, we each moved into position, back to back. The chickens neared. Several of them looked familiar. They had their eyes on me and they were lit with a fervent hope for payback. Apparently they were pissed I'd killed one of their friends. Warble pushed to the front of the flock, a pistol in his hand. He lifted it. Trained it on me. He looked super ready to pull the trigger.

Awesome.

"What now, Galahad?" she muttered.

I shrugged. "Feel up to a chicken fight, soldier?"

She stilled. I felt her muscles bunch against my back. "You know?"

"I know you can kick ass when you want to."

She snorted a laugh. "Well, okay then, hero-boy. Let's kick some ass."

And the melee ensued.

The first thing I did was drop Warble. He fell with a squawk. The other birds stared at him and then ruffled their feathers and rushed in.

It didn't take long for me and Angel to get separated—there were far too many opponents for us to hold our position—but I tried to keep a bead on where she was so I wouldn't accidently shoot her. My pistol was going off at a pretty rapid clip though, with a *pop, pop, pop*. And when it ran out of juice, I switched to my Glock, and when that ran out of bullets, I used it as a bludgeon. That and my fists.

I was vaguely aware of her skirmishes. They were all hand to hand. I tried not to be ticked that she finished off her attackers first and had to come and help me. After all, *I'd* had the weapons.

But damn, it was wonderful watching her work. Poetry

in motion. If I hadn't been a little preoccupied with my own fights, I would've loved to stand there and watch. She moved like a psycho ninja on crack, leaping and dancing, lyrical, flowing. She'd snap a neck, garrote a windpipe, and then flip through the air and roundhouse another three birds.

Amazing.

They sure as shit didn't know what hit them.

Before long, the warehouse was littered with bodies, some still moaning; feathers danced on the air. She glanced at me as she brushed the down from her latex—I tried not to drool—and she shot me a grin. "That was fun."

Fun. Right.

She cracked her neck to one side and then the other. "I do like a little cardio in the morning."

I asked the question that had been burning on my brain. "How the hell did they capture a badass like you?"

Her eyes narrowed. She glared at the bodies. "They caught me by surprise," she muttered. "Damn sneaky birds."

I glanced around the room and shot her a smile. "Well, too bad there aren't any eggs. We could have breakfast."

She laughed at that. A sweet lilt. It knocked me off my game. It made me lose focus. It made me completely forget to distrust her.

Before I knew what had happened, she had casually bent down and picked up the pistol Warble had dropped. And trained it on me.

My pistol was empty. Pretty sure she knew that. I let it fall. Fuck.

I just couldn't catch a break with this one.

"So . . ." She studied me for a long moment. "Where do we go from here, hero-boy?"

Ah, you shoot me and walk away from a damn-fine looking corpse?

I stiffened my spine. "What do you mean?"

"I'm not letting you take me in. You gotta know that."

"I do." *And thanks for the warning.* "But I wasn't planning to take you in."

She snorted. "Do you think I am a complete moron?" The tiny hint of disappointment in her tone caught me by surprise.

"What?"

"Come on, sweetie. Back there, in the Greek House, when you mentioned you had a Skeeg?" She crossed her arms and glared at me. The move took the gun off me. I could have rushed her at that moment, but didn't. Couldn't. Besides, I needed her to trust me. For some reason, women had a tendency not to trust men who rushed them and overtook them with sheer brute force.

Instead, I dropped down onto the rack. Fiddled with my dead pistol so I wouldn't have to look at her. "And?"

"And the only folks who run with Skeegs are munis. And munis run for Granny."

I met her gaze. Stared into those beautiful green orbs. "I am not taking you to Granny."

She tipped her head to the side. "Riiight."

"I'm not. Look. Call me sentimental, but I don't want to see you carved up—"

She stepped closer and jabbed me with the pistol. "What do you mean?"

My throat worked. "I mean, they'll cut you open to get it out."

Her exquisite face paled. She dropped down on the rack next to me. A hint of horror danced over her features. "Get . . . *what* out?"

I gestured to the vicinity of her chastity belt. Even that seemed profane. "That. Whatever you're carrying."

She stared at me. Tension hummed. I could see her brain

working, the thoughts flickering through her mind. And then she tipped to the truth. "I'm not the first nove you grabbed."

"You're the first *I* grabbed." It felt important to clarify. "Not the first Granny has grabbed."

"Oh God." She slumped down, but when I moved to comfort her, she snapped back into position, holding the gun with two hands, pointed it right at my heart. "How many?"

"I—"

"How. Many?"

"Just one."

"*Just* one?" A snarl. Her expression was ferocious. Her finger tightened on the trigger. I might have leaked a drop. Yeah. Not my best moment. "Is she alive?"

I shook my head. Just a little bit. Her features tightened.

"Look, I'm sorry. I—"

"She was my sister. My *sister*. Do you understand?"

"Yeah. I do. I didn't hurt her. Hell, I never even saw her. I was disgusted when I found out they killed her. And that's why I'm not taking you back there."

She snorted derision all over me. "Then why are you here?"

"I want to help you escape. Get out of town. Get to the Hive."

Whoa. Her look of utter disdain cut me to the quick. She waggled the gun up and down. "You?"

"Yes, me." No one else could do it. Would do it. Mia probably knew that. That was why she'd called on me. It was clear now. "I . . . know people. Places. Secrets." Every rotten corner of this town. "I can get you out."

"And what about Granny?"

"What about him?"

"Come on, muni. You work for him. He'd pull out your fingernails and feed them to his hatchlings if you betrayed him."

"Probably." My smile was a little forced. "But I can't take

you back there. I just can't. Our only chance is to blow out of town, as quietly as we can. If anyone else finds you . . ." A shrug.

"Okay. All right. I'll buy that."

I glanced at her hopefully. She believed me. It was a start.

She lowered the gun onto her lap. Another scrap of encouragement. "How much does your boss know?" she asked through tight lips.

"About what?"

Her eyes narrowed. The gun whipped up again. "Don't play dumb, copper. I'll splatter you."

I sighed, and edged the barrel down with a cautious finger. "All I know is what they told me."

"Who?" A jab. "Who?" Another.

"Granny."

Her features puckered up, like she'd sucked a lemon or something. "Right from the trout's mouth?"

"Yeah."

"And what did he say?"

Honestly, there was no reason to lie to her. No reason to prevaricate either. Besides, this might be a chance to get a little information—or confirmation—of my own. "The Sisterhood is building something. Some weapon. He wants to know what it is."

For some reason, she relaxed at that. A little. It incited me to continue.

"He has a piece of the machine."

Should have shut up. She went right back on point.

"What?"

"Something that looks like a cog."

She went preternaturally still. "A . . . cog?"

"Yeah. Weird piece of metal."

"Hmm. And he showed it to you?"

"Yeah."

Her features curled into a smirk. "Right. And where was this, exactly, over tea and cookies?"

I frowned. "In his office. It was in his desk."

She dropped the gun, her shoulders slumped. "Damn."

I stifled the insane urge to wrap her in my arms and comfort her. She was still holding the gun, after all. "What is it?" I asked.

She scraped her hair off her face and blew out a sigh, offering me a shaky smile. "That thing Granny has? It's not what I thought it was."

"What do you mean?"

"If it was what I thought it was, no one, not even Granny, would leave it lying around in a desk drawer. He must have been bluffing."

"Why would he need to bluff me?" *Shit.* I *worked* for him!

She stilled. Studied me. "You're right. You're right." She huffed a sharp bark of a laugh. "Son of a bitch. He is one devious Creel."

"What do you mean?"

She waggled the gun. "He set this all up."

I looked around at all the dead chickens.

"Not this, but he knew you would find me. He probably suspected we'd have a conversation like this."

"Right." I didn't understand a bit of this. But I didn't want her to think I was, you know, a complete idiot.

"You were supposed to mention that cog to me, see?"

I did not. I did not see. "Why?"

"Don't you get it?" She stared at me. Her eyes wide and limpid.

I reminded myself how she'd played me before. Reminded myself to take everything she said with a grain of salt. Maybe a shaker of it. I reminded myself not to let her bamboozle me with that wounded, innocent crap. Let her seduce me with her smile or deceive me with those wide green eyes.

It was kind of tough to remember.

"Get . . . what?"

She set her hand on my knee. Her heat scalded me. Made my blood boil, and not with anger. With something else. "Don't you see, hero-boy?" This time, she said the epithet softly, warmly, without a hint of derision. Her tone made my skin ripple. My cockles surged. "He knew I was an operative, didn't he?"

Yeah. He did. I nodded. Scrubbed my face.

"He knew I would fight like hell not to be captured. And he knew I would best any man he sent."

"Gee, thanks."

She waved off my feeble umbrage.

"He knew you didn't have it in you to serve me up. He knew you would never drag me back to his station to be . . . shredded."

"Then why the hell did he give me this assignment?"

"He sent you here to tell me all this. To make me think they had something. To tease me with the information."

I shook my head, my lips working. I had the feeling she was living in one universe, with one set of knowledge and understanding, and I was living in another. "Why?"

"Because he knew, if I thought that piece in his desk really was . . . if it really was one of the items we've been carrying, I would never leave this town. Not without getting it back first. He was hoping this info would trick me into delivering myself right into his slimy little hands."

Well, crap. That was devious. "Sounds like Granny." I hated that he knew me as well as he apparently did. I tried not to stub the cement with my toe. But . . . "How do you know it's not the . . . thing?"

She laughed. It was a harsh offering. "These pieces we're carrying? He'd never leave one in a desk drawer. No way. It'd be in a safe. A containment field at the very least."

I gaped at her. "A containment field?"

She smiled and held up her fingers, a wee bit apart. "Just a teeny, tiny bit radioactive."

"Right." I scrubbed my fingers on my duster. Just in case. I had touched it, after all. "Okay. So . . . where do we go from here?"

She drew in a deep breath. I tried not to notice how it lifted her chest. "Are you serious about helping me get out of town?"

"I am."

She sidled closer. Her fragrance danced to me. "Seriously?"

"You'll never make it out of town on your own." I glanced at her bloodied fists. "I don't care how good you are."

She preened. "Did you really think I was good?"

"Yeah." Damn good. "But there are a lot of people looking for you. All Granny's munis, probably. The rest of the Swans. God knows who else."

"Okay." She offered a small smile. "You know this planet. What do you suggest?"

Relief gushed through me. Was she really? Was she really willing to let me help? "We should hole up somewhere safe. Wait 'til it's dark before we move." It was a lot easier to skulk in the shadows. "I know a safe place. We can wait there." And at the same time, I could get the papers we might need to pass through any checkpoints if Granny had set any.

"Okay." She nodded and held out her hand. "Partners?"

Partners?

God, that sounded nice.

I slipped my hand into hers. Our palms kissed. "Partners." A whisper.

Our gazes tangled. Silence riffled. Heat hummed.

Her attention flicked to my lips. "What did you say your name was again?" she murmured.

My chest swelled. Something else too. "Tig."

"Tig." I shivered at the sound of my name on her lips.

"And what do I call you?" I whispered.

Her response was a small smile. She cupped my cheek and I shivered again. And when she leaned closer, I nearly melted. And then I did. Because her lips brushed mine. Soft. Sweet. Delicious. A skein of delight danced through me, body and soul. "Thank you, Tig. You really are my hero."

We stood then, together. I picked up the cloak and tucked it around her shoulders. Tied it around her neck. When she was fully veiled, we headed back out to my skimmer—stepping over the chicken carcasses on the way.

One threat down.

Now all I needed to do was get her to safety before all the others descended on us in a flaming conflagration.

SEVEN

We headed straight to Gaelen's place because I knew, of all my PIs, she was most likely to be off Granny's radar. Gaelen was a pretty little humanoid/succubus shifter with a kickass figure and vibrant red skin, who had started out as a hooker and clawed her way out of the trade.

Literally.

Clawed her way out.

I'd only seen her dark side a couple times, and I never wanted to see it again. Watching that sweet, cherubic mien morph into a snarling mouthful of fangs kind of humbled a man. She was usually pretty good at keeping the demon at bay, but if she got cornered or wounded—or got her period—all bets were off.

She lived in a nice, quiet neighborhood that was off the grid and kept her nose clean. Plus her place was close to Chickentown, so I figured it was probably the best place to go. Besides, Skinny's shop was just down the street. Two birds, one stone.

With apologies to the Cluckers for the metaphor.

Gaelen was happy to see me. Not so happy to see me arrive with another woman. Her lower lip pushed out. "Tig." A whiff of discontent.

Seriously? I'd told her, time and time again, it was over.

I pressed a kiss onto her forehead. Making that point. "Gaelen, this is Angel. Angel, Gaelen." I ignored the face Angel made at the moniker, but seriously, she hadn't told me her name so I was calling her what I wanted to. And she looked like an angel. "We, ah, need a place to crash for a while. Do you mind?"

Gaelen opened the door and ushered us in. "Not at all. You in trouble again, Tig?"

I shot her an unrepentant grin. "Business as usual." Trouble, deep.

"Some things never change."

I chuckled. Then I turned my attention to Angel. "We got into a . . . kerfuffle with some chickens. She's got some cuts. Do you have any styptic?"

Gaelen winked. "You know I do."

Yeah. She did have a tendency to scratch and claw in bed. Especially when she was on the feral side of the moon. She headed into the bathroom and returned with a first-aid kit. I was fully prepared to help Angel, you know, tend to her wounds, but she shot me a sardonic look and snatched the kit away.

Gaelen's perky nose wrinkled and she snorted a laugh at Angel's disdain toward me. Apparently, she liked that. "You kids hungry?" she asked.

My stomach growled. "Starved."

"I'll make you something. Just relax, okay?" With a smile, she headed into the kitchen.

Angel tracked her with a hard gaze. She glanced at me. "You trust her?" she asked in an undertone.

I sat next to her on the couch. She let me. "Yeah. She's good."

She glanced at the curvy little fiend, docilely making sandwiches in the kitchen like Donna Fucking Reed. "A . . . thing between you?"

"History."

Her response was a snort. She peeled back the latex and started zapping her cuts, letting the styptic close the wounds. I was fascinated by the opalescent, translucent quality of her skin. My fingers flexed of their own accord.

I yanked my attention away when Gaelen came in carrying a tray. She set it on the coffee table. "You need anything else?"

I held up my laser pistol. "I'm out of juice." What a piece of crap. "You have a charger?"

She took it and checked the make. Snorted. "Yeah. In the back. I'll get this amped up."

I stood and gave her another kiss. "Thank you, baby."

She stared me in the eye. "You know I got your back, Tig. I always will."

"Yeah. I know."

She nodded to Angel and stepped back. "I'll give you two some privacy. Let me know if you need anything."

"Okay. And thanks again."

She shot me a sweet smile and headed back to her bedroom.

As the door closed, Angel snorted.

I frowned at her. "What?"

"You just gave a felon your weapon."

"We're all felons here."

I didn't understand her expression. "Are we?"

Kind of the point of a prison. "Pretty much. Do you have a point?"

She shrugged. "That's a lot of trust."

"Gaelen and I go way back."

"Right. But you're asking me to trust her too. And I don't do trust. Not very well." To underscore the message, she pulled out Warble's piece and set it on the table next to the styptic, within reach.

"We're not going to make it through this if we don't trust someone. We can't get out on our own."

She totally ignored that. With two fingers, she rotated the pistol until the barrel pointed at me. "You're asking me to trust you too. That's asking a lot."

"I know. But I told you why I'm doing this."

"Yeah. Because you don't want to see my ass carved up. You expect me to buy that? Really? Tough, badass, heartless muni? Willing to give it all up? Walk away from his world? Risk his life? For a woman he just met?"

Annoyance rippled through me. Something in her tone dug at an old wound. "Give it all up?" I threw out my arms. "Give it up? The luxurious life of a muni? All the parties and champagne? The infinity pools and movie stars? I live in a shithole apartment in a shithole part of town. I squirm under Granny's thumb. I'm a convict on a brutal prison planet with no parole. No reprieve. No escape. No way out but death."

She looked at me from beneath her lashes. Damn, they were long. "That's a little melodramatic, don't you think?"

"Is it?"

"Point is, you work for the guy who wants me dead."

"He doesn't want you dead. He just . . . wants what you're carrying."

"He's not getting it."

"Of course not."

"And yet, you work for him."

"Not by choice." None of this was my choice.

Her eyes narrowed. "You're his stooge."

"I'm no one's stooge."

"Why don't I believe that?"

"Because you're not paying attention."

She barked a laugh.

"I saved you from the goddamn Swan Cartel."

"Because you want to deliver me to the enemy."

"That is not—"

"I. Don't. Trust. You."

There it was. Simple. Pure. Heart-wrenching.

My expression must have made my chagrin clear. She huffed

a breath. "Nothing personal, muni. I'm just trying to survive here." Yeah. Me too. "And I know nothing about you. Nothing."

I dropped into a chair. Threaded my fingers together. "Fair enough. What do you want to know?"

She gaped at me. Her lips worked. My attention stalled on them. No idea why.

Hunger bubbled up. It took some effort, but I shut it down.

"Ask away." I forced a smile. "Open book."

"I . . . ah." She lapped at her lips. Again, lust slashed at me with greedy claws. "Okay. Let's start at the beginning. Why are you here?"

"Why?"

"Who did you piss off?"

I shook my head. I didn't understand.

She sighed. "Look, the Fed doesn't incarcerate everyone in the KU. If they did, they'd need a lot more prison planets. Who did you piss off on your HP?"

Um . . . everyone? No one on Earth appreciated an honest cop. Not anymore. Not since the Fed moved in. "The PTB, I guess."

She glared at my vague response. "The Powers That Be, huh? What did you *do*?"

I shrugged. "Didn't follow orders."

Her eyes narrowed. "As simple as that?"

"It was . . . a big deal. Went against the grain. I refused—"

"No one refuses the Fed."

"I did. But then, that was all new." The Fed had just moved in. We were all a little clueless about them back then. Still optimistic, idealistic and shit.

"Right." She fiddled with the styptic, just to have something to do with her hands. "Let me guess. You thought they were going to cure cancer and bring world peace."

"Something like that."

"Your world leaders just handed the reins over."

"Hmm."

"How long did it take for the other shoe to drop? How long did it take for you to realize what they really were?"

"Not long."

"And you had no way of fighting back."

Not a hope. Not a chance. I shrugged. "Just what I did."

"Refusing to follow orders?"

Yep.

She gored me with a glare. "Did it feel good?" Nope. "Pushing back against them? Because each time you push them, they shove."

"Yeah." I raked my hair. "I figured that out."

"All right. Whatever. So then you find yourself here. How did you hook up with Granny's crew?"

"Just lucky, I guess."

"Look, Tig—" she snapped.

"Hey. I was only trying to survive. Align with the most powerful force I could. That's as far as my loyalty goes."

"And as far as I'm concerned?"

I flicked my gaze over her belly. The scratches were already starting to heal. "My humanity is not completely dead." There was still a shred of it left. "I want to get you out of town. Get you somewhere safe. And then maybe . . ."

"Maybe?"

"Rest."

Damn, but that sounded good.

"You do know the Sisterhood is not going to take you in. And if they did—shelter you—you wouldn't like it."

"Yeah. I get that." I glanced at her. Looked away. She was too stinkin' pretty for my eyes. Gave me thoughts. And no one wanted that.

"So, where do you go when this is all over? Assuming we make it through alive?"

I shrugged. Let my weariness show. "Don't really care."

She studied me. "A man who doesn't care is a dangerous ally."

My pulse thrummed in my ears. I knew what I was contemplating was some crazy-ass shit, but I couldn't resist. I had nothing left to lose at this point, and if she killed me, hell, I'd be out of it.

I leaned closer. Set my forehead against hers. Our gazes bore into each other's. Energy sizzled between us. "Then give me something to live for," I whispered.

I stilled as something hard and metal pressed against my side. Part of my brain recognized it as Warble's pistol. "Come any closer and you won't live for long," she said sweetly.

I pulled back and stared into her limpid eyes. Something I saw in them made me smile. Something like . . . warmth. "Are you really going to shoot me?" I asked.

"Probably." It was heartening that her lips quirked.

Gently, I enclosed her hand with mine, and edged the pistol away from my heart. I leaned closer, until I could taste her breath on my tongue. And then closer still . . .

"Ahem."

She jerked away at the interruption, dropped her gaze. But her breath was heavy, hard, lifting her breasts with each pant. I was kind of gaspy too. I forced myself to turn to Gaelen. She held my laser pistol in her hand, but casually, cradled in her palm. I should consider myself lucky it wasn't pointed at my heart too. She did have jealousy issues, after all.

She forced a smile. It didn't reach her eyes. "All charged up."

I stood to take it and holstered it with practiced moves. The laser pistol was a symbol of my office, so I tried to use it, but honestly, I preferred my revolver. Probably because it was more reliable. And illegal. "Thank you, darlin'."

"Yeah." She stared at my neck, unable to meet my eyes.

I forced her chin up. "Gaelen?"

"Yes, Tig?"

"I need to go visit Skinny."

Her head bobbed.

"Are you okay with Angel staying here? Because if you're not, we'll go somewhere else." Where? I had no clue. But I needed to know Gaelen would keep her safe while I was gone. Needed to know my ex-lover wouldn't rat her out because of some twisted, covetous snit.

Her smile wasn't sincere. "Of course."

I pulled her closer, met her eyes. Bored in. My expression was stone-cold serious. "Baby, without her, I'm a dead man. You understand?"

She licked her lips and studied my face, saw what I was telling her. At least, I hoped she did. It was the truth.

"I need her to get through this alive."

Gaelen slumped against me. Her brow knit. "Yeah. Okay. I . . . understand."

"Aw, baby." I pulled her into a hug. "I knew you would. Thank you," I whispered into her hair.

When she headed back into the kitchen, Angel gored me with a suspicious look. "Skinny?"

I nodded and picked up the cloak. "Forger. Does papers."

Her brow rippled. "Will we need papers?"

"Probably."

"Won't they be watching for you at places like that?"

Probably. "Nah." My plan was to sneak in the back door anyway. "I'm going to leave you here with Gaelen. She'll keep you safe."

She snorted.

I leaned closer. Murmured, "Don't be fooled. She's a shifter."

Angel's brow lifted. "Really?"

"Really."

She looked me up and down. Her lips quirked. "Didn't take you for a kinky boy."

And damn, I liked the flirty tone in her voice. I grinned. "Back soon."

"Have a nice day at the office, honey."

And yeah. I liked the snark too.

There was a lot of water under the bridge between me and Skinny. A freaking tsunami of water. I'd saved his ass a thousand times and he'd saved mine in return. I trusted him as much as a guy could trust anyone on this planet.

Still, I was cautious as I slipped out the rear door of Gaelen's apartment and made my way through the back alleys to his shop. Fact was, it wasn't just Skinny I had to worry about. I had to worry about the entire world right now. One bad eye on me and it was all over.

The leper cloak helped. I hunched lower and moaned with each step.

People had a tendency to turn away from things they didn't want to see. I figured that could work in my favor as well as Angel's. And the only one who knew about the cloak was my partner, so that narrowed the viable threat down to one in 7.5 million. I could live with those odds.

Fortunately, it was dark outside, which helped with my skulking. Though it was the middle of the day, there was a raging sandstorm howling over the dome. When the storms hit, they hit hard, with savage winds kicking up tons of acidic kaling dust that consumed everything in its path and blocked the light from the suns.

While no one was precisely thankful to live in Kaww Settlement, we were all pretty lucky to live beneath the protective dome. Outside, in the Barrens, there was no protection from the ferocious weather on Viridian, and if it wasn't a sandstorm, it was a deluge of rain and raging floods that occurred with utterly unpredictable regularity.

Everyone ignored the fact that the dome would eventually fail beneath Viridian's fury. All we cared about was the fact that we were protected now. To hell with the future.

It didn't take me long to make my way to Skinny's because it wasn't far, and, aside from piles of garbage and the occasional dung beetle, the alleyway was deserted. His front was a dingy liquor store. He probably made a decent percentage, considering the fact that most of his product fell off a truck somewhere in the Swank District, but his real profit came from doing high-end deals with gangsters who needed to disappear for some reason. In this shithole, someone was always pissing someone else off. Someone always needed a new identity. Skinny was the witness protection of Viridian. His new IDs were top of the line. A lot of powerful people owed him big.

What I liked best about him was the fact that he didn't trade on those debts. He didn't sell out. He lived simply, wallowing in the squalor of the ghetto. Spent every day serving his customers and staring at the craptastic wallpaper peeling at the edges of his life.

There was probably a story there. I never asked.

I tapped on the glass of his back door and waited. The back door was guarded. Skinny was protected, but not stupid. Collum, his lieutenant, a big-ass Trog with muscles like granite, opened up. He grimaced as he took in my cloak. A grimace was kind of funny looking on a Trog because their stony features hardly moved. Still, he made his revulsion clear. "Tang off, leper," he snarled and shut the door in my face. Or tried.

My foot stalled the slam.

Damn, it hurt. I tried not to wince.

I hunched deeper. Collum knew me, knew my face, but I wasn't about to let him see it. "I need to see Skinny," I whispered. "Tell him it's an old friend." I slipped a card through the cloak—an old, established message. One we always used when we needed to reach out to each other. The symbol on the card was one only he and I understood. I made sure to let the Trog see my fingers. And how they were *not* covered with scabs.

He took the card with a grunt and flipped it over, then he frowned at me. "Wait here."

When he closed the door again, I let him. I knew he'd be back. I studied the cluttered alley as I waited, scanning the overflowing dumpsters and discarded barrels oozing with filth. The tart scents of rotting offal and urine burned at my nostrils. But not a creature was stirring. Which was comforting. Although if someone was watching the place, I would probably never know. Not if they were good.

And a lot of them were good.

It occurred to me, once again, how handy it was to be invisible.

The Trog opened the door and cocked his head. "Come in," he said.

I did. Made it a point to shuffle slowly. He took me to a storage room littered with crates, boxes and, paraphernalia of the trade. Not Skinny's office, but I was okay with that. This whole transaction needed to be on the unadulterated down-low. And not just for my safety. I needed to keep everyone whole here, and the only way to do that was make sure no one found out I was here. No. One.

Skinny pushed into the room, holding the card between his thick fingers. Yeah, Skinny wasn't skinny. But he wasn't fat. He was a Rhino—six hundred stones of pure muscle and a huge, bony horn. His tiny eyes narrowed on me and he held up my message. "Where'd you get this card?" he asked in a gruff, throaty growl.

"I think you know."

His features relaxed as he recognized my voice. He kicked the door shut and blew out a breath. "Nardnoodles, Tig. I nearly shot you."

I dropped back the hood and grinned up at my friend. We clasped hands. Man hug. "Hey Skinny."

Damn, it felt good to feel safe. Or at least, relatively so. Unlike so many others on this rock, I knew Skinny could be trusted. I'd met him through Big Jogn, the Ferrod who'd set me up with Granny. I'd closed hundreds of cases over the years based on his flawless intel. Skinny'd always had my back, and I'd always had his.

I couldn't imagine anything that would make him turn. Except maybe an obscene amount of money.

He gave me another tight squeeze, one that nearly crushed my ribs. "So, what the hell is going on with you, Tig? You wouldn't believe the buzz on the streets."

Yeah. I would. "It's . . . complicated."

He settled himself onto a crate. It groaned volubly. "I bet."

"I need to get out of town."

"You surely do. Whatchu need from me?"

"IDs. Two. Male. Female."

"Specs on the female?"

"Blond hair. Green eyes." *Lush, verdant, simmering eyes.*

"HP?"

I opened my mouth. Snapped it shut. I had no idea. No idea where she came from. "Let's say Earth." She was close enough to pass for a Hume. And damn, we were definitely DC.

"Earth?" Skinny lifted a brow. "Really?"

We both knew there were no Earth-born women on this planet. No Earthies other than me, as far as I could tell. The general consensus was that humans were too soft to survive. "It would give me a reason for sneaking her out of town."

"That it would." He studied me for a moment. "Everyone wants her, you know. Contract's out."

Yeah. I figured. The confirmation still sent a roil of acid through my belly. That hatching ulcer woke up and squalled. "What's the bounty?"

"Seventy-five."

Shit. "Mil?"

Skinny shook his head. "Bil."

Holy shit!

That was an obscene amount of money. A mind-blowing fortune.

Was it enough to tempt Skinny? God, I hoped not.

But really, it didn't matter. I had to trust him. What other choice did I have? What other friend did I have?

He leaned forward, his small black eyes intent. "Someone wants you dead, my friend." His sincerity soothed my trepidation. Well, somewhat.

"Granny." It had to be Granny. Who else would—?

"Oddly, no."

I blinked. "Ah . . . who then?" Who wanted Angel bad enough to offer that much? It was a freaking fortune.

Skinny's leathery gray skin folds twitched. "That's the thing. No one knows. But the word is out. All over the streets. Someone wants you and wants you bad."

Right. The wheels in my head turned. The gears clicked in place. Comprehension snarled through me. Someone wanted me bad enough to offer an exorbitant bounty . . . or someone wanted to force my hand. To ensure I got this package to the Hive. Give me an incentive I couldn't afford to resist.

Gotta wonder who that could be.

If I ever saw Mia again, I was gonna kill her.

Skinny blew out a breath. "Every skim shooter and draw-head gonna want a piece of the two of you. Better get scarce, or I may be tempted to clip you myself." This he said with a chuckle, which sent a gush of relief through me. I hoped he'd never turn on me, no matter the bounty—too much history between us—but a guy never knew for sure. The fact that he was joking about it put my mind at rest. At least about him.

"Can you help me?"

He nodded. "I might have something on hand. Let me check the safe."

Thank God. There wasn't time to wait for him to draw up new papers. "We're on a tight clock."

"Yeah." A chuckle. "I'll go get them."

"How much?" Because, hell, I was flat busted.

Skinny opened the door and leaned on the jam. "Brother, this one's on the house."

Aw, man. "I owe you." So totally.

He nodded with a grin. "You got that right."

"Thanks, man."

"Sit tight. I'll be back in a jiff."

I let myself relax—first time in hours, days, it seemed. I'd been riding high and hard on adrenaline and God knew what else. It was about time I caught a break.

I probably shouldn't have relaxed.

A shout, a shot, from the hallway rocketed through me. *Shit.*

I yanked out my pistol, pulled down my hood, covering my face, and skittered to the door. More yelling. More shots. Hell. I had no idea what I would be walking into, but I knew I had to react; if this was what I suspected, I'd be cornered. Aside from that, I couldn't not have Skinny's back.

There was a real good chance I'd brought this down on him.

I cracked the door and peered out. I could see Skinny at the end of the hall hunched on the floor, pinned down behind the counter by the register, with his Trog at his side. Beyond them, a clutch of masked men, holding their guns high. I counted five.

This could be a random robbery, but I doubted it. Far too coincidental for comfort. And most street thugs knew better than to hit this liquor store.

They weren't real smart, whoever they were, because they were wide open, at least from my angle. I took aim with my Glock and popped off one of them. He flew back and crashed through the window onto the street. The blast from my pistol echoed through the room, followed by an acrid sulfur bouquet. Nothing was as efficient as a laser pistol for killing a man, but there was nothing in the universe as satisfying as pulling the trigger on a good, old-fashioned handgun. Skinny shot a grin at me and lifted his piece as well—a gorgeous Colt 45. Seemed we both had a thing for old-fashioned weapons.

As I took down another of the bastards, Skinny tapped a third. The other two got wise and dove for cover, returning fire. Wide, wild shots. Blind response.

While they were busy playing Rambo, I ducked down and slipped through the hall, circling around the far side of the counter. While I was getting in position, Collum covered me and popped the fourth guy. Brains splattered in an explosion of creamy white goo speckled with feathers.

At least we knew who they were. Blood never lies.

The Swan Cartel had found me.

Skinny and I shared a look. He held up three fingers. I nodded.

Three.

Two.

One.

In tandem, we rose up and laid down suppressive fire. One of us nailed the last guy. Tough to say which one of us had scored, as there were so many bullets. No doubt we'd argue over bragging rights over a beer or two for years—

One more shot resounded through the room.

And then, to my horror, Skinny fell with a dull thud. The floor shuddered with it.

I stared at him in shock as the scene rippled through my mind, trying to take root. Slowly, I lifted my gaze.

Collum. His weapon still pointed at Skinny. Smoke trailing from the barrel.

Rage clouded my vision. Without even thinking, I whipped up my pistol and filled him with lead.

The fucker. The fucker.

The absolute fucker.

My last shot hit him in his beady Trog eye and he dropped with a thud.

I ran to Skinny's side. My heart hiccupped at the hole in his chest. Gray blood bubbled from it. He wheezed a breath. "Tig."

I took his hand in mine. The pressure nearly crushed my bones. "Jesus, Skinny. I'm so sorry." I'd never meant to bring this down on him. Never imagined . . .

Well, hell. I should have imagined.

No doubt Collum had recognized me. Knew how sweet the reward was. Called in the Cluckers as a distraction and then gunned down Skinny to get to me. He knew Skinny would never give me up.

And now, here was my friend. One of the few people I trusted. One of the few I even liked. Trying to breathe through the blood filling his lungs.

Jesus.

He looked up at me. I cradled his head. There was nothing I could do for him.

Nothing.

"Do ya . . . do ya ever think about it, Tig?" he rasped.

"Think about what, Skinny?" A whisper.

"Getting back. Goin' home?"

Something in my soul lurched. No. Not anymore. Too damn painful. Once a convict, always a convict. That ship had not only sailed, but it also had hit an iceberg and sunk. "There's no going home."

"But . . . what if we could, man? What if there was a way off this rock?"

"There ain't." The Fed had this place locked up good. Any convict who tried to cross the shield would fry. Even if they had a ship. Even if they had guns. Even if they were stupid enough to try.

He grabbed my shirt in a tight fist. Death clutch. I'd seen it before. Something in me wailed. "What if there was a way. I mean . . . what if there was?"

"There ain't."

"Would you go home, Tig? Put it to the bastards who set you up? Would you . . . Would you. . ."

His grip loosened. His words gurgled in his throat. His breath rattled.

I watched the light flicker from his eyes. Saw them cloud over. Saw his expression go slack. He was a con and a hard ass, and more often than not an asshole, but he was my friend.

I hated leaving him there, like that, but I knew I had to skip. This place was too hot. In a New York minute, there'd be munis crawling all over the place. With one last look, and taking a moment to wipe something annoying from my eye, I stood and headed for his office. His safe was open. A pile of IDs were scattered over the desk. I quickly flipped through them, grabbed two that would work, and then, for good measure, emptied the contents of his strongbox into the pockets of the cloak.

God knew where this benighted journey was going to lead me. I needed every advantage I could get.

The cloak served me well on my way back to Gaelen's. I made sure to shuffle and moan as I moved away from the scene of the crime, even as the muni units screamed in, sirens blaring. No one even glanced my way.

Still, it was hell walking away. The darkening shadows and the howl of the sand overhead only mocked my mood.

I was swamped with the knowledge that if I'd never gone to Skinny, he'd still be alive.

At least, now, he was a free man.

I tried to hold on to that, but it was a slippery thought.

My steps were heavy as I climbed the stairs to Gaelen's apartment, weighed down by some impotent guilt. I stilled as I rounded the landing and noticed that the door was ajar.

Hell.

I took a moment to center myself, polish off my razor-sharp senses, and pull my piece. I ain't gonna lie. The thought that Gaelen might suffer because of this nightmare, same way Skinny had, did whip through me. It was a cold wind. I didn't know how much guilt I could carry before I broke with it.

I made a solemn resolution to do the rest of this, whatever it turned out to be, all alone. I couldn't take the risk of anyone else paying the price.

My pulse pumped as I pushed open the door, scanned the room. The couch, where I'd left Angel, was empty. There was no sign of a struggle, which was heartening. Kind of. There was also no sign of my collar. Or my ex.

I quartered the living room and moved into the kitchen. Nothing. Bathroom? Clear. That left only the bedroom. Slowly, I eased open the door.

And shit.

There was Gaelen. Tied to a chair with a gag in her mouth.

Her eyes were wide. Her skin rippling. Spines were beginning to prickle on her neck. She was getting ready to turn. If she did, I knew I wouldn't be getting any answers for a while.

I might get savaged though.

I made sure no one was skulking in the shadows before I holstered my weapon and hurried to her side. I caught her gaze. Tried to send her calming energy. "Baby," I cooed. "I'm here. Are you okay?"

It took a minute for her to realize it was me. She was already slipping over to the dark side.

"Breathe. Breathe." I'd tried to teach her Zen at one point, when things were still fresh between us. She'd never mastered it, but at least she tried. Her nostrils flared as she fought back the change.

I didn't release her until I was sure she had it under control. I wasn't stupid.

And then, I just untied the gag. "Baby." I kissed her. "Are you okay?"

"Yes." A whimper.

"What happened?"

"Bitch knocked me out," she snarled. Spikes bristled on her cheek.

Okay. Maybe I should have waited a bit.

"Hey. It's okay." I stroked her hair. "It's okay. I'm here. You're fine."

"She came up behind me in the kitchen, Tig. I was making her coffee," she spat. Spittle flicked on my face. I wiped it off.

"I'm sorry, baby."

At least Angel hadn't hurt her. She could have just snapped her neck.

"Do you know where she went?"

"How the hell should I know where she went?"

"Did she say anything? Anything?"

Gaelen sent me a derisive frown. "Only that she wanted coffee."

"Aw. Baby." I kissed her forehead. "I'm glad you're okay." I stood and tugged on my gloves.

She gaped at me. "Where the hell do you think you're going?"

"I gotta go find her. It's not safe out there for her." Angel had no idea how bad it really was.

"What about me?" A wail.

"What about you?"

"Are you going to untie me?"

I forced a smile. "Are you going to turn?"

She growled in response. But it wasn't too feral.

"If I let you go, you promise to stay inside tonight?" I suspected the whole town was going to blow up over this and I didn't want Gaelen exposed. There could be a lot of collateral damage before all was said and done.

She glowered at me. "I have to work."

"Call in sick."

"I can't do that."

"I'm serious, baby. It ain't worth it. Not tonight."

It was a relief that she listened to me. That she relaxed into her bonds and then, after a moment, nodded. "Okay."

"Okay." I kissed her again—one for the road—and then untied one hand and then the other. Her feet, I left tied. It would take her a minute to work free, and that would give me a chance to split without her following me with some misplaced intention of protecting me from the hellion I'd brought to her door. "Be safe, baby," I murmured and then I turned to leave the room.

Her curses followed me out the door.

EIGHT

I had no idea where to turn now.

No idea.

Angel could be anywhere, doing anything.

Hell, she could have been captured already.

To make matters even more super awesome, I was being hunted by every fucking con on the planet. Kind of hard to track someone down when you yourself couldn't be seen. Thankfully, I knew lots of quiet places. Places I could think.

The public library was one of those places. It was an old, rundown hulk on 85th that was frequented by homeless bums and lepers. It served as a kind of shelter for the disenfranchised and was run by the Ēostrevarians. They operated a soup kitchen in the back and had bingo on Thursdays. If a guy was willing to listen to a sermon, it was a good place to crash.

Everyone there was refuse. Lost.

I fit right in.

There's something to be said for hiding in a crowd. No one would notice one more leper.

I thought.

I was sitting alone at a table, forcing myself to swallow the swill some old geezer had handed me, running through my limited options, when someone took the seat across from me.

A familiar scent teased my nostrils.

My gut clenched.

"Fancy meeting you here." A mocking murmur.

I lifted my gaze and huffed a humorless laugh. Apparently leper cloaks were in fashion again. "What do you want?"

"Same thing I've always wanted." Mia sighed. "You just can't seem to keep your hands on her, can you?"

"Your shit isn't helping."

"My shit?"

"The bounty? You can't tell me that didn't come from you. No one else has that kind of scratch."

She chuckled. "It's not like anyone was going to actually collect, Tig."

"They don't know that. I'm public enemy number one. You cut my maneuverability in half."

Her shoulder rose. "If that."

I glowered at her. "Skinny died because of you."

"No. Skinny died because of *you*."

Bitch.

"How the hell am I supposed to do this?" I snarled. "How am I supposed to get her out of town now? How am I supposed to find her if I can't even go to my PIs without worrying they'll plug me?"

"Aw, Tiggy. You don't need your PIs."

The hell I didn't. I—

"You have me."

My heart thudded. Once. "You . . . know where she is?"

Mia leaned in and smiled sweetly. "Of course I do."

"Then why don't you collect her?" I muttered. I was about over this shit.

"I told you. I'm keeping a low profile." Her snotty smile made the hairs on the back of my neck riffle. She sighed and checked her watch, though she wasn't wearing one. "You better get going." *Go? Where?* "Time is ticking. It'll be shift change soon."

Aw, hell. Exasperation and trepidation scoured my nape.

"She went to Granny's?"

"Mmm."

"Why the hell would she go there? Knowing what he wants to—" Oh. Right. "Shit."

Her voice, soft, sincere, and a little too seductive—as she assured me the piece Granny had found wasn't important—drifted through my brain. I didn't know a lot at that moment, but I was pretty sure I was a patsy—again. No doubt Angel knew it too.

She'd had every intention of going to the station and reclaiming that cog all along.

And I'd told her right where to find it.

If I didn't die in all this, I deserved to. The jury was in. I was officially TSTL. In the common tongue: Too Stupid To Live.

"Well?" Mia tapped a finger on the table.

"Yeah. Right." I pushed to my feet and shot a look at her. "Before I go . . ."

"Yes, Tig?" Why she fluttered her lashes at me, I had no clue.

"Is there anything else you're not telling me?" Anything else that could get me killed?

Her smile was sinful. "Bunches." A wink. "But this is all you need to know. Now, do me a favor? Get your ass in gear, get to that station," she stood and patted me on the cheek, "and save your girl from certain death, will you?"

I glared her down once more.

One more for the road.

And then I whirled away and stormed out of the shelter.

Totally forgot to shuffle.

No one noticed me anyway.

What kind of nimrod breaks in to a police station? I wondered as I stared at the façade.

Kind of pathetic that my life had devolved to this. But it was what it was. As always, I just sucked it up and did what had to be done to survive.

But this wasn't just about me.

It was about saving her impetuous, foolish, sorry ass.

Irritation snarled in my gut. Annoyance at her idiotic stubbornness and the fact that I had to risk my life to save her from herself.

A pity I didn't have the luxury of time to wallow in it. Instead, I pushed it back down and focused on the task at hand: Get into the station without detection, find her, and—somehow—whisk her back out.

I knew the leper cloak wouldn't work as a ploy to worm my way in. Munis had a tendency to shoot first rather than scratch later when it came to Scard infestation. One of my options was to waltz through the door, face Doris head on, and hope she wouldn't taze me for the bounty—or the fun of it. But there were too many people who wanted me dead to risk it. I knew I had to go in covert. Somehow.

A van hummed past the station, then turned and pulled into the back lot. The logo on the side was from some laundry. Probably had the bedding contract for the Skeeg dorm. Considering how much they seeped, that was probably a hefty contract.

Regardless, it gave me an idea.

I kept my head down as I crossed the street, then stealthily rounded the corner and scuttled to the back behind the station. I waited until the driver stepped into the service entrance, and I headed to his cab. I balled up my cloak and tucked it behind the seat, then snagged a cap and pair of overalls and hefted a load of sheets.

I held them on my shoulder, obscuring my face, and followed in after the driver, trying to look like a laundry guy. Keeping the bill over my features, I nodded at the guard. "Where to?" I huffed.

He didn't even glance up from his newspaper when he poked a thumb at the stairs. "Three."

"Thanks." I bounded up and dumped the load on two. And, that easily, I was in.

Question was, what did I do next?

I didn't know if Angel was here, and if she were, I didn't know where. I couldn't risk searching the holding cells or the other nooks and crannies of the station house.

But I did know something. I knew she was a badass, and would figure out a way to get in somehow. And I knew she would eventually head for Granny's office.

My best bet was to slip in and wait for her there.

If I wasn't already too late.

I took the stairs because the elevator offered too much opportunity for exposure and no exit strategy. I didn't want to get boxed in. Besides, most of the munis, staff, and hangers-on were too lazy for the workout. The stairwell was deserted. My footfalls echoed with each step. It was a long way up.

The top floor of the station house was Granny's. His suite included his private apartment, his office, and a large conference room. There was a lobby too, by the elevator, with a desk where a guard was stationed. It was also where Scale hung out when Granny was in residence.

Since it was a secure location, I had to use my keycard to get past the stairway door. As I swiped it, I crossed my fingers that no one had thought to set an alert for my encoding. Thankfully, no alarms went off, though that might not mean a lot. Granny was a sneaky bastard sometimes. Best to work quickly.

I eased open the door and scanned the lobby. To my surprise, it was empty. No guard. No Scale. No anyone. I wasn't sure if I should be thankful or worried. I decided not to give a damn. It was an approach that had worked for me pretty well up until now.

There was no way I could avoid the security cameras. My only chance was not snagging the attention of anyone who might be watching by looking suspicious. So, acting like I owned the place, I swaggered down the hall toward the double doors leading to Granny's office. As I was about to slip through the doors, something in the corner of my eye captured my attention. A flash of color at the guard desk. Under it actually. Crammed into the foot well.

A body wearing Granny's colors. The guard.

Well, that answered one mystery.

And told me something else.

Angel had already arrived.

Damn.

If she'd snagged the cog and made tracks, I would probably never catch up with her.

Steeling my spine, I pushed into Granny's office and . . .

Oh. Hell.

Yeah. She was still here. So was Scale. Holding her at gunpoint.

She glared at the Dargum, who had her backed up against the wall. She had the cog clutched in her fist.

"Am I . . . interrupting anything?" I asked.

Dargum hearing isn't the best because their earholes are so freaking tiny, so I surprised Scale. He whipped around and pointed his gun at me.

A mistake.

First of all, we were supposed to be on the same side.

Second of all—as I'd learned—you never turn your back on Angel.

Before I could react, she beaned him over the head with the cog. It only stunned him—his skull was like a rock—but it distracted him enough to cause his aim to veer. I took the opportunity to pull my pistol posthaste. Meanwhile, she wasn't done. In fact, she moved so quickly, I couldn't get a bead on the Dargum. She made some kind of gravity-defying, ninja-slash samurai move, leaped through the air, and scissored her legs over his outstretched arms.

There was a snap—which was impressive, considering the composition of Dargum bones—and a howl. His gun went flying. But he wasn't Granny's number one by accident. A broken arm wasn't enough to stop him. He spun around and ran at Angel, barreling into her and slamming her into the wall. She hit and hit hard. I could tell the blow stunned her.

To my horror, he reared back and did it again. Pile-driving into her, sandwiching her between a literal rock and a very hard place. She gasped. Blinked. Dropped the cog; it fell with a thud. A surprised expression flitted over her face, and then . . . and then her eyes drifted closed and she slumped to the floor.

My first thought was that he'd killed her.

I don't know why such a rage swamped me, but it did. And it was undeniable. Unstoppable. With a feral growl, I lifted my weapon and, walking toward him, fired. The bullets hit him and hit him good, one after the other. They didn't exactly bounce off his lizard hide, but they didn't do much damage either. That was one of the reasons so many Dargums were munis. They were almost indestructible.

He did do me the courtesy of flinching at least.

And then, when my clip was empty, he hauled back and slugged me.

The blow was stupefying. I flew back across the room until I came to a halt against the side of Granny's mahogany desk. A shower of really pretty lights danced before my eyes, blurring my vision. A curtain began to drop. And I was ready to let it.

I was pretty sure if I let myself sink down, when I woke up, I'd be dead.

And I was cool with that.

But then something happened. As I stared at Angel across the room—crumpled against the wall facing me, under the shadow of Scale's enormous body—her eyes opened. Our gazes tangled. Something rose up in me. It might have been my will to live.

I knew that if I died, so did she.

Scale reached down and lifted her up, by the neck, until her toes were dangling. He leaned closer and whispered something to her. I couldn't hear it, but hardly needed to. It was probably some tired, old chestnut like, *Now you're going to die*, or some shit. He wasn't very clever.

But it was true.

Hell, the sounds of her rasping gasps made me think he might not even bother with the torture. He might just choke her out, right here and now.

Then he might as well choke me too.

Crazy-ass-ninja-bitch or not, I suddenly realized that, for some incomprehensible reason, she made me feel alive. More alive than I had felt in years. The sight of her made my pulse sizzle—and not only with exasperation. Her presence awakened something in me, invigorated my soul.

I didn't think I could stand going back to the way I'd been, half-dead and cold inside.

What that realization really meant was beyond my comprehension at the moment. I resolved to explore it later—if there was a later. At the moment, it hardly mattered.

Scraping together my tattered strength, I struggled to my feet and staggered toward him. I stooped to pick up his gun and unloaded it into his back.

With a sigh, he dropped her again—she sucked in a heaving breath—and he turned to me. I knew of only one thing that could drop a Dargum for good, and that was a slug right in the eye, where the skull wasn't as thick. But you had to get it just right—in the inside corner, next to the bridge of the nose—or you'd end up with a one-eyed Dargum who was really pissed off.

I raised the weapon and aimed, making sure to sight it carefully, and squeezed the trigger.

Click.

Yeah.

Fucking. Click.

The goddamn gun was empty.

Scale's chuckle shivered through the room. He cracked his knuckles and fixed his ominous gaze on me. "This," he growled, "is going to be a pleasure." Or not. "I always hated you, Hume."

I sighed. "I assure you, the feeling's mutual." I scanned the room, looking for some kind of weapon. Anything. Another pistol. A paperweight. A letter opener. Nothing.

"Know what I'm going to do?" he asked. I assumed it was a rhetorical question. "I'm going to break your legs." Ooookay. "And then your arms. Your dainty little bird-like fingers. I'm going to snap you into pieces. But I won't kill you. Not right away. I'm going to let you watch." Watch? "Watch while I flay her alive. Let you hear her scream. Plead. Beg for death—"

A strange sound zinged past me, a whisper, a whizz. Scale stopped this rant abruptly. Stilled.

I stared at him, waiting.

A black tear eased from his eye, dribbled down his cheek, along his nose, then dripped from his lips to the floor. He made a noise, like a sigh, and fell to his knees with a resounding thud. And then, after a second, fell full on the floor.

I whipped around—holding my empty pistol—and stared at the doorway.

One Eye stared back with a smoking laser gun in his hand.

Before I had time to react, before I could even process what had just happened, he nodded to me and holstered his weapon. Without a word, he loped over to Angel and helped her to her feet. She found her balance and then cast about for the cog, picked it up and tucked it into a satchel she'd probably stolen downstairs.

I gestured to Scale's lifeless body. "You realize Granny will kill you for this?"

One Eye grunted. "Scale was an asshole."

That he was. But this was more than just clipping a mobster's number one. I didn't think One Eye really had a firm grasp on what he'd just done. "Helping us is not good for your health." It needed to be said.

He stared at me for a moment. His lips quirked a little and he tipped his head. "You're my partner, Tig," he said, his low, Froggy voice filling the crevices of my soul. He slapped me on the shoulder. "I got your back."

Well hell.

And I'd been such a dick to him.

"Thank you, brother." I held out a hand and he took it. I hardly minded the goo.

A call echoed from the hallway. One Eye glanced that way and frowned. "Need to go," he croaked. "Now."

Uh, right.

"Follow me."

He didn't head for the hallway, which was confusing because that was the only way out. I didn't have much of a choice though. I nodded to Angel, and we both took off after the Skeeg as he pushed into Granny's private apartment.

I'd never been through these doors. No one had—it was absolutely forbidden—so it came as a shock. The residence was like a freaking rain forest, with potted plants, draping vines, and algae-covered ponds here and there; a drizzle drifted down from sprinklers in the ceiling, and the scent of earthy loam clung to the damp air. The cadence of unfamiliar insects chirped in the background, punctuated by the occasional call of a water bird.

It was probably designed to mimic his HP, but I gotta say, it was a weird thing to find in a penthouse.

One Eye seemed to know his way. He threaded through the warren of rooms, each designed with a slightly different topography, but all of it damp. Then he led us through a back door and into a utilitarian service area. He stopped next to a large door on a swinging hinge, midway up the wall.

"What is this?" I asked.

"Laundry chute."

I eyed it. It was large. Large enough for me. Certainly large enough for Angel. But I hesitated. I didn't know what was at the bottom. I knew the laundry guy was making deliveries and picking up old sheets. What if he'd emptied the bins below already? Or worse, what if he'd rolled the full bins to his truck already. Or, hell, what if—

Angel, apparently, wasn't a thinker. She heaved up and levered her legs over the lip, pushing through the swinging door and easing into the chute.

"Wait—"

Should have saved my breath. She was gone.

Damn it all.

One Eye winked at me. "Fear of falling?" he jibed as he crawled in as well.

"Fear of landing," I muttered. But when One Eye disappeared into the chute, I knew I had to follow. For one thing, I didn't want to give Angel another chance to escape my protection. And for another, I didn't want to stay here and be slaughtered.

You know. Priorities.

With a deep breath, I put myself in position, feet first, in the too-narrow cold, metal tube and released my hold.

Holy. God.

It was a hellish plummet in the dark, whipping down and down, picking up speed, totally out of control. It was all I could do not to squeal like a little girl.

Okay. I might have squealed a little.

My run ended sooner than I expected, and still not soon enough. I emerged into the light and landed on a soft pile of sheets with an *oof*.

Or not.

Not a soft pile of sheets so much as a soft, warm female.

Coming face to face, chest to chest, groin to groin with her was a shock. I lay there, speechless, reveling in it, staring into her eyes. They narrowed, her eyes. She growled in her throat. And then, when I still didn't move, she grabbed my wrist and forcibly yanked my hold free.

I guess I'd had a hold of her boob.

Can't imagine how that happened.

She arched up. It was marvelous.

"Get. Off."

"What?"

"Get off. You're heavy."

Reluctantly, I rolled to the side in the large bin. I caught One Eye's grin; he was lounging on the other side. I blew out a breath and heaved myself over the lip, then fished for my hat, which had fallen off sometime during the fall.

Angel sat up and thrust her hand at me. I think that meant she wanted me to help her out. Hard to know because no words came along with the command.

But there wasn't time.

Voices resonated from the hallway. Someone was coming.

Without thinking, I tossed one of the sheets over her head. One Eye nestled down beneath the covers as well.

I tugged on the brim of my hat and looked up as the laundry guy, a fat, bug-eyed Polarian, shuffled in, studying his clipboard.

"Evening," I said with a nod.

He glanced up. The tentacles around his mouth flailed in greeting. "Evening."

"Still on duty?" I asked. It was nearly dark.

He snorted through both proboscises. "Rough day."

"Tell me about it."

"Almost done though. Just this monster, and then the sign-off on the delivery. Then I'm off duty."

"Sounds good."

"Don't I know it." He shot me a gummy grin, then tossed the clipboard onto the sheets and began rolling the bin toward the door. The bin with Angel and One Eye.

Ah, hell!

"Damn," he muttered as he tried to maneuver the enormous basket through the turn. "I swear these mothers get heavier every day."

Ah. Right. I skittered to his side and gave it a push. "Let me help."

"Much obliged."

Together, we pushed the bin to the laundry truck and up the little ramp on the back. Again, I appreciated the benefits of being invisible. Though there were munis crawling all over the place—looking for something, I guess—no one even glanced at the "laundry crew."

When the bin was settled and the wheels locked, the driver grabbed his clipboard and nodded to me. "Thanks," he said with a salute.

"Sure thing," I said. I followed him out of the truck, but when he headed inside the station house, to get the signatures he needed, I hopped back inside. "We're clear," I hissed.

One Eye's stalk popped up. He glanced around.

I tried to push him back down. "But there are muni everywhere. It's probably better if we stay here and let this guy drive us off the lot."

The sheets riffled as Angel fought her way out. She frowned at me. "We don't know where he's going," she snapped.

I leaned closer. "We know he's not going to a police station." Anything else would probably be easy to handle.

Her frown darkened, but she relented. With a huff, she pulled the laundry over her head. One Eye did the same. I could have crawled in as well, but I thought it was probably better, from a strategic perspective, to have one of us hunkering in the back, watching where we were going and keeping an eye out for trouble.

Besides, I didn't think I could handle accidentally brushing up against her again. That had been way too disturbing.

Not long after I took my position, the driver came back, lowered the rolling door with a clang, and climbed into the cab. I stayed down, so he wouldn't see me over the seat. The truck powered up, rose on its anti-gravs, and took off. They stopped us at the gate, but it was only so the guard could give the driver a tip on the next race at Godolphin.

And then, after that, we were on our way.

I didn't know where. And didn't care.

We rolled through the dark streets for a while. I tried to figure out where we were based on the thrumming music and the occasional call, but only because it was entertaining. It didn't really matter. Wherever we stopped, it would be our bouncing-off point. We would head for the Bronson Gate. At the Ēostrevarian soup kitchen, Mia had mentioned she was holding it open for us—no doubt she had some other poor screw under her thumb. I could only hope it was still open when we got there.

When the truck stopped, it wasn't at the laundry. I could tell by the blaring red lights that flooded through the windshield as the truck eased from the street and into a parking lot. Red lights meant one thing, here and on Earth.

Hookers.

And this particular house of comfort was also a restaurant. Everyone knew how much Polarians loved to eat and tang. Then tang and eat. The driver would be busy for a while.

And while I hated to do it to him—he seemed like a nice, hardworking stiff—I really needed his truck. So after he got out, I waited a minute or two and then slipped into the driver's seat, broke open the ignition, and pulled out the wires.

"Ahem."

I tore my attention from my work to glance over my shoulder. Angel had extricated herself from the bin and stood behind me.

"Yes?"

"There's an extra set of keys under the visor." Her tone was dry as the Sahara.

I shot her a grin. "Where's the fun in that?"

Still, she leaned over—God, her breast brushed my cheek—and flipped the visor down, dropping the keys into my lap. Unfortunate that. Something else had risen there.

I didn't meet her eyes, just cleared my throat and fit the key into the slot—trying not to think of fitting something else into something else—and started her up.

Angel levered into the passenger seat and One Eye settled in behind me, standing at my back and holding onto my seat. He took this *I-have-your-back* thing literally, apparently. "Where to?" he croaked.

"Bronson," I said, putting the truck into gear and easing back into the seat. Trying not to think about the fact that I was committing a felony. As sins went, it was the least of mine, I suppose.

"Bronson?" One Eye murmured.

"Yeah. I got intel that the gate is lightly guarded."

"And who gave you the intel?" Angel asked, crossing her arms and propping her feet on the dash.

I shot a look at her. It was smart for her to be suspicious, but I wasn't telling her this. "Someone who wants me to get out of town alive." At least, I hoped. I hoped that was Mia's plan, that she didn't have some other plot ticking away, ready to blow up in my face.

But hell, what was I thinking?

This was Mia.

She always had some convoluted intrigue in play. I'd never really understood her. Never really trusted her.

But at this point, I didn't have a lot of options.

So I sped up onto the flyway and headed west, for the Bronson Gate.

Hopefully, not to my doom.

NINE

My tension started kicking up as we approached the gate. I saw it looming in the distance long before we reached it. The wall around the city was a bulwark. Along with the dome, it served the purpose of keeping the residents contained, but also protected us from the screaming storms beyond the walls.

Though all the gates were guarded 24/7, it was merely a formality because no one really wanted to go into the desert. The only poor souls who lived out there were those who had really pissed someone off and been exiled to one of the mining colonies. And those who really wanted seclusion. Like the Sisterhood.

I figured the latter was as good an excuse as any.

We all knew it would be smart to keep Angel hidden, so as I approached the gate, One Eye helped her back into the laundry bin and covered her up. He then took a seat next to me, and huffed in a deep breath. I knew he was bloating, couldn't miss the swelling from the corner of my eye. I just didn't understand why, until he leaned to the side and issued a high-pitched hiss that reverberated through the cab.

And then the stench hit me.

My eyes watered. Bile rose in my throat.

Oh, holy God, if Skeegs could do one thing really well, it was stink up a joint.

I glared at One Eye.

He grinned.

"What is that smell?" A wail from the back, from beneath the linens.

"Welcome to my life," I muttered.

I pulled up at the barricade and tugged on the bill of my hat. I tried to look casual when the guard ambled over, a bearded Porcine with ominous tusks and enormous nostrils tipping his whiskered snout. He knocked on the window and I unrolled it.

His eyes crossed and he reeled back as a noxious cloud engulfed him, and shot a wary look at One Eye. "Power down," he grunted.

Hell. I'd hoped this would be a simple flash and roll.

I nodded and turned off the engine; I left the keys in the ignition.

"License and registration."

I nodded to One Eye, who fished around in the glove box as I pulled the fake ID I got from Skinny from my pocket. When my partner handed the registration over, it was caked with ooze. And Skeeg stank. I passed the documents to the guard, trying to hide my smirk. "Here you go."

He grimaced and held up the documents with two fingers, pretended to survey them, and then handed them back. "And what's your purpose in the Barrens?"

Right.

"Ah, damn it all to hell. I pulled this shit duty. Gotta make a delivery to one of the outposts. Gonna take all night."

He stared at me for a while and then nodded. I let out a breath—

"But I need to inspect your load."

Hell.

"Sure thing."

I opened the door and eased out, catching One Eye's gaze. He nodded. We were both on point. If we had to, we would take this guy out and run the blockade, guns blazing. I just hoped we didn't have to because the gate had mounted laser cannons pointed right at us. And we didn't have a whole lot of guns to blaze.

I headed around to the back and rolled up the door, following the guard inside. And damn . . . the pungent odor of a Skeeg in musth hit me like a wave. My eyes burned, lungs seized. I fixed a smile on my face and turned to the officer. He wasn't doing any better, poor guy. With his long snout, this had to be even worse for him. His cheeks pooched out as he held his breath. But—bless his heart—he persevered, peeping under the piles of folded sheets and then poking at the dirty laundry in the bin. Fortunately he didn't poke too deeply.

When he couldn't take it any longer, he blew out his breath and launched himself from the truck. He bent over, setting his hands on his knees and gasping for breath. "Jesus," he muttered as I rolled the door back down. "How do you stand it?"

I blinked. Probably to blink the tears from my eyes, but whatever. "Stand what?"

"That smell?"

"Oh. Right." I nodded. "You get used to it."

He shot me an incredulous glance. "No. You don't."

I shrugged and pointed to my nose. "Sinus condition. Can't smell a thing."

He snorted. "Lucky you. Well. You're clear to go. Just be careful. We have word there's another heavy storm coming in from the South tomorrow. You should find cover before it hits." He walked me back to the cab and then nodded. "Travel safe," he said. His tone was a little odd, so I glanced at him. His expression was odd too, for a gate guard just passing through a laundry truck heading for a mining colony.

I didn't ask.

If he was Mia's warthog, he'd never tell me anyway. Just like I'd go to my grave before telling anyone I was working for a Fed.

It was like asking for someone to shiv you. I wasn't that stupid, and neither was he.

I nodded to him though, before I hopped back up into the truck and started her up. The guard waved to whoever was manning the barrier and it lifted. The cannons went off point, and we rumbled into the tunnel that led to the broad, barren desert surrounding the city.

After we passed through, and I turned onto the road heading south to where I believed the Hive to be, I tossed over my shoulder, "Okay. All clear."

"Pflerg," Angel snarled as she fought her way out of the bin. "Someone, open a fucking window."

We followed the south road until the looming wall of the city was out of sight, and then I pulled over and shot a look at Angel.

She frowned at me. "What?" She was still a little perturbed by the smell in the cab, even though we had the windows open. Probably because the blowers on the undercarriage of the skimmer kicked up a hell of a dust cloud. In the city, you never even noticed the blowback necessary to keep us aloft—hell, it kept the streets clear of refuse—but out here, it was a problem. Especially if you had a farting Skeeg with you and wanted the windows open.

I ignored the wave of dust that caught up with us when I stopped. "I don't know where we're going," I said. No one really knew where the Hive was, just that it was in the desert. And this planet was mostly desert.

She stared at me, her face curiously blank. "You don't?"

"Don't you?"

"Uh . . ." She frowned. "No."

Well, hell.

"What do you think, One Eye?" I asked, shooting a glance

at my partner. He didn't respond because he was playing with the GPS, punching random buttons and murmuring to himself. Skeegs were fascinated with electronics. Probably because they didn't have them on Creel. Something about electricity and water being a bad mix. I knew we'd lost him for a while.

I looked out the windshield at the vast expanse of nothing. A couple red-ish crags mounded on the horizon. We could drive for days, weeks, and never find anything if we didn't know what we were looking for.

The city took up about a quarter of the surface of the moon, and I knew most of it like the back of my hand. The rest of this rock? Not so much. I'd never even been outside the walls. All I knew was what I'd been told. It was barren. Desert speckled with rocky monoliths. It ranged between bone-dry sandstorms to cloudbursts that bordered on deluges, flooding every flat surface. Within a day, the downpour would sink into the sand and it would be desolate and arid once more. Nothing indigenous lived out here except the sand beetles and the raptors that ate them, and even the transplants had a tough time staying alive.

The mining colonies were based in the Stony Buttes in huge caverns seated up high so the flood waters, when they came, could not swamp them. I had a vague idea of where they were located. Other than that, my impression of the Barrens was just that. A vast, empty expanse on a map.

"You sure you don't have any ideas?" I asked Angel.

She wrinkled her nose. "All they said was, 'head for the Keys.'"

What the hell was that supposed to mean? One Eye pressed a few more buttons on the GPS. The beeping was starting to annoy me. "How were you supposed to get to the Hive?" I tried to keep the impatience from my tone. Probably failed.

"I was supposed to be met by an escort." She huffed a breath.

"They found him stuffed in a trash can by the depot." Mia, no doubt. "'Head for the Keys' was my plan B."

"But we don't know what the Keys are."

She shrugged.

"Any plan C?"

"There's always a plan C."

"And what is that?"

"You won't like it."

"Probably not." I didn't like much lately. "What is it?"

"Flare."

"Flare?"

"Send up a signal."

She was right. I didn't like it. "That would notify everyone where we are."

"Exactly. And all we could do is hope the Sisterhood got to us first."

"Thin hope." Not knowing where the hell they were and all.

"We have to do something," she said. "The guard said there was a sandstorm rolling in."

I nodded. No one and nothing survived a sandstorm on the Viridian Barrens. The winds were unbelievably powerful, and the sand itself was caustic. When wind and earth whipped together in a frenzy like that, it was lethal. That shit would eat through the metal of our truck in two ticks. And then eat through us. Taking shelter at a mining colony was out of the question—no doubt Granny had put out an APB on us by now. Our best bet was to find a cave somewhere and sit out the storm. The upside was, the sandstorm would cover our hover tracks. "We'll head for those mountains." I nodded to the horizon.

"Wait." One Eye. A croak. He handed me the GPS module.

I stared at the screen. Then stared at him.

Holy crap. He'd plotted a route to a rock formation called . . . *the Keys*. And yeah. It was in the opposite direction than we would have been heading. "Good job, buddy," I said, clapping him on the shoulder. I rested my hand there for a moment, and then peeled it off. He was getting sticky.

I scrubbed my palm on my pants and started up the truck, turned it around, and headed north. We would have to go off road for this trek. I only hoped the sand wasn't too abrasive on our rotors, or didn't clog our fans. It would suck to break down out here. But it wasn't like we had a choice.

The GPS indicated the drive to the Keys would take nineteen hours, so I figured this would be a good time to get some rest. It felt like I hadn't slept in days, and God knew when we'd have a chance again, so I locked in the course and flicked on the autopilot.

Angel riffled through a locker bolted to the floor and found the driver's food stash. Apparently he was a binger—hardly a surprise; Polarians were known for their excessive, ahem, appetites. There was a lot of revolting stuff like squid mucus, larva paté, and protein bars. But he had other foods that were actually palatable, an eclectic selection that would last us for a while. I grabbed a sandwich and a beer for myself and thrust another at One Eye. He waved me off with a grimace. Yeah, sandwiches weren't Skeeg fare, by a long shot. They preferred algae. "You gotta eat." He really wasn't looking well. His skin was seeping something fierce, and he had swelled up even more. I was worried he might burst or something.

"Not hungry," he grumbled.

Whatever.

But when I handed him a bottle of water, he sucked it down in one gulp. Then he settled himself in the passenger seat with a sigh and retracted his eyestalk. It wasn't long before his snores rippled through the cab.

I settled next to Angel and shot her a tentative smile. I was gratified when she smiled back. This was hardly a date or anything, but damn, it felt like one.

I guess, despite my attempts to remain detached, I had it pretty bad.

We chowed down in silence and then leaned against the wall of the truck, relaxing to the hum of the skimmer. After a while, she set her hand on mine. I tried not to flinch at her touch, but it sent an electric jolt through me.

Yeah. I had it bad.

I glanced at her. Her green eyes seemed to lance right through to my soul. "Thank you, Tig. For this."

A ripple of guilt rose. I pushed it back down. "Yeah. Sure."

Silence again, but different this time. I could tell she was staring at me. Felt it. I locked my focus on the opposite wall because I couldn't meet her eyes.

"So what did you do?" she asked.

"Hmm?" I had a sense of what she was asking, but figured clarification would be advisable. Wouldn't want to voluntarily spill my guts about something else on accident.

"What did you do on your HP?"

"I was a cop."

"Dirty cop?" I didn't like the acid in her words.

"Don't need to be a dirty cop to end up here."

Her eyes narrowed. "Prison is usually for criminals."

"Usually."

"So why are you here?"

Ah, the question of the hour. "Here?"

She huffed an annoyed breath as I danced around the query. "You said you're here because you didn't follow orders. What orders didn't you follow?" Right. "What did you do?"

"It's what I didn't do."

"And?" Damn, she was relentless.

I gusted a sigh. Scrubbed my face. "Didn't kill a kid."

Conscience. Yeah. It'll get you every time.

She grunted. "For who?"

"The Fed." Who the hell else was there?

"Why did they want this kid dead?"

I shrugged. "I dunno." I did.

"So you refused the orders and they sent you here?"

"Not exactly. I didn't obey orders, they killed the kid anyway, and set me up to snag the credit." I kept staring at her because I knew, if I closed my eyes, I'd see that scene again. And I didn't want to see that again. The fuckers had made me watch. The screams still haunted me.

"Lucky you."

"I've always been a lucky guy."

"So . . . here you are."

"Here I am."

"A good cop on a shit planet. Surrounded by criminals who want to feast on your innards."

I attempted a grin. "Only some of them. And what makes you think I'm a good cop?" That was quite a leap.

"Any other flatfoot would have delivered me to Granny. Let me get carved up by Scale."

"Maybe not all of them."

She snorted. "You put yourself at risk, helping me. They wouldn't have done that." Probably not. She turned a bit; her gaze became steadier. "Why?"

I stared at her exquisite face. Swallowed. My pulse thrummed. She was far too close. I could smell her breath. Feel her warmth. That old familiar ache swelled. "Haven't you figured that out yet?" A whisper. No need to say it out loud.

Besides, hell, I'd just figured it out myself.

"I—"

Didn't let her finish. Didn't want to hear. Couldn't bear it if it was some kind of gentle rebuff.

I leaned forward and silenced her with a kiss. A soft one. Gentle.

She didn't pull away.

And I took her then. Took those lips with mine. Let every vestige of my need and hunger flow through. Every scrap of my soul.

She stiffened as my lips touched hers, but then, as the kiss continued, she breathed a soft sigh and leaned into it, responded, dabbing her tongue against mine. It quickly became something else. Something wild and fragrant. Something corded with hunger and angst and need. Her fingers raked through my hair, nails nested in my scalp. She consumed me.

And I consumed her.

Our lips clung.

Her taste suffused me, filled my brain. Elated me. Made me whole and left me empty at the same time. Left me longing for more. I knew it couldn't happen. Could never happen, but that didn't quash my hunger. My hope.

It crossed my mind that she might be playing me. She had before, pretending to be all soft and helpless, but at the moment, it seemed genuine. And frankly, I kind of didn't care if she was putting on an act. It was a damned tantalizing kiss.

She pulled away and gazed into my eyes. "Guess I'm pretty lucky too," she murmured. And then she nestled closer and laid her head on my chest. I froze. And then, when I could manage it, curled my arms around her and held her.

And tried to ignore that annoying ripple of guilt.

We slept for a while, and then ate something and slept a little more. Occasionally, I wandered up to the front to check on the route. Made sure the autopilot was still on track and checked where we were on the GPS. Night had fallen again, so there wasn't much to see as we hummed through the dark desert. It was a good thing the truck had a self-charging proton battery, so we wouldn't need to juice up. There weren't many power stations in these parts. The only thing I had to worry about was the temperature of the engines. If the filters were crap, the rotors would clog with sand and eventually grind to a halt, but so far, everything looked good.

One Eye was quiet, curled up in a ball in the passenger seat.

Seriously. A ball. He had his knees up to his chest—as close as they could get over his bulging middle—and he had his arms wrapped around them. His goo was starting to harden into a crust. I wasn't sure what that meant, but it probably wasn't good.

His eye peeped out and blinked at me.

"You okay, buddy?" I asked in an undertone.

He grunted.

"Need some water?"

Another grunt.

I grabbed a bottle from the stash and handed it to him. He tipped up his face, expectantly, so I opened the bottle and poured the water into his mouth. But he closed his mouth. The water dribbled all over his face. He sighed.

And I got it.

He was drying out.

I dumped another bottle over him and he shivered in pleasure, but I had to be careful. We didn't have a lot, and I didn't know how long it had to last. And, God forbid we broke down in the desert, we'd need it. It would be the difference between life and death.

About dawn, the alarm went off. I woke with a start, surprised to find myself alone in the back. Angel and I had spent the night curled together—sleeping. It was a shock to wake up alone. I wasn't sure why.

I hefted to my feet, brushed the wrinkles from my clothes,

and made my way up front. Angel was in the driver's seat, and One Eye was by her side. He looked much better this morning, but still a little crusty.

"What is it?" I asked over the blare of the claxon.

"Sandstorm alert." Angel frowned. "We've been running ahead of it for the past ten hours, but it's catching us. We need to find shelter."

I leaned over her and glanced in the rearview mirror. A large, dark cloud roiled in our wake.

Hell.

I scanned the landscape. Pointed at some lumps on the horizon. "Can we make those?"

Her expression was harsh. A muscle worked in her cheek. "We'd better." Then she shifted into seventh gear and the truck surged forward. It was a wear on the engines. I could hear them wail, but we didn't have a choice.

It was a damn shame the proximity alert hadn't given us a little more time.

I hoped to hell there was a cave in those rocks, or we were all going to be finely polished bones.

We barely made it. The engine was chuckling and billowing smoke by the time those rocks loomed up before us. And the raging cloud was almost on us. Thank God Angel was at the controls. She was much sharper than I was. She spotted a dark recess, a crevice in the stones, and with a wail from the engines, made a 90-degree turn and jetted us into a cave.

We still weren't safe. Depending on the direction and ferocity of the wind, the storm could still eat us. Only slowing a bit, she followed a tunnel, deeper and deeper into the cave, until it became too narrow for the truck to pass.

We shuddered to a halt.

"Come on," she called. Grabbing her satchel and opening the door, she sprinted for a smaller tunnel leading off at a backward angle. One Eye and I followed without demur. We had to get out of the reach of the shrieking winds. The more twists and turns we took, the better.

I could hear the storm approaching. The rumble of a freight train, the scream of an anguished bird. And fury. Definitely fury. I could only imagine the hell that was unfolding outside. But then, I didn't want to. Following the beam of light from the torch Angel had snagged from the cab, we headed down the slope into the bowels of this rock. Gradually, the howling faded.

Another sound rose over the echoes of our footfalls. An incessant drip, drip, drip.

One Eye went on point.

When we came to a fork in the tunnels and Angel paused, trying to decide which way to go—we didn't want to head back into the maelstrom—One Eye nudged her aside and padded into the left passage. His nose was high, quivering. His stride, determined.

I glanced at Angel. She shrugged. We followed.

He led us into a cavern, lit by some phosphorescent diatoms. It was a cool blue light, emanating from a serene pond and rippling in waves over the stony walls. Stalactites and stalagmites kissed here and there, and the walls were speckled with large, glowing crystals. The cave had a pleasant, damp-earth scent.

Angel blew out a breath. "Wow."

Right? Who knew such beauty existed beneath the harsh surface. Judging from the erosion patterns on the walls, the cavern filled up when the rains came. There had to be a crevice or two leading to the surface.

One Eye didn't pause. Unbuckling his holster, he let it drop and made a beeline for the water. He walked right in, all the way to his neck—his low moan bounced off the walls—and then he submerged. Bubbles tracked his passage.

Angel chuckled as she dropped her satchel on a stone

outcropping. "Well, he's happy." Her voice echoed off the stony walls.

"He deserves it. He's been a trooper through all this."

"Yeah. He has. Considering." She shot a grin at me and then sat on a flat rock. I sat next to her. "Why do you think he did it?" she asked.

"Helped us?"

"Yeah."

"I like to think it's because he's loyal to me."

She patted my hand. "That's cute."

"You don't think so?"

Her lips twisted. "He turned on a Creel. That doesn't happen."

I lifted a shoulder. "Maybe I'm just that awesome."

Her expression was sardonic. "You hold on to that thought, Skippy."

"What? I am." I eased closer. 'Til our thighs touched. I was gratified she didn't pull away.

"I'm sure you are," she said. "But you Earthies don't exactly have a firm grasp of KU politics."

True. That fact had slapped me in the face more than once during my internment. I'd had to take a crash course on the various species of the Known Universe and their history when I arrived, just to stay alive. There were some gaps in my knowledge.

"How long has it been since the Fed annexed your planet?"

I looked away. Shrugged. "'Bout ten years."

"And how long have you been here on Viridian?"

"'Bout ten years. You got a point here?"

"Yeah. My point is, you're a nube. Oblivious to the basic understandings the rest of us have. When I tell you a Skeeg would never turn on a Creel, you should believe me."

There was a hint of irritation in her tone and I didn't like it. "Okay," I said. "Will you explain it to me?"

Her eyes glittered in the strange light of the pool. One Eye's bubbles blurped. "Okay. Creel is a bi-denizen planet. That means two dominant species evolved at—"

"I know what bi-denizen means." I wasn't a complete rube.

"All right. But did you know the two are symbiotic lifeforms?"

Hell. I hadn't known that.

"They need each other to stay alive. Aside from that, in the ecosystem, the Skeegs are the submissive organisms. A Creel might betray a Skeeg, but never the other way around. They just aren't wired that way."

I glanced at the pool. One Eye was now floating and doing the backstroke. I lowered my voice. "So you think he might be playing us?"

"I think, if he's helping us, it's because that is what Granny wanted him to do. Regardless, we need to keep an eye on him."

I nodded. One Eye flipped over onto his stomach and began to cruise through the pond with his mouth agape, hoovering up the phytoplankton. Damn, he must have been hungry.

Silence cloaked us as we both indulged in our own thoughts. Mine were dark—memories, curiosities, regrets. After a while, I asked the question that had plagued me for a decade. I don't know why I put words to it. It was, after all, a moot point. "Why do you think they came to Earth?"

"The Fed?"

I nodded. "Yeah. After a millennium of leaving us be."

She huffed a laugh. It held no humor. "They left you alone because you weren't a problem. It was only when you emerged as a threat that they made their move."

"Hell, we were hardly a threat." All we'd wanted to do was smoke weed and watch cable television.

"You *weren't* a threat. The KU considered Earth to be nothing but a backwater of ignorant savages. Occasionally, some peckerwood would do a drive-by, abduct some Illinois house-wife, and slip her an anal probe . . . but they were only dicking with you."

"Why?"

"Because you were clueless. You had no idea there was a whole cosmos of civilization just beyond your borders."

"And what changed? What brought them to us?"

She shrugged. "Some Earth genius decided to send out a probe. *Voyager*, I think they called it. It landed in a system that was opposed to Earth inclusion in the Alliances, so they kept it under wraps. But the Fed eventually found out. That put you on their radar. And when you guys developed space travel . . ."

"Yeah?"

"That put you on a watch list. You do not want to be on a Fed watch list."

"Why?"

"Two reasons. First of all, it adds you to the equation. A planet with interstellar travel capabilities will always be a concern to the Fed, the régime with one goal: to control the KU. Second of all, given your level of technology little more than two hundred years ago, there's no way you could have made the jump to light speed on your own. Someone had to be helping you. Feeding you info. Slipping you schematics. Tech."

"Yeah. I got no idea what you're talking about."

"Think about it, Tig. When did things change on Earth?"

I shrugged. I was hardly a historian. Probably something to do with all the weed and cable television.

"The atom bomb that ended your World War II? Standard mining tech on Gnomus Prime."

"I don't even know what that is."

"Doesn't matter. Point is, the tech didn't originate on Earth. And then, in '47 ET—"

"ET?"

"Earthtime. There was an incident in New Mexico."

"Roswell?" A squawk. "Are we talking Area 51 shit?"

She sighed. "Drunk drivers. Point was, they crashed, and some curious Hume scientists got their hands on technology they shouldn't have. Started the ball rolling." Her expression darkened. "There are some who believe it wasn't an accident. That it was intentional."

"Who would want to give us tech that could kill us all?"

"Someone with noble intentions, probably." Yeah. In my experience, that was usually the kiss of death. "Someone who knew the Fed would eventually come and thought you deserved a fighting chance, maybe."

"They would have come?"

"Of course. All this just moved up the timetable. When you sent a man outside of your system, they knew they had to make their move. Nip it in the bud."

"Nip what in the bud?"

She shot me a commiserating look and shook her head. "Look at you. Your species. Your nature. You have a don't-give-a-goddamn attitude. You're naturally rebellious. You like to kick up dirt. They couldn't have that."

"So they invaded."

"Technically, it was an annexation."

I snorted a laugh. "That what they're calling it?" A military invasion? Wave after wave of Blue faces carrying laser rifles? Locking down the cities and states? Martial fucking law? Bodies everywhere?

She leveled me with a solemn look. "That's what they are calling it. It's how they roll. Peaceful assimilation."

Peaceful, my ass.

"You should consider yourself lucky."

"Like hell."

"You had a childhood, free of slavery—"

"Slavery?"

"Yeah." She squeezed my hand and huffed a laugh. "You really have no idea what they are, do you?"

"I've been busy." Been here almost since the start. The only Blues I'd ever interacted with were the assholes who'd set me up on Earth and the guards here. Neither experience had been stellar.

"You didn't grow up under a Blue thumb. You don't know what it's like to spend your childhood in fear. Enslaved. You have no idea what they do. You have no idea what's happening on your planet right now." I had a pretty good idea. I didn't like to think about it.

"Where are you going with this?"

She shot a look at One Eye, who was rolling around in the algae. "I was . . . just curious, is all."

"Curious about what?"

"Everything I've heard about Earthies. I just was wondering if it was all true."

Umm . . . "What have you heard?"

"That you're savage. Defiant. Stubborn." She glanced at me beneath her lashes. "That you have a rebellious nature. A strength of character that can't be crushed."

Had to wonder what kind of fairy tale she'd been reading. "They crushed us."

"Hmm." A grunt. "And look at you. You're not crushed. Not crushed at all."

I gaped at her, I begged to differ. I'd watched them die. My whole family. My friends. The people I thought were my enemies. Everyone. I was pretty freaking crushed. I would kill or die to have any one of them back.

She glanced at my hands, which had curled to fists. Her lips quirked. Her look said, *Toldya so.*

"What are you trying to say, Angel?"

"Nothing." *Right.* "Just, there aren't many species in the

KU with a backbone left. Most of their spirits have been beaten into the dust."

Something in her tone snagged my attention. "And . . . the others?"

We both spoke softly now, our gazes locked on One Eye, who was literally in his element, practically in orgasmic raptures.

"The others . . ." Her voice dropped a notch lower. "Still fight."

"Fight the Fed?" Was she kidding me? Judging from her expression, she was not. I straightened up. Hit her with a sharp glare. "What are you talking about?"

"Other systems, thousands of them, are tired of being ground beneath the Blue boot."

"Are you talking . . . rebellion?" Hell.

She lifted a delicate shoulder. "Bound to happen. As dictatorial as they are." She blew out a breath. "Of course, I'm talking theoretically here."

"Of course."

"If there were such a rebellion, it would be a lonely battle." She shot a look at me and added, "I'm sure they would . . . appreciate another ally. Someone defiant. Stubborn. Savage."

I don't know why my heart trilled with excitement. Maybe the thought of finding a way, any way, to strike back at the Fed. I hated those bastards. I really did.

"If there were such a rebellion, would you . . . be interested?"

Fucking A. "Might be."

I liked the way her lips curled.

I liked it a lot.

One Eye rose up out of the water and shook off. Algae splattered everywhere. His grin was wide as he padded up to us. Damn. His skin was a vibrant green, and there were little brown speckles all over his flippers. Some plankton dribbled from his chin. He flicked out his tongue and slurped it up.

"Feel better?" I asked.

"Yup." A deep, throaty croak. He held out a hand, full of blue goo. "Want some?"

"I, uh, think I'll pass."

He grunted, sat down next to us, and began to lap. Angel shot me a grin.

"Any idea how long the storm will last?" I asked.

One Eye shrugged. "A day?"

Angel nodded. "Depends on how big it is. I'll head up and check after a while. But, in the meantime, we should rest."

I wasn't tired, but she was right. Who knew what tomorrow would bring?

TEN

I liked that when I laid down, using the cloak as a pad, she curled up next to me. It was a little distracting, having her ass pressing up against my groin, but when I curled my arms around her, she didn't smack them away. So I was cool with being distracted.

One Eye slept in the pond.

I guess he figured he needed to take this opportunity to soak in as much water as he could. He was probably right.

Somehow, I drifted off. I was in the middle of a dream, featuring a beautiful, green-eyed siren, on her knees before me, when something woke me. A gentle, probing touch. The stroke of her toes against my ankle. I grinned to myself, a sleepy offering, and tightened my hold on her. I was on my back, with her on my chest. It was a nice weight. She murmured something indistinct and sighed against my neck.

Her toe moved higher. Curled around my ankle. Coiled up my leg. I liked where this was heading . . . until it occurred to me that toes, generally, didn't coil. By the time I realized it wasn't her at all, it was too late. The tentacle tightened on my leg and yanked.

I bellowed and lurched up and gaped at the thing that had a hold of me, even as it dragged me toward the pool. *Shit!*

It was too much like a snake for comfort, long and slimy, and it was corded with muscle. I scrabbled at the rocks as I passed, even got a good grip on one, but I couldn't hold on for long.

"Jesus!" I howled as Angel leaped to her feet and cast about for a weapon. She scrabbled for a pistol and aimed. "Shoot it!"

She hit it dead on. The sound of the blast bounced off the walls. The creature—whatever it was—screeched and released me. And the limb whipped back into the water.

I stood, panting, and scanned the pool. My heart was in my throat. My ulcer babies were in an uproar. "Where's One Eye?" I cried. I didn't see him. I didn't see him anywhere.

A fountain of water erupted from the pond as One Eye surfaced, with a nasty-looking squid-thing in his grasp. The two thrashed and splashed. Angel took aim, but they were moving too fast for her to get a bead on that thing without taking a chance of hitting One Eye.

In a flash, they submerged. Bubbles and waves rippled through the pond. My pulse pinged, muscles bunched. If this didn't go our way, we had to be ready to run.

I should have known better.

I should have trusted my partner, who'd been born and raised in water.

After a long, long moment, One Eye burst to the surface with a loud gasp, and then he walked to the shore, dragging a limp jumble of tentacles behind him. He dropped it at my feet and grinned. And then, he croaked, "Dinner."

I gaped at him.

Dinner?

Really?

But we scraped some dried algae from the rocks and piled it up and started a fire while One Eye sliced up his kill, which he then roasted over the flames. His expression was proud as he handed me a chunk.

I held it between two fingers and studied it. "Seriously?"

Angel nudged me with her shoulder. "Gumvar. It's a delicacy

on Vanit." She popped a bit into her mouth and moaned. "Scrumptious."

I eyed her suspiciously.

"Go on. Try it."

I did. A lick. When that didn't make me gag, I took a nibble. Okay. It wasn't heinous. Kind of like . . . calamari.

One Eye grunted and lit in. I guess he was still hungry. Maybe the plankton had been only a salad or something.

It was kind of horrifying watching him eat. He slurped and snorted and even growled a little as he consumed slice after slice of Gumvar. Little bits of it dangled from his teeth when he shot me a grin. "Gooood." He nodded.

"Yeah. Good." It filled my belly, at the very least.

And best of all, I was eating it. Rather than the other way around.

After we finished our meal—such as it was—we decided to head back out and check on the storm, you know, in case there were any more Gumvars lurking in our cave. One Eye assured me this one was a youngster, which meant there were probably parents somewhere around.

If this one was a youngster, I didn't want to tangle with one that was fully grown.

My partner was a little gloomy as we plodded up the tunnel, away from the pool. He might have glanced back a time or six. It occurred to me once more how rough it must be for him to be incarcerated on a dry planet when his whole world was one big swimming pool. As hard as it was for me to be here, at least there was oxygen.

We came around the corner into the main tunnel, and I stumbled on a hummock of sand. One that hadn't been there before. I could tell the storm had passed because the howling had ceased, but I wasn't prepared for what I saw. A mound, blocking the passage. It took a moment for me to realize it was our truck. Buried.

Kind of humbling because we were parked about a mile in. I couldn't imagine the damage the storm would have done had we been exposed.

It took a couple hours to dig out. We piled the sand behind us, so we wouldn't have to fight it getting out, and then we took a little extra time to clean out the fans, filters, and rotors. Finally, we got the truck ready to run again.

Before we left, we all went back down to the pond to wash off the sand. It was everywhere, in my hair, my clothes, my nostrils. I wasn't even a Skeeg, and it was grating on my every nerve. And I have to admit, as brackish as it was, the water felt good. I didn't mind seeing Angel get wet either.

The GPS said we still had a couple hours to go before we reached the Keys, but we were all well-rested, refreshed, and filled to the gills—forgive the pun—with Gumvar. It was a relief to turn the key and feel the engines rev, the skimmers lift the truck. We were immediately surrounded with a cloud of dust, of course, so I went slowly as I maneuvered through the maze of tunnels. I hadn't been paying attention when we rushed in, but the GPS had a *69 to reverse the route.

I nibbled at my smile as we rounded a bend and harsh daylight flooded the cavern. It took a sec for my eyes to adjust. That, and the dust curtain probably accounted for the reason I didn't see them.

The thump-thump-thump was the first indication that I was hitting something.

I eased off the gas, flicked on the wipers, and peered through the windshield. And—*thump*—hit another. This one plastered against the glass for a second, his face frozen in a surprised expression before he slid beneath the truck, so I got a good look.

Tiny, piercing eyes.

Flat beak.

Feathers.

Damn.

Cluckers.

A flock of them.

I gunned it, plowed through the throng attempting to block us in. When we burst out of the mouth of the cave, I eased off on the throttle to let the dust—and the feathers—settle.

And hell. There were birds everywhere. They surrounded us in a malevolent arc.

One Eye bristled. Which surprised me. I'd never seen his spikes before. He scanned the flock and nodded to the biggest one, a rooster. "Crow," he snorted.

Aw, hell. Warble's boss. No doubt he'd followed us to exact revenge for our earlier massacre. But—

"How did he find us?" Angel voiced my question.

One Eye frowned and then pulled out his scanner, waving it over his arm, his belly, his leg. It beeped.

He grimaced and took his knife and then sliced himself open. I gaped because seriously, what else do you do when a dude pulls out a knife and opens his own leg? Also, his flesh beneath the skin was some kind of gelatinous goo. He fished around and pulled out a small bug with a blinking light. He narrowed his eye and crushed it beneath his heel.

"Must have put a tracer in you when they captured us earlier," I muttered.

Hell. They'd been tracking us all along.

One Eye snorted and then stood and grabbed me by the scruff, levering me out of the driver's seat. I really didn't have a choice. He was a lot stronger than me and, apparently, pissed off. If he wanted to drive, hell, who was I to stop him?

Crow stared at us, puffed out his chest, waggled his comb.

One Eye revved the engines.

Then the rooster lifted his piece and aimed.

One Eye gunned it.

I could have sworn he chuckled as our truck zoomed forward. Crow dodged out of the way, but the hens weren't quite so quick. We caught a couple with that first pass. They squawked as we bowled them over. Then, instead of taking off and jetting toward the Keys as we probably should have, One Eye turned us around and came at the flock again from another angle, sending them all scattering. The smart ones ran for the cave.

Apparently One Eye had a bone to pick with the birds. He probably hadn't gotten over the fork thing. Or the licking. I could hardly blame him, but seriously. "I think that's good," I assured him.

He ignored me. He took another pass, then came around again and crashed into their skimmers, which toppled, one after the other.

It occurred to me that if we kept this up, we'd wreck our own transport.

It also occurred to me that I probably should never piss off One Eye.

"That's good," I repeated, but he didn't let up until Angel set a hand on his shoulder.

"We should go," she said.

One Eye stared at her, then nodded. He yanked on the wheel and sent us careening off, out into the open desert, away from Crow and his thugs.

They would probably try to follow, if they could, if their rides weren't too trashed. Our best bet was to put as much distance between ourselves and the Avian Nation as we could.

We didn't get far before the engine started chunking. Not as far as I would have liked, at least. It was an ominous sound. "Pull over," I said, and One Eye nodded. He headed for a monolith to our left and parked in its shadow. This one was a tall, craggy column, not like the looming mound where we'd found shelter. There were no caves pitting the surface, nowhere to hide if someone found us.

But we had to check the engine. Fix it if we could, or we would never make it to the Keys. According to the GPS, they were still several klicks away. Too far to walk in the blistering heat, for sure.

Figuring it was probably a surfeit of sand clogging the engine, I grabbed a brush and crawled under the front end. "Aw, hell."

"What is it?" Angel called.

"Feathers." A plethora of them. Enough for a pillow at least. They were mixed with what I could only presume were chicken guts. Nice. I grabbed handful after handful and yanked them out of the rotors, manually turned them and did it again, until they were clean. Then I gave everything a good brushing. While I was down there, I checked the pistons and the fans as well. They weren't in the best condition, but they were serviceable.

I was sweating by the time I crawled out.

Sweating and covered with feathers. I didn't appreciate One Eye's chuckle. I glared at him, but there wasn't a lot of heat in it.

In an unspoken accord, we all took a short break to eat and relieve ourselves before we crawled back into the cab. It also gave the engines a chance to cool down. And it gave me a chance to think. I was annoyed that the Cluckers had slapped a tracker on One Eye, and it made me wonder if they'd tagged me too. I didn't like the thought that they might still be able to follow us. So I turned to One Eye and held out my arms. "Sweep me."

He blinked.

"Go on. Sweep me. We need to make sure none of us are tagged."

He nodded, slow and silent, and pulled out his scanner. As he made a pass over my arm, it beeped. *Crap.* Last thing I wanted to do was slice myself open and—

The scanner beeped again. Over my leg, my chest, my head. *What the hell?*

"In the bloodstream," Angel murmured, staring at me with a pitying look, one that curdled my gut.

"Not Cluckers," One Eye added.

"Not . . ." But who, then?

My stomach knotted.

Right.

I should have figured Mia would never let me leave town without some leash.

"Well, hell." I scrubbed my face.

Angel tipped her head to the side and studied me. "Why would the Fed be tracking you?"

My heart leaped—yeah, fucking leaped—into my throat. "What makes you think it's the Fed?" This, I practically stuttered.

"Seriously, Tig?" She crossed her arms. "They're the only ones with this kind of tech. They're the only ones allowed to use it." I didn't like the shadow that crossed over her face. Didn't like it one bit. "Are you working for the Fed?" A whisper, wreathed in disenchantment. It nearly gutted me. That, and the way One Eye took a step back and fingered his pistol.

"No!" When they merely stared back at me warily, I added, "I'm not. I hate them."

One of them in particular.

"We all hate them, Tig. That's hardly an endorsement of sincerity. They are nasty, duplicitous, manipulative creatures. They have ways of turning people. Trust me. I know."

"I am not working for them!" I wasn't. I'd made the decision long ago that if I had the first chance, I would screw Mia over, any way I could. That she was probably tracking me, even now, was horrifying. For one thing, it made me an accomplice to anything that happened to Angel. And I couldn't bear anything happening to her. Not now.

Her gaze narrowed. I had the sense that she was staring into my soul. And she might have seen something. Her expression hardened. "But they approached you."

Shit. I slumped down and scrubbed my face. "Yeah."

"You'd better tell us everything."

I glanced at them, from one to the other, and sucked in a deep breath. "Okay. Yeah. One of them asked me to help you escape the city."

"Asked?"

Well, *asked* was hardly the word for it. "She . . . has something on me."

Angel snorted. "They usually do."

"I knew if I helped you get to the Hive, I'd be betraying Granny. If I didn't, they'd execute me. Either way, I was in deep trouble. So I agreed. I didn't have a choice. But I didn't make up my mind which way I would go until . . ."

"Until what?"

"Until I met you." I thought my tone was sincere, but she didn't seem convinced. "And then, I found out Granny was planning to—"

"Carve me up?"

"Yeah. I couldn't let that happen. But I swear, I didn't know Mia was tracking me." She must have injected the microbots when I was unconscious in Maltby's Rat hole. Bitch. No wonder she'd been on me the whole time.

Angel stilled. Her expression went blank. "Mia? Mia Dia Ous Inkley Dominios?" she forced through stiff lips.

I nodded. "Tall? Slender? Blue skin?" Built like a brick

shithouse? Screams when she comes? "You know her?" I could tell from the look in her eye, she did.

"What . . . ahem . . . what is your relationship with her?"

Heat crawled up my neck. I didn't want to admit it—not that I'd slept with the enemy, not to the woman I wanted to be next on the list—but I knew I had to. "We, ah, had a thing."

"Had?"

"It was a long time ago. Over now." I slashed my hand to make a point, though I don't know how it mattered. It wasn't as though this was something Angel could forget. Or forgive.

She blew out a breath. "It's never over with them."

Ella's face flickered in my mind. My heart clenched. "It is with her."

Angel waved at my person. "But she still has her claws in you."

I firmed my jaw. "Not by choice. She . . . betrayed me."

A harsh laugh fluttered from her. "What a shock. A Blue not keeping a promise?"

"I was a nube, remember?" I'd had no idea what she was capable of back then. No idea about much, really. Still don't.

"Let me guess. You were flattered she was interested in you." *Kinda.* "She promised to keep you safe. She offered you special deals. She gave you small, innocuous jobs to do." *Pretty close.* "She drew you in. And then, she seduced you."

Okay, right on the money.

I nodded. I couldn't meet her gaze. One Eye stared at me, clucking his tongue and shaking his head. I wasn't sure which disillusionment mortified me more.

"Look. I'm—"

"Don't. Don't say you're sorry."

But I was.

Angel turned away and stared out at the desert. She raked

her fingers through her hair and gusted a sigh. "We just need to decide what to do now."

What to do? "Uh, what do you mean?"

She turned to my partner. "Do we take him with us, or leave him here?"

Leave me here? In the wilderness? All alone? I nearly eeped.

The Skeeg nodded in agreement and my pulse surged.

"What do you think?" she asked. "Do you trust him?"

I tried not to give him the puppy dog eye as he thought it over, but, hell. I didn't want them to leave me. I really didn't. It was a death sentence. A—

"Yes."

I never loved the sound of his throaty, Froggy voice more. I nearly collapsed with relief. Which was foolish because he was only half the banishment equation. I shot a look at her. She didn't appear welcoming, with her legs braced, her arms crossed. She drummed her fingers on her bicep. Studied me for far too long.

Then she blew out a sigh.

"Come here," she said in a tone that sounded a little too full of disgust for comfort. But really, I didn't have a choice.

As I approached her, she opened her arms. My steps slowed. It looked like she was offering a hug, but part of my brain knew that wasn't normal in this kind of situation. I shot her a curious glance.

"Here," she repeated. So I stepped into her embrace.

To my shock and delight, she curled herself around me in an intimate clinch and held me tight. I was about to chuckle and say something pithy when an odd sensation rose within me. It felt like little bolts of electricity zinging along my nerves, dancing through my veins. A sparkling cloud swelled around us, speckled with beautiful, tantalizing lights. "Close your eyes," she muttered. And I did. But through my lids, a caught a bright flash of light, just as a huge wave of energy surged through me.

It knocked me to my knees. She let me fall. I clambered to my hands and knees, gasping for breath. That had been . . . brain scrambling. And, if I was being honest, highly erotic. I was fully erect. Which was stupid of me. Because *that* wasn't getting play anytime soon.

I glanced up at her. "What . . . what did you just do?"

Angel grinned. "I cleaned your clock."

What the fuck?

"Demagged your trackers."

I boggled. "You . . . what?"

"All of them." She batted her lashes. "Now poor Mia doesn't have a clue where you are."

Wow. Just, wow. I was too befuddled to even process this. Or maybe her electrical field had fried my brain a little too.

I glanced at One Eye. "Scan me," I said. He did. Ran the reader up and down my body. Not a blip.

Holy hell.

Angel tapped my temple. "Got your con chip too."

I swallowed. Each con had one. They were implanted on intake. It was a cross between a brand and a kill switch. Without it, I was free. Free.

Kinda hard to wrap my brain around.

"How do you do that?" I asked when I could manage it.

She shrugged. "I'm electrogenic."

I had no idea what that meant.

Obviously she could tell. She sighed. "Some of the people on my planet have the ability to create and use electric current. It comes in handy as a weapon, or . . ." She waved at me. "When an EMP is necessary." She wrinkled her nose. "Your cell is fried, by the way. Sorry."

She didn't sound sorry at all, but I didn't care.

Hell. My con chip was dead. The threat that had loomed over my life for ten long years, just gone in the blink of an eye.

Angel frowned. "Why are you looking at me like that?"

Was I? Looking at her? Like that?

"Is my con chip really gone?"

"It's not gone. It's still in your brain. But it's fried."

"Why did you do that?" I asked.

"Don't you know?"

"No." Jesus. Could it be because she had feelings for me? The kind I might be growing for—

"We can't have the Fed following us."

Oh. Yeah. Right.

"We should probably get going," I said, but only because I couldn't think of anything to say that wouldn't make me look like a mooning, lovelorn swain.

One Eye turned to her and opened his arms. "Hug me too."

She chuckled and did so, and this time, I had the privilege of watching, of seeing her light rise and shine.

I probably shouldn't have watched because it was a really bright white light, and it filled my vison with little back dots, blinding me. I blinked a bit to clear it, but it didn't work.

So it was equally horrifying when a shot whizzed past my head just then. I didn't see it coming. Literally. By the grace of God, it smacked into the monolith behind me, sending down a shower of rubble. And I had no idea who was shooting at me, at us, until Angel bellowed, "Cluckers. 2:00."

I pulled my pistol and pointed it toward the sound of approaching skimmers. Then I squeezed the trigger and fired.

"Oh, pflerg!" Angel yelled. At my 2:30. "Watch where you're shooting!"

"I can't see," I responded.

"To the left, flatfoot."

I readjusted and fired some more, blindly splattering our

attackers with round after round. I was gratified to hear a war-bled howl and the sound of a collision as the skimmers crashed, but I wasn't sure if it was my bullet or someone else's who'd hit home. But it hardly mattered. I just kept firing.

As Angel called out the positions of the birds, and I shot blind skeet, the wind picked up, bringing in the acrid scent of blood and a gentle rain of feathers. They surrounded me in a cloud of fluff. I spat several from my mouth and then snorted one out of my nostril. Apparently the distraction turned me around because the next time I fired, Angel bellowed, "Watch where you're shooting!"

"Have I mentioned I'm blind?" I bellowed back.

"Can you hear my voice?" she snapped. Well, I could hear the disgust in her voice. "Try shooting in the other direction."

Fine. I pivoted and focused on where the laser blasts were coming from. One sizzled past my cheek. Close. Too close. But it gave me a pretty damn good idea where to shoot and I let off a round of bullets, along with a manly primal scream.

All of a sudden, I realized I was the only one still shooting. Angel set her hand on mine and I lowered my weapon. "They're dead," she said. "You can stop."

Right.

I felt her palms cup my cheeks, knew she was staring at me, but couldn't see shit. Her breath huffed over my face as she sighed. "Did you watch?"

"Yeah." My lips quirked. "It was pretty."

"Dumbass." There was no heat in the word. "Come on." She hooked her arm in mine and led me to the skimmer . . . and then stilled. I stumbled to a halt beside her. "Oh my God." Horror threaded through her tone.

"What is it?"

"One Eye was hit."

Fuck.

"Is he okay?"

"He's . . . foaming."

Not good. Not good at all. "Let's get him inside. We need to get moving," I said. "We can put the skimmer on autopilot and tend to him." God knew, I couldn't drive or see to him. I couldn't see to anything.

Angel led me over to my partner, and together, we helped him to his feet. His moans were indistinct and feral. I hated that I couldn't see him. Couldn't help him. Not really. "How long will this blindness last?" I asked, fumbling for the door.

"No idea," she muttered as she rolled up the door and we helped One Eye inside and settled him with a thump on the floor. Well, she helped One Eye. I mostly flailed around. "Depends on the photo receptivity of your retina. I've never flashed a Hume before."

"Wow. I feel so honored."

She grunted. "Stay with him." The door rolled down again, and she went around to the driver's side. The engine powered up—thankfully with no more clunking—and we shot into motion. As I waited for her to return to the back, I did a quick check of One Eye's body, feeling for wounds. She was right, he was foaming. Covered with a thick coating of it that clung to my fingers like mucus. His pain must be pretty bad. I found the bullet wound—mostly because he recoiled when I touched it.

"Sorry, buddy." I was.

Sorry that I'd hurt him.

Sorry that he'd been shot, probably because I was a dumbass.

Sorry that the wound was to the chest.

I didn't know much about Skeeg physiology, but most creatures have their critical organs in the chest. I had no idea how bad this was. And because I couldn't see, and because everything felt wet, I had no idea how much blood there was.

Angel settled down beside me with a sigh.

"Well?" I asked.

She did a quick survey as well. "Not good."

Damn.

"Our best bet is to let him foam up and get him to the Hive as quick as we can."

"Let him foam?"

"It's how Skeegs heal." Though I couldn't see it, I felt her gaze on me. Her energy practically hummed through me. "He's your partner. Didn't you know that?"

"Uh . . . no." I didn't know much about him at all. I'd never cared enough to find out.

Like I said, I was a dumbass.

"Well, it is," she said gently. "They foam and then it turns into a crust. Like a chrysalis. It allows them time to regenerate. If the wound isn't too severe."

"And if the wound is too severe?"

Silence.

The worst sound I ever heard.

"I'll clean it the best I can, so there's no chance of infection, and then we need to let him rest. Although . . ."

"Yeah?"

"Some water wouldn't go amiss. Aside from the wound, dehydration is a serious risk for him because the foam draws fluids from his cells."

"I'll get some." I crawled over to the locker and felt around for a bottle. She took it and cracked it open. I could hear the dribbles. The sighs.

"There. That's about all we can do," Angel said. "Why don't you get some rest and I'll keep an eye on the road."

Sure. Okay.

"And, Angel?"

A heartbeat.

"Yeah?"

"I'm sorry. About this. About . . . everything."

She blew out a breath. "Yeah. I'm sorry too."

"I really had no intention of delivering you to Mia."

"I know."

"Do you?"

"Yeah."

And I believed her.

The alternative was untenable.

ELEVEN

My vision cleared after a couple hours. I made a mental note not to look into the light again. I checked on One Eye—he was in a full cocoon, a hard, waxy shell that rose and fell with each breath—and then I made my way up to the front and dropped into the passenger seat.

Angel glanced at me. "How's he doing?"

I shrugged. "Goddamn birds."

Her features tightened. "Should have known they'd follow us."

"Shoulda, coulda, woulda." I huffed a breath and raked back my hair, staring out the windshield. It was getting dark again, which was weird because it wasn't close to sunset, but I could see more monoliths rising on the horizon. I hoped to hell they were the Keys. "Gotta wonder why they were so . . ."

"Tenacious?"

"Yeah. Following us all that way." Cluckers weren't known to fly far from the coop.

"Lots of reasons. The bounty for one."

"That's a lot of birdfeed."

"Revenge."

I grinned. "We did kick some ass in that warehouse."

"And then there's the most likely reason."

Something in her tone made the little hairs prickle at my nape. "Which is?"

"They want the Shuffle."

Okay . . . "What's the Shuffle?"

She glanced at me. "It's what I'm delivering to the Sisterhood. Something so important, so powerful, no one who even *knows* about it is safe. Everyone on this planet would be after it. Everyone."

"Including the Fed?"

"Especially the Fed."

"What is it?" I asked, though I wasn't sure I really wanted to know.

She shot me a look. "It's going to change everything, Tig," she said in a low tone. "Everything."

Before I had a chance to ask—or decide if I wanted to ask—our proximity alert sounded. I glanced at the dash. "What is it?"

"Pflerg. Rainstorm. Coming in from the East."

I should have guessed, the sky was filled with heavy, angry, glowering clouds. *Damn.* It didn't rain much on the Barrens, but when it did, it totally fucking did. And skimmers didn't run on water because of the electricity required for the anti-gravity boosters. If we tried, we'd fry. "How long before it hits?"

She tapped the monitor. "An hour."

I eyed the monoliths in the distance. "Can we make it there?" It was our only hope.

"With time to spare . . . if we don't break down again." She revved up and the skimmer leaped forward.

God, I hoped we didn't break down again.

I was standing over One Eye when she pulled the skimmer to a halt and came to the back. She stilled when her gaze landed on the motionless cocoon. It had gone even crustier, turned a discomfiting shade of gray.

"Do you think he's dead?" she asked in a soft voice.

I shrugged. "Dunno. Probably."

She leaned down and felt for a pulse. Slumped. "No heart-beat. And he's not breathing." Hell. Beyond that, his eye was closed. I'd never seen his eye closed. It did something funny to my chest.

A well of grief and regret rose in me as I stared at his crusty sarcophagus.

He'd been a good guy. A good partner. And damn it all, it was just wrong for him to die dry.

"Damn." Angel blew out a sigh. "Well, there's a cave up on the bluff. Looks to be above the water line. We should head there before it starts to rain."

I nodded. "But we should probably bury him first." I glanced at One Eye, assessing his proportions. "Gonna take a hell of a hole."

She opened the toolbox and pulled out a power shovel. "Then we better get digging."

"We could just leave him."

She glared at me. Damn, she was ferocious. "For the raptors?"

"I meant in the truck." What, did she think I would just dump him in the dirt?

"The truck will be underwater. Probably float away."

Ah, hell. I hadn't thought of that. "We should anchor it." And waterproof the damn engine too.

"First things first." She tossed the shovel at me. I caught it, because if I hadn't, it would have hit me in the face. "Get digging."

It was a hell of a thing, burying my partner. He was a big guy. And he'd swelled even more after the shooting, but it was even more than that. As I worked, memories of our times together filled my mind.

I'd been kind of an ass to him.

And he'd always been a class act in return.

Never seeking retribution for my nasty comments about

his floppy feet or his ooze or his tendency to fart. Never taking me to task for my contemptuous attitude toward him. Never failing to have my back.

Always treating me with a calm, cool respect. A reverence almost.

Yeah. I was a jerk of epic proportions.

It was humbling.

I'd been on this rock nearly a decade, and all I'd ever thought about was staying alive. I hadn't cared about anyone but myself, not really—even someone like Skinny who was willing to die for me. I mean, I had cared about him, but not enough to really get to know him. I hadn't bothered to really know anyone.

That sad truth was reflected in the undeniable fact that I knew almost nothing about my partner. I'd never bothered to ask about his hopes, his dreams, his Home Planet. I didn't know if he had a mate, or if his species just ate them when they were finished tanging. I knew nothing.

And now, it didn't matter.

It was one galactic moot point.

We finished the hole—not as deep as I would have liked, but there wasn't a lot of time before the storm hit—and I dragged his cocoon over and lowered him down. It was awkward because he was large and unwieldy. The chrysalis broke open with the movement and foam oozed out.

"Aw, shit."

Angel looked up. "What's the matter?"

I wiped the foam from my face. "I got some in my mouth."

No idea why she snorted a laugh.

Nothing funny about any of this.

We covered him up quickly, too quickly—I would have liked to have a moment of silence or something—but fat raindrops were starting to fall, and we still had a helluva climb up to that cave.

As I chucked on the last shovelful, Angel looked up at the sky. "Better get going. Rain's coming."

I nodded. The plain would be a lake bed in less than an hour. It could take days for the water to soak in. "Let's grab some supplies, anchor the skimmer, and get moving."

She nodded and headed off, but I stayed behind. Just for a moment, I needed it. Some kind of closure. Some time to grieve.

With a feral growl, tinged with regret and remorse, I planted the shovel deep into the mounded sand.

He'd been my loyal partner.

He'd died dry and would spend eternity in the clutch of this arid desert.

At the very least, he deserved a marker.

I was in a pretty pissy mood as I climbed up the rocky out-cropping—burying someone you cared about would do that to a guy. The insistent patter of raindrops on my head and shoulders didn't help.

We passed several pockets in the stony wall, but I knew we had to get to the one above the water line, so we kept going. I peeped into the ones we passed and saw the water stains. I knew those would flood during the storm, and we needed one high enough to avoid a swim.

It was a tough climb to begin with—nearly vertical—but there were lots of handholds and, of course, there was the view. The magnificent vista of Angel's ass as she scrambled in front of me.

It distracted me from my discomfort, from my woozy head, from the bitter, numbing tinge in my mouth. It distracted me from her constant barking at me to hurry up, too.

I had no idea why she was in such a rush. The rain was going to do what the rain was going to do. As long as I kept ahead of the rising waters, I figured I'd be okay. Still, I tried to keep up. That view and all.

We both carried backpacks loaded with survival gear from the back of the truck. Thank God it was required in any vehicle rated for travel in the Barrens. We could be stuck in that cave for a while, and even though we'd sealed and anchored the truck, who knew what condition it would be in when the storm abated.

I hoped to God we wouldn't get to the top and find some other creature living there; it would suck to have to fight for turf after the day we'd had.

It seemed to take forever before we clambered over the lip and into the cavern. I dropped my backpack on the ground and looked around. It was large, dark, and completely empty. I tried not to collapse in relief. Maybe it was the effect of such a challenging climb, or the fact that I'd been on the go for far too long, practically living on adrenaline, but my knees were weak.

Then again, maybe it was the pglet—hallucinogenic crap—because my mind was a little bleary too. I turned around and stared out of the mouth of the cave at the desert below. It stretched for mile upon endless mile into the distance. The truck looked like a derelict junker, all banged up as it was from One Eye's rampage. And his grave . . . hell. I didn't want to think about his grave.

I leaned against the wall of the cave and gazed down at his sandy barrow. Something pricked at my eyes. Emotions welled within me. I sniffed.

"You okay?" Angel asked from very far away, although she was right behind me.

"He was a good p-partner." A wail. I had no idea where this was coming from. I'd never been a drama queen. Emotion was weakness. I buried it deep. It had to be the pglet. It had to be.

"I know he was." She put her arms around me and tried to lead me into the cave. I didn't want to go. I wanted to stay here, needed to be here. To see him. It was like we were together again, on some ephemeral, cosmic—

She tugged on my arm. "Come on, Skippy. Let's lie down."

My brain hiccupped.

Lie down?

With her?

Oh. That caught my attention. All thoughts of everything else—of One Eye, the Cluckers, the rainstorm, and the guilt at that I should be feeling—was swept away by a tsunami of lust. Or perhaps my brain ceased functioning because all the blood in my body suddenly rushed to another point.

I whipped around and stared at her. Then I followed her into the cave like a dog in heat. I was transfixed by the wiggle of her ass. It was all I could do to keep my palms to myself. I so wanted to cup that latex. To my muffled surprise—everything was a little muffled—I realized she'd laid out our bedrolls. Right next to each other.

Promising.

I rubbed my proverbial palms together and, when she guided me down onto the mat beside her, I followed. Leaned in. I ached to taste her again. It had been far too long, and she was ripe for a kiss.

I have no idea why she dodged my approach, but I ended up face first on her mat. Guess I'd been coming at her with some velocity. I pushed back up and stared at her. Our gazes met. The light in her eye sent a sizzle through my groin. Obviously she wanted me. I couldn't help but grin.

"So . . ." I huffed, as I leaned suavely back against the wall. Or would have . . . had the wall been there. I was about a foot short, so I careened back and bonked my head on it, but I quickly scrambled back up and struck a studly pose.

Her lips quirked. "So."

"Here we are," I gusted.

"We are here."

I waggled my brows. "All alone."

"Yup."

"Just you and me."

"Right."

I leaned closer, but something stopped me. It took a moment for me to realize it was her hand. I stared at it as I tried to sort out the physics of that. It was beyond me. But I thrust the conundrum aside and shot her a hopeful look. "You know, novitiates don't have to be chaste until they take their vows." I felt it prudent to remind her. "And we are DC, after all." I was pretty sure of that. Also, I was pretty sure I didn't care. I wanted one thing and one thing only. And she wanted the same. Or I thought she did.

It was kind of lowering the way her lips tweaked, her eyes danced. Like the thought of slipping between the sheets with me was funny or something. I must have pouted or some shit because she cupped my cheek and leaned in. The scent of her breath made me woozy.

"I know," she whispered, and then she kissed me.

Oh, not the kind of kiss I'd been strumming my cock to. This one was soft and sweet and saturated with . . . meaning. It made my blood simmer.

She pulled back and smiled again, that slow, sexy slide of lips, one that made visions flood my head. And the visions made my pants tight. "You, my friend," she cooed. "Are as high as a kite."

"I—what?" I gaped at her.

"Skeeg foam will do that to you."

"Do what to me?" A squawk.

She snorted a laugh. "Make you . . . amorous."

"I'm always amorous for you, baby," I whispered. Then I fluttered my lashes seductively. For some reason, she chuckled.

"Just lie down and close your eyes. It'll wear off in a while."

"I don't want to lie down and close my eyes." Yeah. Definitely a pout. "I want to make love to you. And you want to make love to me. I can tell."

"Can you?" A thread of humor wove through her tone.

I put out a lip. "Don't you?"

She sighed. "It hardly matters—"

"It really matters."

"Not at the moment."

"What do you mean?"

"Oh for heaven's sake, Tig. You swallowed a mouthful of Skeeg foam."

"And?" I listed a little to the left, though I was pretty sure I was steady. She righted me.

"It fills a man with . . . intention. And completely suppresses the ability."

I had no idea what she was saying. The words just didn't make any sense. It was babbledygook. She glanced meaningfully at my lap. I couldn't help but follow her gaze.

Suddenly, I realized what she was trying to tell me.

All my passion was in my head. There wasn't a bit of it anywhere else. Not. A. Bit.

Shit.

She patted me on the shoulder. "Besides, did you forget the belt?" She waved at her groin. I grimaced. I had. I had forgotten. She cuddled close, too close, and whispered, "And I don't take advantage of men who are under the influence. It goes against my principles." Damn. Of all the women in all the worlds, I had to have a crush on one with principles. What were the odds? "Now, lie down and close your eyes."

"Will the room stop spinning?" Because that would be good.

"Yes, of course it will." And then she muttered, "After a while."

I let her press me down onto the mat, and I let her cover

me with a blanket. I even closed my eyes. But I didn't rest. I couldn't. Not until I knew.

"Angel?"

"Yes, Tig?"

"What if I weren't high?"

"What?"

"What if I weren't high? And you weren't a novitiate? And there weren't a belt? Would you make love to me then?"

She didn't answer right away. In fact, her hesitation was so vast, I figured she didn't plan on answering at all. I lived a lifetime of hope and despair in those moments, and it was at that point I realized she was probably right.

I was definitely stoned.

But then, after an eternity had passed, she leaned over me and pressed a gentle kiss onto my forehead. My lashes fluttered open and our gazes tangled. Her lips quirked and she whispered, "Go to sleep."

It was as good an answer as any.

And, apparently, it was the only one I was getting.

I woke up with one hell of a headache.

Also, I was alone on the mats. I sat up and looked around. My gaze landed on Angel, standing by the mouth of the cave, staring out at a curtain of gray. It took a moment for me to realize it was rain.

I scrambled to my feet, then clutched at the cave wall as my head took a whirl. I sucked in a breath and steadied myself. Hell. What a night. I'd been visited by the weirdest dreams. They still haunted me, clung to the edges of my sanity.

Angel glanced over her shoulder and grinned. "Good morning, Sunshine."

I grumbled something in response. Not sure what it was,

and it hardly mattered. I shuffled to her side and stared out at the ocean the desert had become. There was water as far as the eye could see. The truck was completely submerged, as was the small mound of rocks to the East. It had been raining all night. And still, the downpour raged.

"How long will it go on?" I asked.

She shrugged. "Hard to say. As long as it does. And then, it will stop."

"And how long to soak in?" How long before we could move again?

"Depends on how dry the ground was. Could take hours. Could take days."

"So we're stuck here."

"Yep." She shot a look at me. "How do you feel?"

"Like hell."

There was no call for her to snort a laugh. "Next time, try not to swallow, okay?"

I glowered at her. She thought that was funny too.

The rain wasn't terribly fascinating, so I headed back into the cave and rummaged in our packs. "You hungry?" I asked.

"I could eat."

We'd gone through all the fresh food in the driver's stash; all there was left were zip packages of freeze-dried food. I wasn't sure what any of it was, but it didn't taste horrible, and it filled our bellies, so I didn't care. Angel and I sat on the floor and nibbled and sipped on the water bottles we had. We didn't talk because there wasn't much to say, and I was still grappling with the trails of those dreams. They'd felt so real.

One of them bubbled to the surface, and I tried to grab it, hold onto it. It was tough, but I had a vague impression, like a blurry vision, of myself in a balmy place surrounded by palm fronds. Angel was in the dream too, but she was different. Warmer. Closer. When she looked at me and smiled, it felt like she meant it. There was someone else too. A girl. A girl with enormous green eyes. I knew she was important to me, but I couldn't remember why. We were safe there, among the palm fronds, yet . . . not.

"What are you thinking?" Her voice surrounded me, startled me.

I glanced up. "Trying to remember a dream."

Her lashes flickered. "Good dream, or bad one?"

"Good one. I think." I shot her a grin. "You were in it."

Her lips quirked. "Was I?"

I leaned forward. "You were nice to me."

"I'm nice." The outrage in her tone was feigned.

"You weren't nice last night."

She stilled and shot me a frown. Again, not terribly sincere. "You were looped out of your mind."

I met her gaze. Held it. "I'm not looped now." Yeah, she wore a chastity belt that kept me from heaven, but there were . . . other options.

Her eyes glimmered. "No. You're not."

"And we are DC. Aren't we?"

Her lashes fluttered. "We are."

"And you haven't taken your vows yet."

She looked away and my gut clenched.

"Have you?"

"I . . . no." Something in her tone snagged my attention.

"Angel?" I prompted.

She blew out a sigh. "Well, the part about me being a novitiate was kind of a fabrication."

"What?"

"Yeah." She lifted a shoulder. "They thought it would help me pass through all the intake bullshit easier."

My pulse fluttered in my throat. Excitement simmered. "And the belt?"

"Fake."

Oh. Excellent.

"It comes right off."

Very excellent.

What was even more awesome was the way she looked at me. It reminded me of the way she'd looked at me in the dream, all sweet and goo-goo eyed.

It befuddled me, bedazzled me. Made me stupid. Probably the blood rushing from my brain to my cock or something like that. Because, damn.

Damn, she was beautiful.

Damn, her expression was sexy and welcoming.

And damn, she went onto her hands and knees and closed the distance between us. Her breath skated over my face, warm and fragrant and damp. Anticipation sizzled through me. Her lips were warm too as they danced over mine.

"And, Tig?" A whisper.

"Ahem. Yeah?" My libido was definitely not suppressed now.

"The answer to your question is *yes*." And she kissed me. Kissed me again. This time like she meant it.

I had no idea what question she was referring to, but at that moment, I figured it really didn't matter. Not in the least.

Oh. Holy. God.

She drained me.

More than once.

She was wild, feral, phenomenal. Our joining was the most mind-boggling thing I had ever experienced—and, I must say, I had experienced a lot.

The thing about Seraphim, at least the ones like Angel, was that when they get excited, they lose control. I mean, really lose control. More than once, as she came apart in my arms, she did that thing she'd done before, with the electricity. If it happened when we were joined—oh man. It was fan-freaking-tastic.

But then, it would have been anyway. No matter what. Because it was her.

I had to admit, even to myself, that I had feelings for her that were unlike anything I'd ever felt. She made me feel strong and weak at the same time, gave me hope and filled my soul. Redeemed me.

It was a scary realization because I'd never cared for someone. Not really. Not like this. Not even Ella.

After we exhausted each other, she curled up in my arms, naked and soft, and I held her as we both struggled to find our center again. Because, yeah, that had tilted the universe on its axis.

I didn't know much in those moments, but I knew I could never let her go.

I could never be without her.

It wasn't love or any sappy claptrap like that. But it was . . . something.

"Tell me more about your dream," she murmured as she nestled closer.

"My dream?"

"Yeah."

I tucked my chin so I could look down at her. "Why?"

"I want to know."

"Okay." I stroked her arm. Long, slow passes. Loved the feel of it. "We're in a warm place with lots of plants. Palm fronds, ferns, that kind of shit."

She leaned up and stared down at me, rapt. "Go on."

"We're . . . together, you and me. And there's someone else there. A little girl. She's laughing."

"A little girl?" Something glimmered in her eyes. She blinked it away. "What does she look like?"

I shrugged. "Can't remember."

"Close your eyes. Concentrate."

"Why?"

"Just do it."

I did. Closed my eyes. Sank in to the memory, the feeling. Let myself float on it. "She has . . ." *Wow.* "Green eyes. Like yours." They were beautiful. "Skin like yours." Pale. Nearly translucent. "Black hair."

"Black hair? Are you sure?" Something in her tone caught my attention. I glanced at her.

"Yeah. And she has dimples." I touched her cheek. "Here."

She touched mine. Stroked the dents that blossomed when I smiled. "Like yours?"

"I . . . yeah."

"Hmm." She tucked her head under my chin, so I couldn't see her face.

I tightened my hold. "Why?"

"I was just curious."

Right. There'd been more than simple curiosity in her expression. "Angel?"

She huffed a sigh and rolled away, but not far. She sat up and took my hand in hers. "Do you know why there's a market for pglet?"

"Because it gets you high?"

"It doesn't get everyone high. Just certain species. And for some . . . it's something more."

I shot a look at her. "Like what?"

"There are those—not everyone, mind you, but some—who have visions when they're high on Skeeg foam."

"Visions?"

"It's in high demand with shamans and healers as an entheogen—"

"A what?"

"A substance used for vision quests. Most people high on

pglet just have hallucinations. But some . . . some have visions of the future."

I tugged on her hand. "So . . . do you think I had a vision of the future or a hallucination?"

She shrugged. Her lips quirked. "No way to know. Until we . . . get there. But I'd like to think it's the future."

I liked that she nestled back down. I curled my arm around her. "Because you want to be with me in the future," I murmured against her brow. Damn, that was good to—

She huffed a laugh and pulled back up. "No . . ."

"No?" Really?

"Because it means we survive, dumbass."

I hardly even minded the epithet because she said it in such an adoring voice. And because, right afterward, she kissed me.

TWELVE

We were stuck in that cave for three days. We ate, drank, and made love. I wish it could have lasted forever. But on the third day, when I woke up, I was greeted by silence. The rain had stopped.

I eased Angel off my chest and resettled her onto the mat, and then padded to the mouth of the cave. Damn. Except for a couple puddles here and there, all the water was gone.

I couldn't ignore the trickle of disappointment that this little respite was coming to an end. But to be honest, we needed to get going. We were almost out of food and water. I could only hope the truck would still run.

I felt her come up behind me. She wrapped her arms around my waist, and I leaned into her. "Looking pretty good," she said. I caught the hint of lament in her voice. It was nice to know she wasn't anxious for this to end too.

"We should wait until the puddles are gone." They probably weren't enough to cause any problems with the electric drive, but it was better not to take a chance.

"Mmm." Her hold tightened.

I turned in her embrace. Kissed her. "How did you sleep?"

She shrugged. "Okay. Someone kept waking me up." I liked her grin.

"Someone kept waking *me* up."

She chuckled. "I meant your snoring."

"I do not snore."

"Ha!" She fisted her fingers in my hair and pulled me down, took my mouth. Distracted me. When we came up for air, she knocked me for six. "So . . . who's Ella?"

The question stunned me. Sent a bolt of horror through me. My pulse thrummed. I stared at her. "No one." Ella was gone. So gone.

Her brow rippled. Her lips turned down into a frown. "Why do you dream about her?"

My heart skipped a couple beats. "Can you see my dreams?"

She chuckled. "No. You talk in your sleep. Who is she?"

"It's . . . difficult to talk about."

"I'm sure it is." Her gaze bored in. Her hold on me tightened. "I think I deserve to know."

Hell.

I suppose she did.

I turned away and scrubbed my face. Raked my hair. "When I first came to Viridian, I was a drawhead."

Angel nodded. So many were. There was no hope here anyway, and the drug numbed the edges. Helped us forget how desperate we were. Helped us forget a lot. And it was plentiful. Hell, the Fed passed it out like candy because it made the cons much easier to manage. Mia had used it to run me. She'd used my hunger for a cheap high as a way to control me. Use me.

Until Ella.

"She was . . . a hooker."

"Hmm."

"Found me ass up in an alley drawed-out to the gills. Twitching. She took me in." Angel embraced me again, held me. Stroked me. Soothed me. "She's the reason I'm clean. She dried me out. Nursed me back to sobriety. Tied me to the bed when I wanted to rail at someone, something. Anything."

"Kinky."

I tried to glare at her. Couldn't. My lips might have tweaked up a bit.

Ella had been. A little.

"What happed to her?"

That, I couldn't revisit. Not now. Not yet. It was still too raw. Even five years after the fact. Damn Mia anyway.

I blew out a breath. "Probably should get going."

Angel stared at me for a moment, then nodded. "Right."

We didn't speak as we packed up our gear. I hoped she understood why I didn't want to share. It seemed like she did. But God's honest truth, I couldn't have admitted it if my life depended on it.

The guilt was too toxic to pierce.

We headed down the side of the cliff—a lot more difficult than the climb up had been—and tossed our gear into the truck. Apparently our waterproofing efforts had worked because there was only a little bit of water on the floor. Angel hopped in and started up the engine. It fizzled and popped a couple times, but then it caught.

We both knew it had to idle for a while, to evaporate the moisture in the e-drive. I figured this would be a good time to say goodbye to One Eye. After all, I'd never have another chance.

My feet were heavy as I plodded over to the marker. But then my throat closed. My gut clenched.

The marker was gone. Washed away by the raging storm. The water had seeped into the ground and had leveled out the mound.

I had no idea where One Eye was buried. Not really.

My chest tightened, and I cleared my throat as some bitter regret swamped me. I pressed it away.

It didn't matter where he was. Not really.

He was dead and gone.

Goodbyes were a waste of breath.

At least the sand was still damp. I wanted to remember him in dampness.

I stared at the horizon and thought about One Eye, all the crazy and funny things he'd done. All the times he'd saved my ass.

I didn't think about the times I'd been a dick.

Angel came up next to me and put her arm around me in a sign of silent support. I tugged her closer.

"He was a good guy," she said after a moment.

"Yeah," I said. "He was."

We stood there for a little while longer. For some reason, I was loath to leave. Then she tugged on my sleeve. "Ready?"

"I suppose." I drew in a deep breath, said my final farewell, and turned back to the truck.

But something caught my eye. A movement in the sand.

My attention snapped back to the spot. The mud shifted.

My heart lurched. My pulse hitched. I stared.

Something pushed out. Something long and green and slender, with a bulb on the end. The bulb fluttered. Then opened.

And shit.

It was an eye.

One. Eye.

It blinked.

All I could do was gape.

Angel came back as well. She stared at the stalk. "What the . . . ?"

"I have no idea," I murmured.

But then another shoot popped up. A second eye. Then the entire barrow began to shiver, lift.

A long-limbed, bright green Skeeg emerged. As he sat up, the caked mud fell from his body. He grinned. "You waited." A croak, but it was a rich, full warble.

I boggled.

Holy hell.

Moving slowly, One Eye extricated himself from the grave, sloughing the husk of his cocoon from his skin. It occurred to me, as he emerged, limber and gangly, that he'd lost some weight. And, apparently, had grown another eye.

I waved in the general direction of his twin stalks. I didn't want to be rude, but I had to know. "How?"

He only grinned wider.

I guess Angel had been right. I guess Skeeg foam *was* regenerative.

Another ripple of movement at my feet drew my attention downward. The entire grave was shimmering. Something else pushed out, something small and slimy and green. It shuddered off the clinging dirt and peered up at me with two round eyes and rasped, "Memat."

One Eye chuckled and picked it up, brushed it off. "No, baby," he said.

The creature turned its attention to him and chirruped, "Memat."

To my astonishment, my partner, a big, bad, take-no-shit Skeeg, brought the Froglette to his lips and smooched it soundly. Then he opened a pouch in his belly—I'd had no idea he even had a pouch—and slipped the baby inside.

Holy shit.

More chirrups sounded at my feet, and I looked down.

I stared at the mass of tadpoles slithering gleefully through the mud. As I watched, one of them sprouted two long, Froggy legs and started hopping.

Holy shit.

I glared at One Eye. He stared calmly back. With *two* fucking eyes. "You were *pregnant*?"

His lips curled up and he bent down again, gently picking

up each of his spawn, carefully wiping them off and securing them in his pouch. There must have been twenty of them. Still, he waited, watching the sand.

Tension riffled.

I had no idea why.

Then he drooped in relief as one more baby pushed through the mud. He cooed as he scooped it up and settled it with the rest. He patted his belly—now quite large—and sighed.

"Is that all of them?" I asked.

His grin widened. He nodded.

"Wow," I said. Just . . . wow. I hadn't seen that coming.

Neither, apparently, had Angel. Her expression made it clear she was as shocked as I was. She gestured at the truck. "We're, ah, getting ready to go. The Keys aren't far. Just a couple klicks."

One Eye glanced at the rock behind us. His nostrils quivered, as though he smelled something delicious. No doubt one of those caves pitting the surface held a pool like the one we'd found earlier. Filled with fresh, cool water.

"You coming with us?" I asked.

He sighed and shook his head, gesturing to his enormous belly, squirming and writhing with a brood of newborns.

"Right." Didn't think so. The plain was drying up, but a secluded pond might stay wet for a while. Hopefully long enough for him to work out another plan. Beyond that, I doubted the Sisterhood would have any use for a Skeeg and his offspring, except maybe dinner. It was probably safer for him if he didn't come with us. "You go. Take them. Get them out of the sun." But damn, it was hard saying goodbye. I thrust out a hand.

He didn't take it.

Instead, he wrapped me in his arms and gave me a big, squishy hug. I didn't expect it, that show of emotion. Not from that tall, Froggy piece of shit. But I appreciated it.

He pulled back and stared me in the eye, and then he croaked, "Tell him I'm sorry."

"Who?"

One Eye didn't answer. His expression was one I'd never seen before. One filled with sorrow and regret. His fingers worked soothingly over his protruding gut. "Tell him I'm sorry, but I have to think of them." And then he clapped me on the shoulder and strode away.

Angel and I watched as One Eye loped off to the cave at the base of the cliff. He turned and waved, and then disappeared inside.

"Do you think he'll be okay?" she asked.

I shrugged. "Probably. He's a tough mother—" We both chuckled at my unintended joke. Because, holy hell. One Eye was a mother. Who'da thunk it?

By mutual consent, we headed to the skimmer and slipped inside. I checked the GPS and then put the truck in gear. Still, I stared at that cave in the mirrors until the big rock disappeared.

I have no idea why.

It didn't take long at all to reach the Keys. In fact, they loomed on the horizon almost as soon as the other rock faded from view. We'd been so close. Probably close enough to make it before the rains.

I was glad we hadn't. For more than one reason.

I glanced at Angel. Shot her a grin. Imagined she was thinking the same thing.

It was easy to see why they called them the Keys. The formation was a collection of rocks, some tall and slender and others mounded about. The three highest monoliths had rounded holes near the top. They were all too perfect, too identical to be natural.

I slowed up as we approached. Though it had seemed tiny from far away, the collection of stones covered acres. "What now?"

Angel shrugged. "We wait, I guess."

That made something prickle at the back of my neck. I didn't like waiting. Out in the open. And in this stone forest, there were too many places for someone to hide. I was probably being paranoid, but I had the sense we were being watched.

Or . . . maybe not so paranoid.

My gut lurched as someone stepped out of the shadow of one of the rocks, his laser pistol pointed at our truck.

Someone large and green, with a ridge running down his back.

"Shit."

Angel leaned forward. "Who is that?"

"Not the Sisterhood." I frowned at her. "Stay here."

She frowned right back. I recognized the stubborn cant to her head. "Who is it?"

"It's Granny."

She whipped out her pistol and checked the clip. I set my hand on hers. "No. You stay here. I know how to handle him."

"Do you? How the hell did he follow us here?"

I shot a look at my erstwhile boss, waving his gun and yelling at us to get out of the truck. He had a couple lieutenants with him, but hardly an army. Still, they had more guns than we did. "He didn't follow us. He was waiting for us. He knew we were coming here. Somehow . . . he knew."

Her brow rippled. "How the hell did he know that?"

I glanced at the GPS. Picked it up, turned it over, and popped open the back to check the data history code and . . . *hell.* "Someone transmitted our destination."

"*Someone?*" Her tone made a shiver crawl down my spine and nest in my bowels. Slowly, I glanced at her. And yeah. Her gun was pointed at my heart.

"It wasn't me." I tried to infuse my innocence in my tone, but probably didn't convince her. Her finger tightened on the trigger. "Angel . . ."

"Stop calling me that." A snarl.

Had to. I didn't know her name. She'd never told me.

I hated that.

I hated more that she didn't trust me. Even more that everything I thought we had, everything between us, could crumble so easily. But then, it was what it was. I raised my hands. "It wasn't me," I repeated. "Must have been One Eye. He's the one who set the GPS in the first place."

She stared at me, her eyes red-rimmed, her expression harsh. "I should have known better than to trust either of you."

Irritation bubbled through my gut. "I'm telling you, it wasn't me."

Her throat worked. "Sure."

"Why? Why would I tell Granny where we were going?" When he wanted, very badly, to kill me?

"So you could work both sides of this?"

"I didn't want to work *any* sides of this."

"Right. But Mia wouldn't let you step out, would she?"

"Angel . . ." She frowned, but I continued on. "We can't turn on each other now. We've come too far. Been through too much. I swear—I swear on all that is holy—I am not letting Granny take you."

She shook her head, snorted, but the gun dropped. And then she scrubbed her face. "You really are a dumbass, aren't you?"

"What?"

She sighed. "Granny doesn't want *me*."

"What . . . ?" My throat went dry. "What does he want?"

"He wants the Shuffle." She turned and glared out of the windshield. "Just like everyone else."

It pissed me off that apparently everyone else knew what

this Shuffle was, except me. But I figured this was a bad time to ask. "Okay. So what do we do?"

A blast hit the front end and the skimmer rocked. Angel lifted a shoulder. "Try to stay alive until the Sisterhood arrives, I guess."

"And how long will that be?"

Another blast.

"Not soon enough."

"Let me go talk to him."

"Go *talk* to him?" She narrowed her eyes. "You don't get it, do you?"

"Get what?"

"You were nothing to him, to anyone, but a means to an end."

Oh, hell. That lanced me to the core.

"If you step out of this truck alone, he'll just put a hole in you." It was foolish of me to think she'd care if he did.

"Was I just a means to an end to you?" My voice was a little more maudlin than I intended.

She stilled, looked away. Her beautiful throat worked.

"Was I?" Because, hell, I needed to know. Even though it would probably slay me, certainly pierce my inflated ego, I needed to know.

"No."

I almost didn't hear her, but I did. The hope that flowered in my chest was unwise. But I couldn't stop my grin. "You aren't a means to an end to me either, Angel," I said softly. "And now, let's go kick some Creel ass."

She studied me for a moment and then she nodded. "All right. But watch your six."

"Yeah, baby," I cooed. "You too."

Angel and I got out of the truck in tandem, with our weapons aimed. Granny and his men pointed theirs right back. I noticed they were all pointed at me.

"Where's the Skeeg?" he yelled across the expanse. His low, throaty voice bounced off the rocks.

I glanced at Angel. She shrugged, then yelled back, "We buried him."

Not a lie.

If One Eye had messaged Granny, known he was going to be waiting here—and he didn't want to see him—that would explain why he hadn't come with us.

What I didn't expect was Granny's reaction to the news.

He staggered. His gun lowered. His expression crumpled. "What?" A wan warble. "What happened?"

"Cluckers attacked us. He was shot."

"Was he foaming?"

I had no idea why this was so important to the Creel, but it was. I nodded.

Granny's relief was palpable, but fleeting. His demeanor immediately hardened. "He's not dead."

I shrugged.

His buggy eyes narrowed on me. "And you left him there?" Practically a screech. Far too emotional for a simple, boss-employee relationship. Something else was going on here. Beyond that, all of a sudden, I understood that One Eye's parting comment had been a message for Granny.

"He didn't want to come."

"What?" Oh God, what a snarl. It made the little hairs on my arms stand on end.

"He said, 'Tell him I'm sorry.'"

"What?" A howl. Granny staggered. He turned his back on us and paced for a moment. When he whirled, his expression was hard. Harder than I'd ever seen it. "Throw down your guns," he bellowed.

"No fucking way."

"Do it," he said. "Or I shoot the girl." He whipped his pistol in Angel's direction. I stepped in front of her, to protect her, but she wouldn't allow it. She stepped around me.

"You're not shooting me, Granny," she said in a cold voice.

His folds quivered as she called his bluff, and then he turned his gun back on me. *Awesome*. "Then I'll shoot him."

"You're not shooting either of us."

"I will. I swear I will. If you don't take me to him."

I opened my mouth. Closed it.

What?

"Take you where?"

"To the Skeeg." He waggled his gun back and forth. "Both of you."

Yeah. I had no idea what was going on here. "It's not far," I said. "You can take the truck yourself."

"I need you to show me."

Not I *want* you to. Or I *demand* you do.

I *need* you to.

"I . . . okay." I hoped to hell I wasn't screwing up One Eye's exit strategy by—

Before Granny could take one step toward the truck, another voice rang out. "That won't be necessary."

All of us—me, Angel, Granny—whipped around, guns raised, and froze in a tableau. There on the rise stood a tall, slender woman in flowing robes—an Ursa, if I wasn't mistaken, given her large furry head, small round ears, and fangs—holding One Eye by the neck in front of her, with a weapon pointed at his temple.

For his part, One Eye stood there, calm and still. There might have been a contrite smile on his lips.

"Don't kill him." The command came in stereo, from both sides of me. Angel and Granny.

The woman tossed her head. "And why not?" This question, she addressed to Angel, as though none of the rest of us mattered. But maybe we didn't.

"He saved my life, Mother. Please—"

Oh. Hell.

"Mother Superior?" I asked in an undertone, and Angel shushed me.

Granny stepped forward, waddled past me. His eyes were wide, his mouth agape. He stared at One Eye, taking in his newly svelte form, his squirming belly, and of course, his second eye. His chins wobbled. "They came?"

One Eye did grin then. "They were early."

And to my shock, despite all the bristling guns pointed hither and yon, Granny stumbled up the rise, fell to his knees at One Eye's feet, and placed his fat cheek against the writhing pouch. He lifted a large, webbed paw and stroked the mound, then gazed up at One Eye's face. His lips rippled, and something damp leaked out of his eye. "How many?"

One Eye puffed out his chest and croaked, "Twenty-one."

Granny quivered. "Twenty-one? Really?"

"Thirteen Skeeg. Eight Creel."

"Eight Creel?" The stroking continued, the soft murmurs. Some kissy noises rose.

And yeah. I stared.

Because, what the actual fuck?

For one thing, this was Granny. The biggest, baddest motherfucker on the planet, burbling at a bellyful of tadpoles.

For another—*what the fuck?*

Angel hooked her arm with mine. "You didn't know they were mated?"

"Hell no, I didn't know." Double hell. Double no.

She gusted a sigh. "You should have done your homework."

Yeah. Maybe I should have.

Mother Superior rolled her eyes. "All this sentiment is making me nauseous." She lowered her gun and pointed it at Granny. "Tell your men to drop their weapons."

With a bit of a surprise, I realized they were all still pointed at me. Nice to be popular.

Granny nodded and stood, but then he whirled and put a plasma blast into each of his lieutenants. They crumpled to the ground.

Even Mother Superior, who seemed pretty damn stoic, was stunned. "I . . . uh . . . why did you do that?" she asked.

Granny holstered his weapon. "They served their purpose."

The nun narrowed her eyes. "Which was?"

"Getting me here."

"There's nothing here for you, Creel."

"Oh, I think there is." His tone was confident, challenging.

I could feel Mother Superior's annoyance riffling on the air. She thrust her chin forward and snarled, "And what would that be?"

Granny smirked. "I think you know."

A sniff.

"And if you're planning to play hardball, which I strongly suggest you do not, be aware I've been following your activities for, ahem, some time."

Mother Superior fixed a blasé expression on her face. "I'm sure I have no idea what you mean."

"I'm sure you know exactly what I mean." Granny waved at Angel. "I intercepted more than one of your packages."

"More . . ." She paled. Swallowed. "More than one?"

"Hmm. Gotta wonder, don't you? How many pieces you're missing?"

Damn. I'd never seen a woman look so pissed.

"It would be a real shame if you discovered you were a piece or two . . . short." He held up a chunk of metal, another weird-as-shit-looking thing.

Mother Superior made a strangled sound. At my side, Angel staggered. Slumped against me. Whispered something that sounded like, "Oh, pflerg."

"And your pieces, coming in as they did? One shipment at a time? Gotta wonder how many deliveries never made it?" He smirked. "What happens when you shuffle without a full deck? Kind of messy, isn't it?"

"You stupid, little Frog—"

Granny clucked his tongue. "Hey. No need to be rude."

"Rude?" Mother Superior's fur riffled. "I should just shoot you right now and take what you have."

This threat seemed to hit home, but I was probably the only one who knew Granny well enough to notice the slight shift in his coloring, indicating his concern. He thrust out his chins. "But you won't."

"I could."

"The only way to assure you have all the pieces is if I give them to you." He smirked. "You just have to trust me."

"Trust you?" She narrowed her eyes. "Do you think we don't know you've been working with the Fed?"

My stomach lurched. Bile rose in my throat. I whipped around and glared at him. "What?"

Granny went white; his fat folds undulated. One Eye stood behind him, silent with an unblinking stare.

Mother Superior chuckled. "Let me guess. Mia pulled you in on some capital beef. Threatened you and your squeeze with termination, then asked for your . . . cooperation on this?"

Granny scowled.

"I'm guessing she made damn sure you knew what we were up to. Hoped you'd lead them right to us. And you probably did." She crossed her arms over her sumptuous chest. "Is it safe to assume she's the one who asked you to task Earth Boy with the escort service?" I didn't appreciate the way she jabbed a thumb at me, but I was too stunned to get all huffy. Besides, my attention was fixed on Granny.

"He was the only one I trusted." Now that was a surprise. Granny glanced my way and grimaced. "I knew you'd wanna tang her, Tig, but I knew you wouldn't eat her. And I knew you'd never sell her to Crow. Or the Fed. Or any other outfit who wanted to put her in service." Yeah. That was true. He smirked. "You're such a fucking Boy Scout."

Or not.

I raked a hand through my hair. "Jesus. I can't believe this. All along? You were working with the Fed?" With Mia? The big Blue bitch of the century?

Granny shrugged. "Not all along. But once she mentioned the Sisters were working on a Shuffle, plerg, Tig. I had to get in on it. It was too great a chance to miss."

"Right."

"This was the one. The one big score. The thing I've been working for, for a long, dry decade."

"And what was that, exactly?" There was no treasure here. No fucking fortune. No power. "What was it that pushed you to make such a drastic play?"

"Don't you know? Can't you figure that out, Tig?"

I shook my head. I guess I was just blind because I couldn't see it. He owned the planet. Ran it all. Had everything. Everyone in his pocket. Total and complete power. What would be worth giving all that up? Walking away?

His answer was soft, whispered. Simple.

"The chance to go home. The chance to live my life in the swamps of Creel . . . with my family. The chance to live wet."

I stared at him, speechless. Because, yeah. What he said.

Not that I wanted to live on Creel, or be wet or any of that shit. But I could relate to that clawing hunger for things to go back to the way they'd been. A simpler time. A time before the Fed moved in and enslaved us all in their bureaucratic clutch.

Too bad. For me, there was no going home. The Earth I had known was gone forever.

"The Shuffle is a way off this rock."

I straightened. A bolt of electricity snarled through my solar plexus.

A dream I never dared to dream.

"Is that what this is all about?" I asked.

Angel hushed me again, but I would not be denied.

"Is it?"

Her nod sent all kinds of delirium though me. "It's a transporter that creates a temporary wormhole through the planetary shield," she said softly.

"Theoretically," Mother Superior added. I ignored her. Because, hell.

Hell.

A way off this rock. I wanted that. I wanted that a lot. Suddenly I understood why everyone was in such a frenzy over this, why they were all so desperate. Why Granny would do anything for it.

He turned to the Ursa and offered something that might have been a conciliatory smile. "Look, Sister . . ." Her glossy fur shivered in what I could only assume was annoyance at the moniker. "You and I want the same thing here."

"And what is that?" she spat.

"A working Shuffle. So here's what I propose . . ."

"You're in no position to propose anything." Mother Superior pushed at One Eye's temple with her gun.

"You kill the Skeeg and you get nothing. No info. No Shuffle. Nothing." He nodded. "Now, do you want to negotiate, or not?"

She made a noise, something like a snarl—and Ursas could freaking snarl—but she nodded.

"Okay. Go on. Release him."

The nun glowered, but she released One Eye, who scuttled over to Granny. They met in a sticky hug. It went on and on. There was some kissing. I stared at them, somewhat transfixed. It was the strangest thing I'd ever seen. And I'd seen a lot.

Mother Superior cleared her throat. "Well? What do you want?"

Granny pulled away from One Eye, and in an oddly chivalrous gesture, tucked his mate behind him before he faced the Ursa. "In exchange for the pieces I've collected—"

"How many?"

"Enough to make a difference."

She huffed a breath. "Go on."

"In exchange for the pieces I have collected, I would like to claim the first casket."

Her beady eyes narrowed. "You're asking a lot."

"Am I? Think about it. I know how many pieces I intercepted. I don't know if someone else snagged any. If there is so much as a bolt missing, the wormhole will be unstable and any transport will either fry or spit out in uncharted space."

Mother Superior shot a look at Angel, who nodded.

Granny set his webbed hands on his hips. "I'm the one taking the risk here. You have to test the Shuffle. Test it on me," something like a croak.

A low moan rose. It came from my partner. For the first time since I met him, I saw a flash of emotion on One Eye's green face. It shook me to the core. I realized then what I'd missed before. What I'd missed all along. They loved each other. *Loved.* They were partners.

And just because it was a relationship that was a little bit out of my comfort zone—hell, a little beyond my comprehension—didn't make it any less poignant. Granny, the hard-ass gangster, was willing to do anything for his lover, even risk his life. Indeed, he'd been doing just that for ten years. Anything to keep One Eye safe. Even pair the Skeeg with a loser like me.

Granny puffed up his chest. "Send me through first. If the Shuffle works, then send my Skeeg and my brood through."

"And if it doesn't?"

He shrugged. "No mess to clean up." A poor attempt at a joke.

Mother Superior snorted. "You're assuming I'm inclined to consider your deal and let you take a ride."

Granny's face went red. "I let your girl live. Without her, you'd have nothing. You owe this to me."

Mother Superior studied him for a long moment. At length, she said, "You're right. I do. But you're not taking one of our precious caskets alone. Your little family is taking the ride with you."

Granny's lips trembled. It was almost riveting to watch. "But . . . the Shuffle may not work."

Her muzzle twisted as she smirked. "If you're telling me the truth, if you didn't screw up any of my shipments, it should." She showed some teeth. "You willing to bet the farm on the hope that all the parts made it?"

Silence wafted the stony plain as Granny processed this co-nundrum. Take a chance to escape—and risk the lives of his family—or stay in this hell hole.

One Eye answered for him. "No. Choice." A desolate ribbit. He and Granny shared a long, dark look.

And then Granny nodded. "No point without you and the little ones," he croaked. "I'd rather we all die together."

Mother Superior huffed a sigh. "Are you finished?"

Granny nodded.

"All right. Let's go down." She waved a hand, and suddenly, an army of women of all shapes, sizes, and species, all wearing the cloak of the Sisterhood, stepped out from behind the rocks. I hadn't even known they were there.

They turned in silence and led the way toward a cave in one of the tall Keys. Naturally, I followed, but as I approached the entrance, Mother Superior held out an arm. "Not him." From her tone, and her glare, I was pretty sure she meant me.

My jaw dropped. I glanced from her furious, furry face to Angel's and was gratified when the latter frowned. "He's with me."

Mother Superior's chin firmed. "We're not taking any of our men."

"He saved my life."

"That doesn't mean you can keep him."

Angel thrust out her chin. "He's. With. Me."

A low growl. "You know the rules."

"I know he broke rules to get me here. Risked his life. And I know I'm not leaving without him. I'm certainly not keying in the code if he stays out here."

A bunch of emotions flickered over Mother Superior's face. Most of them were pissed. "He's a *man*."

"He's *my* man."

Oh damn. I liked that. I liked that a lot. I tried not to grin, but failed. Because, shit. I was her man.

Fortunately, no one was paying any attention to me. The others had filed into the cave, and Mother Superior was busy glowering at Angel. A glowering Ursa is an intimidating sight, but Angel was equal to her ferocity. Tension sizzled as the two faced off. I would have said something but decided it was best to just shut up right about now.

Finally, Mother Superior looked away. "Fine," she snapped. "But he's your responsibility."

"Fine."

As the Queen of the Amazons turned and strode toward the cave, I shot Angel a grateful smile. It warmed the cockles of my cockles that she smiled back. But then her expression froze. She gasped and looked down at her midsection. I followed her gaze and stared, horror curling through me at the sudden welling of blood. It was red. Like mine. The sight burned through me like a fucking Q-bomb, searing me from the inside out.

At the same moment the sound registered in my brain, a sharp, sizzling ping.

Fuck.

THIRTEEN

I caught her as she fell. I yelled something—not sure what, but it howled up from the dark well of my soul. It was accompanied by the percussion of laser shots and bullets peppering the stones around us.

Mother Superior whirled around. Her eyes widened as she fixated on Angel's wound. A cry rose from her throat. Something feral and anguished. She glanced back behind us and her eyes narrowed. The lines of her face tightened, and her lips pulled back over her sharp teeth in a ripple of fury—she was a grizzly mama, ready to protect her cub.

She lumbered forward, placing herself between us and the threat. Although to be fair, she was probably not all that concerned about me. "Run!" she roared, and I did. I lifted Angel into my arms and ran like hell for the shelter of the cave as more shots screamed past me.

From behind me, I could hear bellowing—an appallingly familiar voice. It took a second for the realization, the import to whip through me. It hit me about the same time a phaser bullet slammed into my shoulder.

It was Mia. Yelling. "Cease fire, you idiots!"

The idiots didn't listen.

Another shot hit me in the hip, and I stumbled. It took everything in me to keep going. Clutching Angel to my chest, I ran for the cave. It seemed so far away. All I could think about was the fact that my Angel, my amazing, kick-ass Angel, was bleeding out in my arms.

I couldn't bear it if I lost her.

I don't know why or how or when that had happened, but I could not face life without her.

I loved her.

Jesus, God. Loved her with everything I was.

I would kill or die to save her.

With that thought, it hit me. The final bullet. Smack dab in my thigh.

My body crumpled as the muscles gave out.

I rolled as I fell, so I could protect Angel from the impact. I took it all, and it winded me. Devastated me. It wasn't just the pain, or the force of the blow. It was the realization that I'd failed her.

Failed in so many fucking ways. Not just here and now, but all along the way. Obviously Mia had tracked me here. Obviously she'd used me—again—to her own evil purposes.

That I'd never really had a chance hardly registered. I was too swamped with the bitter knowledge that—albeit, unwittingly—I had betrayed the woman I loved.

Again.

And now, a coterie of Fed agents swarmed us, circled us, captured us, holding Mother Superior at bay with a battery of laser pistols. Her hackles were up. Her lips were still undulating—a sure sign of ursine angst. Flecks of foam gathered at the corners of her mouth. She turned in a slow arc, surveying the enemy. There weren't many—just Mia and her prissy partner and a collection of Trogs—but enough to destroy all hope that we could escape into the cave.

It was a small blessing that they'd stopped firing, but it might have been better to die here on this barren plain than become a captive of the Fed on the eve of our potential escape.

My gut clenched as Mia stepped through the battlement of Trogs. She glanced at me, at Angel who was now motionless and silent, lying on me. I could feel the damp warmth of her blood seeping through my shirt. Mia's gaze flicked to Mother Superior and she said, with some hint of pity, "It's over, Adrena. Surrender the Shuffle."

Mother Superior snarled in response and Mia tsked. "You know you cannot win." She waved at Angel. "Your key is dying. Surrender the Shuffle and I will save her."

I was stunned by the emotions that flickered across Mother Superior's face. Grief, regret, agony, and fury. And finally, with a glance at Angel's still form, capitulation. Her voice broke as she said, "All right. Save her."

"And you will surrender the Shuffle to me?"

Mother Superior grunted out a bitter, "Yes."

Mia's smile made my blood go cold. "Excellent." She turned to her partner and said, "I'll take a team into the cave to destroy the machine. You stay out here and protect the perimeter." It seemed as though her partner was about to object, but Mia glared him into silence. He swallowed and then nodded, waving to his Trogs who took up positions circling the mouth of the cave.

When Mia motioned for the Ursa to proceed her inside, Mother Superior frowned. "First, heal her."

With a gusted sigh, Mia came over to us and knelt beside me. She smiled at me as she rolled Angel off me—some arrogant smirk, I suspect—and then pulled out a med kit. She ran the beam over Angel's back, then turned her over and strafed her belly as well.

Then her beam stalled over Angel's belly, over all the blood. Mia's expression tightened and my heart sank. When she repeated the scan, again and again, with no response, my soul began to shrink. God. Was it too late? Had I lost her?

Mia glanced at me again—an odd look I did not, could not

interpret. She changed a setting on the med scanner and tried again. And again.

"What's taking so long?" Mother Superior echoed my thoughts in a tone that mirrored my anxiety.

Mia frowned. "Hush. There are . . . complications."

"Complications?"

Mia ignored her and continued to scan, pass after pass, as though reconstructing Angel's abdomen corpuscle by corpuscle.

It was a freaking relief when Angel groaned and sighed. More than a relief. There isn't a word that describes my elation and gratitude. Not gratitude to Mia so much as to God, if he was still hanging around somewhere. I sent up a prayer just in case.

While Angel recovered, Mia scanned me as well, over my shoulder, my hip, and my leg. The pain faded, even as my annoyance grew.

The Fed had these miraculous machines, but cons died every day on Viridian from wounds like mine. The bastards kept the miracle to themselves.

How like them.

I turned my attention from Mia to Angel, who was now trying to sit up. I supported her, held her, stroked her back. "Are you okay?" I asked.

She grimaced. "I suppose." I knew what she meant. Though she'd been physically healed, there was the spiritual wound to contend with.

We'd failed this mission.

That we had failed together was no consolation. There was so much I needed to tell her, but I couldn't find the words. And I needed some indication that she didn't blame me. Although she should. My lips met hers.

Her response was warm. That kiss said everything I needed to say and was everything I needed to hear.

"All right. Enough of that," Mia snipped. She'd replaced the med kit with a pistol, which she waved. "Let's go inside."

With a huff, I stood, and then reached down to help Angel stand. She was still a little wobbly, so it only seemed right that I curl my arm around her and help her walk.

Keeping her pistol on Mother Superior, Mia and three of her Trog minions herded us into the mouth of the cave. Her partner and his men shifted to cover any escape we might launch—as though we would. There was, literally, nowhere to go.

As we stepped into a shadowed, cool cavern, Mia glanced around with a frown. It was deserted. Utterly deserted. If I hadn't known better, I would have assumed this was just one more barren cavern on a barren plain speckled with barren caverns. Her eyes narrowed. "Where is it?"

Mother Superior sighed. "Down below. In the vault."

"The vault?" I whispered to Angel.

She nodded. "It's the underground bunker. Impenetrable. Impervious to the sandstorms and watertight."

Impenetrable? That sounded promising. Perhaps when we got down there, separated from Mia's reinforcements, I could rush her—and her Trogs—and save the day.

It was an awesome fantasy.

But, as it usually happened, Mia outmaneuvered me. Mother Superior pressed a nondescript stone by the wall and a hidden door swung open, revealing a large elevator. As we all filed through the door, Mia and her men flanked us, with weapons trained on Mother Superior and Angel. Apparently they didn't consider me a threat . . . or they knew I wouldn't do something stupid for fear of putting Angel in danger again.

Mia's smirk said as much.

Mother Superior pressed a button, and a heavy blast door clanged down before the elevator doors closed. Angel squeezed my hand and shot me a smile. It was a conspiratorial smile, so it made my mood lift, but I had no idea what it meant.

I assumed the blast door was what protected the vault from the floods, but it could have been something more. Something that could keep the rest of Mia's forces out, perhaps.

The descent seemed to take forever. I was certain we were in the bowels of the moon when it finally ground to a halt. The doors opened to an enormous cavern. The members of the Sisterhood were assembled around a huge circle of rectangular stones, fanning out like spokes of a wheel. It took a moment for me to realize they weren't stones at all, but large caskets. In the center, there was a machine, a collection of cogs and microchips, dotted with blinking lights and flanked by a large computer screen.

Mia allowed us all to enter the room first, and then she and her Trogs herded us over with the rest of the Sisterhood. She kept Mother Superior by her side. Her attention fixed on the machine. "Is that it?" she breathed.

Mother Superior nodded. "Most of it."

Mia waved a hand at one of her Trogs. "Collect the pieces."

He grunted and, while the others held the assembly under guard, clomped over to Granny and held out his hand.

To my surprise, Granny had three cogs. I don't know why I was surprised. It's not like anyone actually ever told me the truth.

Angel handed over the piece she'd stolen from Granny's office as well. The Trog delivered the collection to Mia, who waggled her weapon at Mother Superior. "Is that all of them?"

The Ursa growled. "Hard to tell, with so much interference from the Creel."

Granny grinned.

In response, Mother Superior showed him her teeth. "In addition to intercepting our deliveries, he also sent through some decoy pieces. We may not have caught them all."

Mia glared at Granny. "Leave it to a Creel to muddy the waters."

He offered a Froggy smile and bobbed a bow. "One does what one can."

"Go on," Mia said on a sigh. "Plug them in. Let's see what we've got."

With barely a grumble, the Ursa did as she was asked, setting the four cogs in place. She stepped back and surveyed her work, then nodded at Angel.

I wanted to grab Angel's arm and pull her back when she stepped forward, but I wasn't quick enough. To my surprise, she walked over to the machine and set her hands on either side. "Close your eyes," she warned, and because I realized what was coming, I did. I still saw the flash through my lids though.

The machine hummed and chuckled and then grated to a stop.

I peeped out through a squint and saw Angel's shoulders droop. "It's not working," she said; the desolation in her tone knifed me. Although I don't know why. It wasn't as though Mia was going to let us use it.

The bitch.

Mia's expression soured. She studied the configuration for a moment, snorted, and then slowly, steadily, turned her head and leveled a steady gaze on Granny. "Better cough it up," she said.

Granny threw back his shoulders. "I have no idea what you mean."

"I think you do." Mia turned her weapon to One Eye and sent a speaking look at Granny. His brows lowered and he grumbled something beneath his breath.

What happened next was revolting. Granny heaved and hacked until he barfed up a gut full of half-masticated worms. But there, in the mélange, was a metal disc with a flashing blue light.

Mia waved at the Trog, who made a face—which was amusing, considering their expressions were set in stone. He plodded over and fished the disc from the goo and returned it, dripping a trail of slime, to Mother Superior.

"Shall we try again?" Mia asked.

My heart lurched into my throat as I watched Mother Superior pull out a similar looking disc, toss it aside, and then fit the piece in. I waited—eyes shut tight—as Angel attempted to power up the machine once more.

This time it took.

As the Shuffle kicked in, a sizzle of energy and a pulsing thrum surged through the chamber. It made the hair stand up on the back of my neck. When I opened my eyes, I saw the screen had activated and was running through a boot-up protocol. It finished with an atonal beep. And then, one by one, the caskets opened.

"Nice," Mia cooed as she surveyed the display. "Very nice." Then she turned to the assembly and waggled her gun at Granny and One Eye. "All right, you two. Hop into a casket."

Granny, who had been pouting up this point, blinked in surprise. As did I.

"I thought you were going to destroy it," I said before I could hold my tongue.

Mia fluttered her lashes at me. "Call me curious. I want to see if it really works."

"Of course it works," Granny insisted, though there was a thread of trepidation in his tone.

"You'd better hope so," Mia said. "Or you and your little family will be splattered all over the cosmos."

One Eye and Granny exchanged a glance. "How sure are you?" My erstwhile partner croaked.

Granny lifted a shoulder. "Ninety percent? Is that enough for you?"

One Eye set his hand on his belly. "Our babies . . ."

"I would rather take the chance on freedom and die than raise our babies here—"

Mia gusted a heavy sigh. "Really. It's not like you have a choice here." She pointed to an open casket. "Get in."

The two exchanged a glance . . . and a wet kiss. Apparently it went on a little too long for Mia's liking.

"Let's move, lovers. We don't have a lot of time," she barked.

Slowly, Granny and One Eye got into the casket. Each casket was designed for four, but Granny took up most of the space, folding himself into each corner. Still, One Eye's belly was too large for the lid to close. He opened up a flap near his grotum and their little Froggy babies slithered out, settling themselves in with their parents. The truth was clear now that they were growing, sprouting: Half of them were round little Creels and the other half, stalk-eyed Skeegs. They were cute little fucks. Angel poured some water over them all, and a musical chorus rose as the babies chirruped.

Mother's lieutenant stepped up to the console and punched some buttons. "Any requests?" she asked.

Granny took One Eye's hand and kissed it. "Please. Send us somewhere wet."

"Right." A snort.

"Safe travels," Angel said softly as she shut the lid. It closed with a clang.

"Everyone stand back," the lieutenant commanded, and we all stepped off the pad; I was gratified that Angel came to my side. My heart drummed as the Shuffle began to hum. An odd light surrounded the casket, shimmering and flickering, as though the pod were phasing in and out of existence. Then, in a flash, it disappeared. Mother Superior turned her attention to the screen, which now showed a map of the KU. Silence hovered, filling the room.

I think we were all holding our breath. No one moved a muscle as we waited for something.

Long moments passed. Long, long moments.

Mother Superior shifted her feet. Angel took my hand and held it tightly. I could see the stress on her face as the screen remained utterly blank. I could see the growing desolation in her eyes as the suspicion rose . . .

The Shuffle had failed.

And a family, our friends—well, at least One Eye held that title—had disintegrated as they passed through the moon's deadly shield.

I pulled Angel into my arms. Kissed the top of her head. Waited, although I knew there was nothing worth waiting for. Nothing but confirmation of my worst fears.

But then . . . a beep. Then a series of them. A blip appeared in the Creel System.

Angel slumped against me, and I blew out a sigh of relief.

"Well," Mother Superior gusted. "It looks like the Shuffle does work after all."

Her relief enraged me, and I glared at her. "You sent them out there, not knowing if it would work at all?"

She shrugged. "We hoped it would, but the Fed changes the algorithms occasionally. We weren't sure."

Not sure? That casket had been filled with innocents. Innocent baby Frogs, but still, they were the only true innocents on this rock. "You are heartless, you know."

"Yeah." She patted me on the chest and shot me a toothy grin. "I know." She turned to Mia and lifted a brow. "So. Have you seen what you needed to see?"

Mia nodded. "Indeed, I have."

I flinched as Mia turned then and lifted her pistol, pointing it at my chest. Her lips curled. The moment hung in the air. And then, to my surprise, she pulled the trigger.

Oh, it didn't surprise me that she pulled the trigger. What surprised me was that she let off three quick shots—at her Trogs. She hit them dead in the eye. One by one, the three stony monoliths fell to the floor with a slight wheeze and a resounding thud. She shot me another grin as she holstered her weapon.

I gaped at her. My mind spun.

And then, as though all that weren't bemusing enough, Mother Superior folded Mia into an enormous—dare I say it—bear hug. "Welcome home, sister," she said.

Mia smiled at her and kissed her cheek, but then all tenderness disappeared. She morphed once more into the cold and heartless Fed agent. "All right, ladies," she barked. "Let's move quickly. Once my partner realizes we've locked him out, he'll assume you have overpowered me and he'll be sending troops in."

Even as she spoke, a muted blast from above rocked the cavern; a shower of dust and stone drifted down.

Mother Superior clapped her hands, and the sisters filed toward the circle of Shuffle pads. "Let's move. We don't have unlimited time here. Our door won't hold forever. Then they'll be in."

My heart hiccupped, and then I said in a tone that could have been interpreted as a complaining one, "I thought the vault was impenetrable."

Mother Superior looked at me as though I were an annoying gnat. Then again, I probably was. "It is impenetrable. No one gets in unless we want them to get in."

"You want them to get in?"

Her smile was a little scary. "Of course we do. The only people who know a Shuffle exists are in this room, or up above."

Angel gasped. "Oh my God," she breathed. "You're going to detonate."

Mother Superior lifted a shoulder. "It's clean."

"But everyone left behind will be annihilated."

The Ursa snorted. "They're just servants. Mostly men."

Angel's expression firmed. Her body trembled. "They *served* us."

"That they did, but don't forget, they're cons."

"Some of them are cons for the same reason we are cons."

I glanced at Angel, trying to figure out what she was really saying, but her expression wasn't forthcoming, except for the rage. It flared when Mother Superior patted her cheek. "You always were a soft heart, my daughter."

"If we are going to win this war, we need all our assets, Mother. Not just the double X."

Mother Superior glanced at me and her nose curled. "Men are too impulsive. Rash, supercilious, arrogant—"

"Necessary."

"Pffft. Men are no more than a sperm factory. They can be replaced."

"Not true." She took my hand. Squeezed. "They are not interchangeable." I loved the passion in her voice.

Mother Superior's eyes narrowed. She glanced at the pad, where the last of the Sisterhood were climbing into caskets. "I suppose you are going to insist on taking him then?"

Angel set her teeth. Another rocket rattled the cave. "He's coming with me, Mother. Like it or not."

A heavy sigh. "Are you serious?"

"He saved my life."

"Lots of people saved my life. I'm not taking *them*."

"I owe him."

"I owe lots of people."

"I want him."

Holy shit. That was nice to hear. Better than nice. Mother Superior didn't seem as thrilled with the declaration. But, to hell with her.

She rolled her tiny black ursine eyes and blew out a breath. "I think I'm gonna barf."

Another blast rocked the cavern; rocks and dirt sifted down. "Enough lovey-dovey crap," Mia said. "It's time for you to go."

Mother Superior set her jaw and nodded. "I'll set the final coordinates and initiate self-destruct. We can time it for when they breach the cavern." She headed for the console, but Mia stopped her.

"No, Mother."

The Ursa stilled; something in Mia's tone captured her attention. She turned slowly, her expression tight and filled with horror. "You're not coming." It wasn't a question.

Mia held out her palms. "I can't. Don't you see? I am much more use to the cause if I stay here."

"But the Shuffle? They will destroy it."

A grin flashed across her beautiful blue face. "No, they won't. After you leave, I'll power it down and remove a few key pieces. I'll tell them you sabotaged it, and we need to study it for future reference."

"But your Trogs?" Mother Superior waved a hand and the flinty corpses.

Mia put out a lip, though there was a smile in there somewhere. "You really shouldn't have shot them."

Mother Superior snorted wetly. "No one in their right mind is going to believe we were able to subdue you without killing you."

"Of course they will." Mia turned to me. She had that expression on her face, the one that was half-smirk, half-mollification. "Hit me, Tig."

"What?"

"Hit me hard."

"No!" I lurched back in revulsion at the thought. Violence against women, no matter the circumstances, never sat well with me.

"Come on, Tig. I killed Ella, remember?" The way she said it, pleadingly, with a thread of remorse, gave me pause.

"Did you? Did you kill her?" I always wondered. Always wanted to know.

"Of course I did."

I don't know why I didn't believe her. Something about the tilt of her chin. The way her words were forced. The way she wouldn't meet my eye.

"Hit me."

"I can't."

"Think of all the times I screwed you over. Think of how I used you. Think of—"

"Well, hell," a sweet voice snarled by my side. "I can hit you."

And she did. Angel's fist slammed into Mia's face. Hard. In the jaw. Mia spun, but kept her balance—barely. She shot a frown at Angel, but there was little heat in it. "You didn't have to hit me that hard," she grumbled.

Angel sent her a snarky grin. "I wanted to make sure there was a bruise."

Mia rubbed her cheek. "Mission fucking accomplished."

"And I wanted to make it clear, if we ever meet up again . . . he's mine." She nodded to me. "Keep your filthy Blue paws off."

Mia forced a grin. "I saw him first."

Angel stilled. Swelled. A snarling energy surrounded her. I've never seen a Seraph glow quite like that. I've never tasted such fury on my tongue. Her green eyes shifted into red orbs. She reached out a finger and a ball of energy sizzled there howling for release.

"He's mine." Her voice resounded through the room.

Mia might have paled. She definitely took a step back.

"Girls, girls, girls." Mother Superior interrupted the spat with a roll of her eyes. "No time for this. We need to go." She turned to Mia. "Are you sure you won't come with us?"

Mia ripped her attention from the Angel of Wrath—it was probably safe now that her anger was diminishing—and nodded at the Ursa. "I'm sure, Mother. The Shuffle is too important to lose. We must maintain an escape route for other members of the resistance." She tweaked a smile at me. "Even the men."

I could tell Mother Superior saw the truth of it. She gave Mia another long and lingering hug and then hustled us to the remaining casket. The blasts from above had stopped, replaced by another odd hum, indicating that the Trogs had broken through the blast wall and had called the elevator. We didn't have much time to spare.

So it annoyed me when, as we crawled into our casket, the Ursa shot me another dark glance and muttered, "Are you sure you want to bring him with you? It's not too late to change your mind."

Angel just laughed and curled up next to me. And damn, she was soft and warm and fragrant. "Yes, Mother. Yes."

Mia snorted at that and punched the coordinates into the machine, then she came over to close our lid. Normally, I would have felt claustrophobic at the thought of being locked in a confined space with a bear who really didn't like me, but with Angel nestled up next to me—between me and the beast—I barely gave it a thought. Of course, most of my blood had left my brain for parts south.

Before the lid closed, Mia captured my gaze and sent me one last smile.

For some reason, I had the sneaking suspicion it was genuine. Maybe the only one I'd ever seen.

"Safe travels," she said. "And, Tig?"

"Yeah?"

"I really am sorry . . . about everything."

And then everything went dark.

FOURTEEN

I knew immediately when we started to Shuffle. It was the strangest sensation. A fizzle in my veins, a hum. Pressure built up in my sinuses to an uncomfortable level. I think the Ursa was uncomfortable too because I could hear her snorting and moving restlessly on the other side of the casket.

We hovered there, in some strange limbo, for far too long.

Panic rose. I was certain something had gone wrong. A suspicion that Mia had played us all once again, that she was somehow sending us to our doom, whipped through me. I must have made a noise because Angel turned toward me, murmured nonsense, and stroked my scalp. It was soothing but not soothing enough.

Because just then, a certain pressure, a tension, clamped down on my chest. Resistance grew, like a rubber band being stretched beyond its capacity to give.

I knew—just knew—we were phasing through the planetary shield. It felt as though the jaws were closing in on us. As though the weight of it would crush us.

"It will be all right," an angel whispered in my ear. I turned to her because if I was going to die, it would be in her arms. She must have felt the same. In the darkness, her lips found mine. Clung.

The kiss distracted me, for which I was thankful.

Even when the intensity of the Shuffle peaked, even when my ears popped and stars danced before my eyes, I didn't stop kissing her.

And she did not stop kissing me.

It was glorious. Fantastic. Transcendent.

Something about hurtling through space with a gorgeous Seraph in your arms made all other concerns fade away. Nothing mattered but this. This moment. This woman. This embrace. I knew then that we would be together forever. Or as long as she wanted me.

I did not want the kiss to end.

But it did.

It was interrupted by a snort of utter disgust.

I cracked open a lid and found myself blinded by a watery light.

Mother Superior sat over us with the open lid behind her, her arms crossed over her be-furred chest, glowering. "Don't you two ever stop?" she muttered.

Angel laughed, some light and evanescent tinkle. She unfolded herself from me—which I did not care for in the least— and stood up from the casket.

I had to follow her. The last thing I wanted was be alone with the Ursa. Did I mention she didn't like me?

As I stepped out into the clearing where our casket had settled, I stilled. A strange sense of *déjà vu* hit me. I felt as though I had been here before.

It was warm; the air was balmy, and we were surrounded by large bushes sporting fat palm fronds. Trees towered overhead, creating a canopy through which I could not see the sky. The calls of various birds and jungle creatures echoed off the mist.

A faint vision wafted through my mind of a raven-haired girl running through these fronds, her laugh dancing on the air . . .

I had been here before.

But I hadn't.

"What is this place?" I asked. "It feels . . ."

"Feels what?"

"Familiar."

I have no idea why her lips curved into a wide, smug grin. I had a feeling she knew something I didn't. She set her hand on her belly and turned to survey the landscape. It was pretty. Green. Flowers and shit. A hell of a lot nicer than Viridian. And Angel was here. With me. I couldn't complain.

She smiled. "It's home. For the time being."

I frowned. "For the time being?"

Mother Superior stepped between us, as though she might have a chance at keeping us apart. She did not. "One day the Fed will find us and we'll have to leave. But for now, it will serve as our base of operations. This planet is far from the center of the KU. It's difficult to navigate, and easy for us to hide our ships. Now that we've perfected the Shuffle, we'll be able to ride the wormhole to anywhere in an instant." She fixed her beady little eyes on me. "We could take you back to Earth."

Was that a hopeful tone in her voice?

"He can't leave."

Mother Superior whipped around and glared at Angel. "Of course he can. He can, and he will be damn grateful to us for saving him. You want to go home, don't you, Earthie?" Practically an accusation.

"I—"

"He cannot go home, Mother." Angel set her hand on the Ursa's arm and they shared a glance.

The bear blanched.

"You're not saying what I think you're saying." At Angel's shrug, the ferocious female turned on me and snarled. I mean really snarled. "You didn't."

"Um. Didn't what?"

"Of course he did." Angel patted the Mother's fur; it didn't soothe her.

"Of course? There is no of course about it," the Ursa growled.

"Um, what did I do?" If I was going to be eviscerated by those flexing claws, I kind of wanted to know why.

The answer came in a feral hiss that made the air around me hum with menace. "You *mated* with her."

Oh. That.

"Well," I said, and unwisely so, "we are DC."

The Ursa's mouth opened and then closed. Then her lips worked. It was almost amusing. But then she leaned closer, so close I could taste her acrid breath, and roared, "You ravaged my baby."

Well, hardly ravaged . . . "It was kind of a mutual thing."

Okay. Wrong thing to say.

She rose up to her full height and bellowed. Her lips rippled over sharp fangs. I have no doubt, if Angel had not scooted around to step between us, she would have mauled me right then and there.

"He did not ravage me, Mother." She shot me a sweet smile. "I ravaged him."

"What?"

"I chose him. I seduced him."

I didn't totally agree—like I said, it had been a mutual thing. But I was wise enough to keep my trap shut. But I did nod a little and mutter, "She did. She ravaged me." I tried to appear wounded and virtuous, but I doubt I pulled it off. Because that ravaging had been pretty fan-fucking-tastic.

Mother Superior crossed her arms and glared at both of us. "It hardly matters who ravaged whom. The point is, Serafina, you've been compromised."

Serafina.

Her name was Serafina.

I liked it. It fit her.

But she was still, and always, my Angel. I loved that she grinned and quipped, "Quite thoroughly compromised."

"How do you expect to fight now?"

My brow wrinkled. How could being ravaged—even by such a stud as myself—keep her from fighting?

Serafina smiled calmingly. "It will be years before the Fed finds us."

"You don't know that. They could be tracking us even now."

"They aren't."

"You don't know that!"

"I do." Serafina's expression was calm, certain. She smiled at me. "I do know. Because he had a vision."

Mother Superior stilled. She fixed her narrowed gaze on me and made a noise at the back of her throat. "What do you mean?"

"He swallowed some pglet and had a vision. Didn't you, Tig?"

"I . . . yes." Yes. That was it. That was why this place seemed so familiar. I'd dreamed it.

"Tell her what else you saw."

"Other than this place?"

"Yes."

"I dreamed of a girl."

The Ursa's fur riffled. Her beady eyes pinned me like a bug. "A girl?"

"With black hair and green eyes."

Her gaze flicked to my hair. "Black hair?"

"Um, yeah."

"Mother pflerging farg—" She scowled at Serafina, then she blew out a breath and stomped away. With no warning, she turned around and barked, "How old was this child?"

I shrugged. "Five. Maybe seven."

"Humph." She shot a contemplative glance at Angel. "So maybe we do have some time."

Angel grinned. "Maybe we do."

Mother Superior didn't respond. Instead, she lumbered away down the path. The damp fronds scraped against her glossy fur, leaving a shiny residue.

Angel took my hand and tugged me in the same direction. "Shall we join the others?"

"The others?"

"The other rebels?"

I grinned at her. "Am I a rebel now?"

"You are. You're stuck with me, after all."

"Am I?" I liked that idea.

"Absolutely. We're mated."

A trickle of unease tightened my chest at the way she said it. Mother Superior had said the word with that same, strange emphasis. "Um, what exactly does that mean, mated?"

Serafina laughed, and again, I felt warmth rise in my veins. "You are such a nube," she said, hooking her arm in mine. "It means we've shared our essence. We are one-in-two." She set her hand on her belly and winked. "Three, really, if I'm being technical."

My knees went a little weak. I stared at her belly, which was, now that I was paying attention, sporting a little bump. "Are you saying you're . . . ? You're . . . ?"

"With child?"

My throat locked. I tried to clear it but couldn't. So I croaked, "Yes?"

"A little girl with green eyes and black hair?"

"Yes."

"If you had done your homework, you would have known that Seraphim always have blond hair. You would also know that we are exceedingly fertile around men we find attractive." Well, that was nice to know that she found me attractive. "And finally—and this is an important point—when we mate, we bond for life. On a cellular level." I gaped at her and she laughed. "You couldn't leave me if you wanted to." Good thing I didn't want to. "You, my darling, are mine forever."

She shot me a brilliant smile, one that warmed the cockles of my heart—and other cockles if I am being honest. Then she led me down the path to join the other rebels. "Honestly, Tig," she said with a sigh, but it was a happy one. "You really should have done your homework."

GLOSSARY

Accords: Some attempt at honor among thieves, these agreements carve up the districts of Kaww Settlement in an attempt to keep everyone happy . . . and alive. But you know those will never last.

Annexation: A word the Fed likes to use instead of "conquer," but everyone knows what it really means. The fuckers.

Barrens: Vast, stony desert to the east of the main settlement.

Bi-denizen World: A planet with more than one sentient life-form; usually symbiotic.

Billygoat: Goatee, horns, braying, the whole shebang.

Bronson Gate: One of six gates leading into Kaww through the wall protecting the settlement from the elements of the Barrens, which range from acidic sandstorms to deluges.

Capuchins: Enormous, monkey-like creatures who are hornier than shit. Watch out for those teeth.

Chickentown: Clucker District. Scrambled eggs are a capital offense.

Chud: Slang for draw.

Cluckers: Bird-like creatures with feathers and a nasty craving for pglet.

C.O.W.: Casualties of War. Hey, it happens.

Crabnuts: Like pistachios with a chewy maggot center.

Creel: A water planet inhabited by Skeegs and Creel—and not in that order.

Cygnet: Tag/tattoo of the Swan Cartel.

Dargumi: Vicious cousins to the Dinks with sharper teeth, longer claws, and sadistic proclivities.

DB: Dead body. Lots of paperwork. Easier to dump them in the Kase.

DC: DNA Compatible—Necessary in a True Mate, or *any* mate. Or the kids come out all squirrelly.

Dink: A reptilian creature that sweats green pus.

Draw/Huff/Chud: An easy, access drug that does not affect the Blues but is like heroin to most other species. Especially those with warm blood. So, naturally, the Fed uses it to control the lockup. It is illegal on all other planets. Fortunately, nothing is illegal on Viridian.

Drawhead: Chud addict.

Earthies: Anyone hailing from Earth, one of the newest Fed acquisitions. Fairly uncommon on Viridian because they have a squishy center.

Electrogenic: Of or relating to the production of electrical activity in living tissue. Take my advice and close your eyes.

Ēostrevarians: Religious fanatics whose goal is to convert the Sullied into the congregation of the Saved. If you visit their shelter, you can expect long, pedantic sermons. But hey, free soup.

Epsy Colony: Prison planet quarked back in ,02 because someone pissed off the wrong Fed.

ET: Earthtime.

Fed/Goon: Short for Federation or Federation Agent (i.e. the bad guys)

The Fed: The Federation, governing body of the KU. Or, if you please, its conquerors.

Ferrods: Furry, two-legged ungulates; males are antlered, with points reflecting their position in the herd.

First Uni: The civilized portion of the universe—and the most brutal.

Gnomus Prime: Craphole mining planet.

Go-jo: Like coffee on crack. Awesome when you need a lift, but watch the crash. It can be a killer.

Goon: Slang for Fed.

Greek: Notorious whorehouse on the Strand.

Gumvar: A calamari-like delicacy on the planet Vanit. But shit . . . watch out for those tentacles. Because those Gumvar would also like to eat *you*.

Harleytown: Dark, dismal district where bad things happen.

Hive: Base of the Sisterhood located at an undisclosed location in the Barrens.

HP: Home Planet.

Huff: Slang for draw.

Huggas: A dismal mining settlement deep in the Barrens. Better to take a swim in the Kase.

Hume: Derogatory term for human.

Intake: Occurring on the Fed space station orbiting the moon, this induction procedure for inmates includes a thorough examination of all body cavities, psychogenic scans, and chip implantation. The process can take weeks, depending on the species, as some have more cavities than others. During intake, cons are held in general lockup. Survival rate on any given transport is less than 25 percent, mostly thanks to the Ozzies who can't keep their fangs to themselves, the bastards. Earthies rarely survive intake.

Kaling: Razor-sharp stones that make up the majority of Viridian. Over the centuries, the massive windstorms have shaved off sharp shards of acidic sand that, in a gale, will eat away at anything it hits.

Kase: A river of antimatter snarling along a groove in the space-time continuum. Awesome place to dump garbage . . . or bodies you don't want anyone to find.

Kaww Settlement: The only habitable spot on Viridian Moon, Federation Prison Planet. Huggas isn't really habitable, and the denizens of the Hive will eat you alive.

Krill: Horny, jumbo, shrimp-like creatures who will stick it anywhere.

KU: Known Universe.

Lepers: Victims of a Scard infestation. They are required to wear special cloaks so others know to give them a wide berth.

Lube: A cross between alcohol and a bullet in the head. Awesome after a long day on Viridian.

Lurian Ease: Best lube ever. Total oblivion.

Millennium Gate: Unguarded portal to the Kase. Unguarded for a reason.

Muni: Enforcer, bagman, cop in a world with no real laws or justice. They all work for Granny, the King of the World, and they have jurisdiction everywhere, except where the accords bar them.

Musth: Skeeg mating cycle. Very sticky.

Nard: Big-ass beetle with vestigial wings. Couldn't fly if they tried. And they don't try. Notorious drawheads.

Novitiates: Pledges seeking to earn membership to the Sisterhood. All virgins. Wear chastity belts. Damn it all anyway.

Oakie: Sentient tree-folk. Don't let the fairy tales fool you. They are mean motherfuckers . . . when they deign to move. Usually they put down roots, but when they pull them up, watch out. They are known to have really sick appetites.

Ozzies: A cross between spiders and vampire bats with long, razor-sharp teeth. They eat anything. Or drink everything. Whatever.

Pglet: The secretions of a Skeeg in turmoil; valued as a hallucinogen and is used in shamanic rituals. Also has healing properties. Not awesome for the libido though. Just sayin'.

Phaser Pistols: Standard, issue Enforcer weapons. Notably unreliable. Always carry a backup.

PI: Private informant.

Polarian: Bug-eyed humanoids with feeding tentacles (and gonads) around the mouth. Polarians are orally obsessed. Be it food or sexual contact, they want it all.

Porcine: Pig-like humanoids with long, bearded snouts and long, sharp tusks. Very sensitive to smell.

Prospect District: Known for riots and days-long parties. Tough to tell the difference between the two. But then. Who cares?

PTB: Powers That Be. Usually the Fed.

Q-Bomb: Quark bomb. World killer. Always a bad thing.

Rats: Tiny-eyed, furry rodents who live in the sewers and collect crap. All kinds of crap. Mountains of crap. A first-uni answer to "hoarders." Suckers for sparkly things.

Ravens: Big, tough birds that don't take any shit from anyone (although they shit quite prodigiously, thank you very much). Most work as munis. Love to peck at roadkill.

Rhinos: Large, slow moving gray bloods. Damn loyal friends. Mind the horn.

Rubberduck: A Fed who comes on planet in disguise to stir shit up.

Scards: Nasty little beetles that crawl beneath your skin and eat you from the inside out. Extremely contagious. See also, Lepers.

Seraph: Beautiful, delicate, glowing creatures with translucent skin, blond hair, and green eyes. They are only fertile around those they find attractive, and then, exceedingly so. They nearly always conceive in such a circumstance. When they mate, they share their essence. Typically, they bond for life. And they are damn hot.

Seventh Gear: Really fast.

The Shield: The electromagnetic field surrounding a prison moon that will zap any bug who tries to flee.

Sisterhood: A clan of women who live in the Barrens. Their hidden base is called the Hive, and for good reason. They keep men as slaves (drones) to serve them and provide the seed for future generations. And occasionally, depending on the species, they have them for dinner (delicious with fava beans and a nice Chianti). Mother Superior is their queen. Novitiates are pledges, seeking to earn membership. And did I mention? Chastity belts. Damn.

Skeeg: Frog-like creature with eyes on stalks, regenerative foam, and pglet secretions. Their feet slap when they walk, and their voices are decidedly croaky. They hail from the planet Creel and have the unfortunate tendency to tell the truth exactly when you don't want them to. Oh, and they fart like the devil. That shit will make your eyes water and your skin peel. Gas mask advised.

Skid: Skeeziest part of town, where cons go to die or just fade away.

Skimmer: A hovercraft operating on a proton battery with an electric motor. Best not to drive in the wet. That shit will fry your ass.

Squig: A landed cod. Lying little fucks. Every one.

Strand: A district dedicated to all manner of sexual perversions. Even straight sex.

Swank District: Where all the rich cons live. Anything goes. If you can afford it.

Swans: A gang of Cluckers. Members are identifiable by a cygnet tattoo. Also, all the feathers.

Trog: A thick-skinned pile of mindless muscle. Spikes running down his spine. Dumber than shit.

TSTL: Just Google it.

Uni: Slang for universe.

Ursa: Tall, slender, bear-like creature.

Vipers: Lower half snake, upper half human. Scary as shit. Spits acid when ticked . . . or when they climax. Or, well, whenever. Extremely horny. But, really? Seriously?

Viridian Moon: Originally developed by a Numarian realtor as a pleasure resort, until a river of antimatter was discovered cutting through the core. Rivers of antimatter can be awkward on pleasure planets but come in useful when dealing with the scum of the universe (i.e. Rebels). The Fed condemned the moon and annexed it as a prison planet, confining the antimatter in a millennium shield.

White: Derogatory slang for Clucker. On account of the feathers.

Wire: A device the Fed uses to record the actions of the cons. You know, so they can blackmail them into doing their bidding.

ACKNOWLEDGMENTS

Thanks to TJ da Roza, for believing in this book, and Lane Heymont and Nicole Resciniti, for fighting for it! And thanks to Sonnet Fitzgerald for her copyediting genius!

ABOUT THE AUTHOR

Blessed (or cursed) with dyslexia and ADD, author Sam York has always loved creating worlds, tantalizing readers, and having complete and utter control over the universe. What could be better than writing snarky stories in a variety of genres?

Under various pen names, Sam has won multiple writing awards and hit the *New York Times* and *USA Today* bestseller lists several times.

Interested parties can learn more at sabrinayork.com/samyork.

Sam lives in seclusion east of Seattle with a really drooly rottweiler.